THE

ELEMENTALS

BOOK ONE
CARNELIAN

MICHELLE KNOHL

To my family- by blood and by marriage, by fate and by love - Thank you. I love you more than anything.

CHAPTER ONE

Wind whips by as the motorcycle roars through the nearly deserted streets. Wanting to pull off the helmet and feel the air on her face, she refrains, satisfying herself by pushing the engine harder. The thrum of the motorcycle's engine hums through her body. Stars in the sky pulse above her, and streetlights flash by. An open road beckons. The freedom, the power, the adrenaline. She slows at the sight of a red light ahead, but as if the fates are listening, it changes color. A shout of joy issues from her lips. She guns it and goes flying through the light. Suddenly, the white headlights of a pickup truck pour in from her side view. Time seems to slow down. The realization they are going to hit is slow in coming. Much slower than the truck.

Brakes screech, glass shatters. Mia, thrown from the motorcycle, lands in a heap on the side of the road. She stands up, a little dazed. She pushes her red hair out of her face. Her eyes dart around, trying to get her bearings. Where is the motorcycle? She hears shouting. Mia turns around to find the wreckage. A man emerges from the truck, unsteady

on his feet. He pitches forward, moving towards the body
in the middle of the intersection. Then he crashes to the
ground, yelling.

Mia can't make out his words. She runs as fast as her
shaky legs will allow. She feels the broken glass eating into
the soles of her bare feet. The pain doesn't slow her down.
The sound of her own breathing echoes in her ears. The wind
she enjoyed earlier seems to cut through the thin fabric of her
blue shorts and tank top. In horror, she watches as the man
opens the visor of the figure's motorcycle helmet. Her Uncle
Anthony's face stares back. His eyes closed; his breathing
jagged. It is then that she starts to scream.

Mia awakened from the nightmare to see her mother crying in her bedroom
doorway. Before Mia could stop her hands from shaking, her mother ordered
her to pack an overnight bag and left the room. It had happened before. The
dreams returning usually signaled another move; Mia sighed. At sixteen, Mia
had already been to a half dozen schools. Now that she had started to take her
classes online, she hoped her dreams wouldn't matter. Obviously, she was wrong.

Mia could feel every bump as her mother's jeep moved down the unpaved
back road leading into an uninhabited wilderness. Her mother was pensive,
not telling her where they were going. They had driven for an hour into a small
hamlet town. Eventually, they turned onto a dirt road. The jeep was ambling
down the road in the middle of the night. Maybe it would be helpful to leave
a trail of breadcrumbs. She wasn't even tempted to pull out her phone. None
of the chat groups she took part in would understand this. She was on her
own… again.

In nervous anticipation, Mia twisted her finger through her red hair. Her
other hand grasped her only piece of jewelry, an old silver star on an antique
chain. Mia's mother claimed it was Mia's father's. Mia wasn't sure she believed
that, but since she knew nothing about her father, she cherished it anyway. She
looked back at the truck bed; Mia's bag was the only one there.

At the end of the road, the car's headlights flashed on a small cottage. Uneven stones covered the front, and the windows were dark. The door was dark purple and rounded at the top.

"Mom… where are we?" Mia finally asked as they sat staring at the house.

"This is the home of Triana Salviano," her mother managed. She reached out her hand as if to put a comforting pat on Mia's arm, but withdrew it quickly without touching her. Her mother winced. "I met her a week or two ago. I think she can help us." Without looking at Mia, she exited the car, leaving the motor running and the headlights on.

Did she mean for her to stay there? Or did she just forget to turn off the car? Mia watched her mother move to the front door and knock. What does this mean? While Mia waited, rooted to her seat, she noticed a large sign in front of the house. Silver letters announced, "Triana, Psychic, Advisor and Medium." Mia exhaled sharply. This is what things had come to.

Lights turned on within the house and eventually the purple door opened. Mia's mother talked to someone. With what Mia assumed was supposed to be a reassuring smile, her mother gestured for Mia to join her, then entered the house. Mia reached over and turned off the ignition, guessing it was distraction that left it on. Taking the keys in her hand, she moved out of the car and paused. She could hear the hooting of owls. A lone howl sent shivers down her spine. She then moved quickly towards the light.

The outside of the house looked homey, but the inside reminded Mia of a carnival. Silk tapestries hung from the walls in a variety of jewel tones. Light issued forth from lamps draped with scarves. In the center of the front room stood a little table covered in velvet with a glass sphere placed on top. Her mother didn't look around, but Mia couldn't take it all in. It was an old-world mystical caravan rolled into a small living room. The place exuded an aura of mystery.

A woman entered the room like a queen deigning to walk among her subjects. She wore layers of skirts and a white peasant top, barely contrasting with her pale skin. Black curly hair framed a heart-shaped face. The hair on Mia's arm stood up.

"This is the girl?" The woman asked without preamble. Mia's mother only nodded.

"W... w... who are you?" Mia stammered. The woman turned her startling blue eyes onto her. Mia was suddenly highly aware of the threadbare Beatles t-shirt, gray hoodie, and ripped blue jeans she had thrown on in the middle of the night. Faced with such a commanding woman, Mia felt like a child. Mia tried not to cringe when the lady's eyes stopped at Mia's hair. The woman's thin eyebrow lifted slightly. Self-consciously, Mia's hand went up to attempt to tame her unruly locks. Finishing her inspection, the woman smiled.

"My name is Triana, but that is not what you are asking." There was a lilt to her voice, like a fortune teller of old. She sauntered to the little velvet table and flared her skirts as she took a seat. "I am the one who can answer your questions, see your future, and find your path." Her mouth twisted slightly. "Come, sit little one." Her arm gestured to the seat across from her.

Mia looked to her mother for approval. Her mother folded in on herself, so small compared to the power of the mystic. A response would not come from her mother. Tentatively, Mia moved forward and sank into a wooden chair covered by a maroon pillow. The old chair groaned under her weight.

"Your mother says you are like me," Triana smiled, clearly doubtful. Mia could only stare at the woman across from her. She was costumed like a fortune teller out of a movie. It would seem like a Halloween joke except for the energy radiating off of her. Triana stared at her as if she could see into Mia's soul and determine her secrets. "Do you see the future?" Triana asked. Mia's heart leapt. She automatically started to deny it. Then she looked to her mom, who nodded.

"Sometimes," Mia responded honestly.

"How?" Triana prodded.

"When I touch someone," Mia replied.

"What do you see?"

4

"It's... different... every time. Mostly it's like a series of pictures in a flip book. They go fast and sometimes one or two stand out," Mia's voice trembled. No one but Mia's mother knew about her curse, and until now her mother had forbidden Mia from talking about it.

Mia's visions started when she was a child. At the age of seven, she announced to a babysitter she was going to die. The sitter passed away in a car crash that very night. That is when the moving began. Her mother had relocated them often, until Mia was old enough to realize what she saw was not welcome knowledge. No one wanted to know what was coming for them nor did they want a mere child to see their past. But Mia saw everything. By the time she turned sixteen, her own mother had been afraid to touch her. Triana held out her hand and Mia flinched away.

"You will not see my future," Triana smiled encouragingly. "Though I may see yours." The 'mystic' didn't believe her. Mia grimaced. She looked at Triana's hand wearily. The easiest thing to prove herself would be to take her hand. But after the heart wrenching dreams earlier that evening, Mia wasn't sure she could take the terror that would appear on this woman's face, the rejection. But she would never see this woman again.

"Go ahead, Mia," her mother whispered behind her.

Slowly, Mia held out her hand and put it in the lady's. As soon as there was contact, the visions poured in...

> A young red-headed woman was kissing a handsome dark-haired man. A hospital room. A red-haired woman with Triana's face crying on the floor. An older man with reddish hair handing a bottle to a young man with features similar to the one who was kissed. The words lanamnas eicne no sleithe. Finally, an older version of Triana, holding out her hand. Suddenly, the connection between Triana and the old lady ripped apart in a moment of agony.

Emotions sang through each image, from joy to heartbreak, and through it all loneliness. The two final images were the strongest... all they held was pain. Mia pulled back her hand quickly, but Triana was already on her feet with a curse. Her posture was defensive, as if Mia would attack her at any moment. Stepping around the table, she grabbed Mia by the wrist. The physical contact sent a shock through Mia's body. Mia looked wildly to her mother for help, but her mother didn't move. Triana pushed up the sleeve of the grey hoodie, exposing Mia's arm. Triana twisted it, examining both sides.

"No, it isn't possible..." Triana muttered as she moved away, never taking her eyes off of Mia. Tears welled in Mia's eyes. Why was she here? Why didn't her mother intervene? "What did you see child?" Triana voice was calm but her eyes flashed. The lilt had disappeared, making her voice hard and demanding.

"I didn't see anything!" Mia's voice was shaking.

"Don't lie to me." Triana was standing far away now, like her mother, afraid to be near her. With tears streaming down her face, Mia replied.

"I saw you kissing a man, you were wearing a white flowing dress, and you had red hair and you were holding a bouquet of wildflowers. I saw a hospital room. The man was in a bed there. He was pale and holding your hand, and...." Mia gulped and looked away, remembering the look of pain on Triana's face in the next images. She tried to swallow the guilt at seeing such personal moments. "And that was it," she lied again. This time, Triana let it go.

They sat in silence for a long time. The high-pitched screech of an owl pierced the moment. Mia huddled down into her hoodie, wishing she could retreat, hide like she always did. If she didn't have contact with the world, Mia could pretend she was a normal kid.

"She should stay here with me," Triana finally announced.

Mia's eyes went wild. "No." She looked back at her mother, who finally turned towards the proceedings. Her gaze locked with Triana's. Mia couldn't understand why her mother wasn't protesting. "No!" Mia repeated. Standing up, Mia knocked over her chair with a deafening bang. The sound made Mia's mother jump and close even more into herself. What was going on?

"You do not have to stay unless you want to." Triana dropped her mother's gaze and turned to Mia. Slowly, she moved forward as if trying to calm a startled animal. "Your name is Mia?" She smiled. "The reason I want you to stay is because I believe you are one of my people."

"Your people? Fake fortune tellers? You want someone to earn you more money?" Mia moved back until she hit a tapestry-covered wall. Triana lifted her hand and pulled off the black wig. Under the wig were red locks, a lighter version of Mia's own. A twisting pattern of braids created a golden crown. Mia's jaw dropped.

Admittedly, Mia looked more like Triana than her own mother. Her mother had dark auburn hair with dark green eyes. Mia's hair was distinctly red. Mia's eyes were hazel, more green or blue based on her clothing, but most days staying a light grey.

This woman was the opposite of her mother. She exuded strength and power. Mia looked to her mother and noticed the haggard expression. The skeletal eye sockets and lines that dominated her face. Everything about her cried out she was powerless and afraid. Mia had always assumed she took after her father, though he was a topic Mia's mother would never discuss.

"You're related to my dad?" Mia ventured.

"I don't know." Triana stopped and looked at her mother. "Who is her father?"

Her mother hesitated. "He said his name was Alan. I met him on a ski trip when I was twenty. I don't know his last name. I was never able to find him again when I found out I was pregnant." She whispered the last sentence.

Mia looked at her mother in horror. "You had a fling?!" Her mother wouldn't look her in the eye. Her mother, the woman who looks at everyone suspiciously, who doesn't even have any friends, who plans her entire life. How could she have had an affair? Had having Mia changed her that much?

"Did his arms look like mine?" Triana asked exposing a sleeve of tattoos that covered her arm. The tattoos were white, gleaming out of her already pale skin. Mia looked at them, half horrified and half fascinated.

"Yes," Mia's mother gasped.

Just below Triana's left wrist was a familiar symbol. Mia pulled out her father's necklace and stared at it. Two triangles on top of each other. They were the same. This woman was related to her dad. At that moment, her mother's cell phone rang. Stricken, her mother took the phone out of her purse.

"Take the call outside," Triana ordered. "I need to talk to Mia." With a hesitant look at Mia, her mother stepped out the front door. Triana sauntered back to the table and sat down gesturing to the other seat. Mia ignored her gesture and remained standing. They regarded each other for a moment.

At some point after Mia's vision, Triana had dropped the Romani accent. Now her voice did not indicate its origin. "I am one of the Aether." At Mia's confused look, she elaborated. "I am an Elemental. We can see the essence of a person. The moments that define them, define their future. The gift is stronger in some than in others. Your gift is rare indeed. Few can read other Aether as you just did." Triana smiled wryly. "As you grow into your gift, you will receive the markers of our people." She gestured to her arm.

"I don't want any tattoos."

"Yet, you will receive them. They are the stories of our life," she paused, considering her next words. "Since your arms are blank, I can only guess at your gift. Our gifted people train as early as five years old to control what they see and how it affects them. You are how old?"

"Sixteen. Almost seventeen."

"Sixteen," Triana sighed on the last syllable as if she was full of wonder. "And with such a gift, it is a miracle you survived. But I assure you, without training you will slowly descend into madness." Her eyes were full of pity, but the words were like steel.

"Can you get rid of it?" Mia pleaded.

"Your gift? No. No one can do that. It is a part of you, part of your soul," Triana frowned. Mia's stomach dropped. Can't get rid of it. *It will ruin my life forever*. She looked at the red-haired woman. She didn't look like a hermit, running away from everyone. She had a sign welcoming people in. Mia pondered for a moment.

"Training? You can teach me to control the... 'gift'?" The word sounded wrong on her tongue. Surely this wasn't a gift. She wasn't allowed near other people. Her only friends were in books.

"I can try... I will teach you what I know... My gift, well, it is not as strong in me. And honestly, I was one of the strongest Aether in my clan. But I promise you, if I cannot help you, I will take you to someone who can."

Mia watched her carefully. Then Triana did something no one who knew her had ever done. She held out her hand.

"Go ahead. If you are as talented as I think you are, you will see my soul and know I tell the truth. The first thing an Aether must learn is words lie, but spirit and intention... those are impossible to manipulate."

Mia stared at the hand. There was danger there. As much as Mia tried to squash the feeling, it gave her hope. Hope that she wasn't destined to be forever different, forever alone. If she could control it, she might stop it or hide it. Mia hesitantly reached out. She winced as she grasped Triana's hand, waiting for more images to flood her. Instead, she was inundated with a sense of calm. She could sense the woman's loneliness and fear of Mia, but also, the woman's honesty. Slowly, Mia released her, overcome with wonder.

"You will find it is hard to lie when you are Aether, for though everyone cannot see the past or the future, we can all see the essence and truth of a person," she smiled.

"Can you read me?" Mia asked.

"I can see who you are. I can see your fear, but also your strength," she paused then added, "I cannot see your future, however. Regardless, you are welcome here." At that moment, her mother walked through the door. Her face was pink with a war of emotions.

"You dreamed of Anthony," she stated, the pain clear in her voice. "He had a motorcycle accident. He's in critical condition in Charleston." Mia's mom braced herself. "Does he die?" Her voice was tentative, unsure if she wanted the answer.

"No," Mia whispered. Relief flooded her mother's face, a sob bursting from her chest. Mia didn't say the rest, for though her Uncle Anthony lived, he would never walk again. Triana stared openly at Mia. If she stays with her mom, Mia knows her mother will stick by her, but she won't trust Mia enough to go to Charleston. Life would go on as it always had.

Mia watched her mother struggle with the decision. At that moment, how much her mother gave up for her became crystal clear. Mia is the reason she has no friends, that she rarely sees her family. For Mia, she has given up living her own life. It is hard to take in, but Mia can feel the truth of it. Guilt tore at her gut. She didn't ask her mom to forsake her family. There isn't anything she can do. But maybe… Mia felt the flicker of hope again as she looked to Triana. After a few minutes of silence, Mia walked over to her mother. "I'm going to stay here." Mia's heart raced with the hugeness of the decision.

Startled, her mother looked up. She reached for Mia, enveloping her in a hug. "You don't have to." Surprised by the sudden display of affection, Mia almost didn't respond.

"I know," came her muffled reply. Her mother pulled away, cupping Mia's face with her hand. Images streamed in.

> Her mother in a simple wedding gown, smiling at a man in a tuxedo who adores her. Her mother holding a baby. Her mother laughing with a family of her own, but one that did not include Mia.

She had never seen her mother's future before. Perhaps she never had it until Mia chose to leave her.

"It will be okay." Her mother reassured Mia and herself. Her mother's love was like a blanket warming her, and for a second, Mia hesitated. Then Mia smiled a sad smile.

"Yes, it will. I can see it." And with that Mia took a step back, releasing her mother to a happier future than she could provide.

CHAPTER TWO

The light turned on, blinding Mia's eyes. "Turn it off!" she squeaked, her entire body recoiling from the light.

"Name three stones to promote healing," a singsong voice came from Mia's right.

"Clear Quartz, Amethyst, and… and," *it's too early for this*, "Lapis?"

"Excellent. You can have five more minutes." The lights turned off. Slowly, Mia opened her eyes, not trusting the lights to stay off. She groaned, flipping her face into her pillow. Triana was a morning person; the type who didn't understand that not everyone could rise and shine at a moment's notice. Stupid sunrise. The book she had been reading when she fell asleep, dropped off her chest as she stretched out under the covers, enjoying the warmth of her bed. Piles of books covered every surface. Triana wanted her to learn so much. The constant influx of information helped distract Mia from missing her mom and being lonely even while living with Triana.

Mia knew it wouldn't even be five minutes before Triana invaded her room again with another pop quiz. Her eyelids felt heavy. Six months of early mornings didn't make a single one easier. She put her pillow on top of her head in an attempt to thwart the evil woman. When the lights went on, it stayed mercifully dark with only a sliver of yellow puncturing her peace.

"What can you use in tea to promote calm?" Triana paused. "I always feel suffocated when I stay under a pillow. My breath is just hot…" *Bleehhhh, she was right.*

"Chamomile, lemon balm and lavender," Mia groaned.

"You get three minutes." Another pause, "and I have a surprise for you, so get up!"

Mia sat up, yawning. A surprise didn't mean something good. She had had several dozen surprises since she started living with Triana. Adapting to Triana's "Aether" lifestyle had been a hard transition. Surprise number one: little technology existed in the house; no video games, computers, or cell phones. Triana only owned a landline, which Mia used to call her mom periodically, and a television connected to a VHS player.

Surprise number two: as she distanced herself, however unwillingly, from technology, Mia noticed her headaches stopped. The constant hum in the background of everyday life disappeared. Things were clearer, more distinct when she stopped to look at them.

Surprise number three: Triana told the truth when she said she could help Mia with her gift. Mia learned every living thing had an aura or energy around it. The aura revealed the type of person she was dealing with, and a flickering color told her what they were feeling. Once she identified the auras, she could control how she received them. Now Mia could block energy to make physical contact with others. She could hold on to an image that flashed in front of her, taking in the details, even the conversations. When she opened herself to it, Mia could sense people's energy, their proximity to her, and their emotions without touching them. And when she wanted to close herself off from them, she could. It was a relief to go out in public and not be afraid of the emotional assault a simple trip to the grocery store once produced. She finally felt controlling her gift might be possible.

Sitting up, Mia ran her hand through her long hair. She heard the radio droning on with the news. The smell of bacon wafted through the air and sent her scurrying to the bathroom for a quick shower. She donned a new pair of jeans and a peach V-neck. Her reflection in the mirror stopped her as she noticed the circles under her eyes had cleared. Her freckles were now the most distinctive part of her face. A little extra weight curved out her thin frame. Triana had made her go shopping for new clothes a few days ago, recognizing more than Mia the changes in her appearance. Mia threw on her familiar hoodie before grabbing her book and following the smells.

Bacon and eggs were already on the table when Mia entered the yellow retro styled kitchen. "Today in traffic, a five-car pileup on..." She slid into a plastic chair and filled up a plate while trying to tune out the news.

"You need to check your crystal grid," Triana stated.

"Why?" Triana had taught her to create a crystal grid under her bed with amethyst and smoky quartz. Her nightmares hadn't returned in months. There was a pause before Triana responded.

"You had a restless night. What are the best stones to use for grounding?" Mia frowned. A restless night? Her eyes *did* hurt more than usual from the sunrise alarm. "Mia..." Mia blinked, focusing in on Triana. "What are the best stones to use for grounding?"

"Quartz, Obsidian, and Rhodium?"

"Excellent!"

"So the surprise?" Mia sighed.

"You have a test today." As Triana spoke, Mia braced herself. "I thought we would go see a matinee."

"A movie? Like in a theatre? Wait, is this why we've been watching all the Charlie's Angels' movies? But won't there be lots of people there?" Her mind jumped from thought to thought. She really wanted to go - but so many people... it might be better to wait for home video.

"I have been waiting for the film to be old enough so the theaters won't be too crowded. It will be a great test. Can you keep up your protection while distracted?" Mia tried to quell the panic lifting in her chest. "You can do it. I know you can!"

15

Mia smiled, doubtfully. Triana had lived alone for years before Mia had shown up. Mia could tell Triana was excited about going to the theatre. Even though she didn't have Triana's confidence, Mia didn't feel like she could say no. The news droned on, "... the Coro epidemic has health officials scrambling to find…"

"No more news," Triana shuddered, turning the radio to a folk music station she liked to listen to. "Don't eat too much, you want to enjoy the popcorn." Suddenly, Mia didn't feel that hungry.

A few hours later, Mia and Triana settled into the red-cushioned seats of the local movie theater. The early matinee had a smattering of people: some teens in the back, a couple holding hands a few rows ahead of them, and a family with a kid a bit too young to be in this particular film. The number was small enough that it took little to no effort to block the feelings and emotions around her, but Mia's hand kept unconsciously moving up to hold the amethyst pendant Triana had given her. Mia popped another kernel of popcorn into her mouth, savoring the buttery flavor. The previews started up, and Mia almost squeaked. Going to the movies was something she had never dreamed possible. Mia turned toward Triana with an excited smile as the lights darkened.

Her face slams into a brick wall. Large, thick fingers have a grip on the back of her neck. Her own hands are up against the wall. Her fingers sport flaking neon yellow nail polish. Before she can process the strange yet familiar hand, she spins around, thrown back against the bricks. Above her is a greasy face with a square jaw, pitch black eyes, and shaven head. The mouth screws up on one side in a half smile. He is enjoying himself.

"Joe," she rasps out, certain the name belongs to the hand that settles on her throat. "I paid you your money."

"But your dad has lost more since our last exchange." He smiles, gazing down her tank with a calculating look. The look is the same one he has always worn when he comes to visit her father at their apartment. It is the look that makes her hide or run whenever she sees him.

"You said you wouldn't let him gamble anymore," she chokes out, clawing at the hand grasping her throat.

"And miss the chance to see you again, Luce?" His breath is so thick and fetid her stomach almost revolts.

"I have no more money."

"Well, that is good news." He leans in. His massive body presses up against her, the stubble on his chin scraping her cheek. "You'll just have to pay me back another way." His mouth envelops her ear, hot and slimy. Suddenly, he uses his foot to kick out her left leg, sinking her further into his choke hold. "Unless, you don't want to see your daddy anymore." The image of her father flashes before her eyes. Not his recent self, the drunk who spends all his time on the couch or out at the races with scum like Joe, but the laughing, loving father from when she was a little kid.

Her eyes dart frantically to the dumpsters, knowing no one will find them behind the theater, not in time. Her blonde hair falls into her face as she kicks and pushes as hard as she can. Wait... blonde hair?! He laughs, but the laughter turns into Triana's voice yelling her name.

"Thank the Goddess," Triana sobbed as Mia's eyes opened. Automatically, Mia began swatting away the people around her. Mia shot up, trying to take in her location. "One minute you were looking at me and the next you just passed out!"

"I'm back in the theater," Mia gasped. The sound of gunfire issued from the screen. A small group of people had converged.

"The alley," Mia choked out. She struggled to her feet, lurching forward. Weaving up the aisle, she grabbed the door to the theater and threw it open. Across the hall, an usher cleaned up a popcorn spill.

"The dumpsters?! How do I get to the dumpsters? There's a girl in trouble." The usher looked up blankly.

"Mia?!" Triana came up behind her.

"THE DUMPSTERS!?" Mia yelled. The usher jumped and moved down the hall. He threw open a door labeled 'Staff Only' and raced down a narrow hallway to a set of double doors at the end. Mia threw herself at the doors. Her momentum almost caused her to fall off the small platform right outside. Not fifty yards away, a blonde girl was fighting off a huge goon's advances. As Mia watched, he slammed her head against the wall to stop her struggling.

"Joe! Stop!" Mia screamed. The bruiser stumbled backwards, landing on the wet pavement. The girl didn't waste any time. Immediately, she took off like a shot. Joe warily got back on his feet.

"How do I know you?" He growled, advancing towards Mia.

"You don't," Mia squeaked, backing up. Mia knocked into Triana behind her. The goon was three times their size, and he was steadily advancing. They were about to become part of her nightmare. "We'll just be on our way."

"Not until you tell me how you know my name!" He was getting too close for comfort.

"Run," she whispered to Triana. Triana grabbed the door handle, but the door had locked and the usher was nowhere to be seen. "Move!" Mia yelled as her heart jumped into her throat.

Mia and Triana sprinted down the alley behind the theater. She could hear the pounding of the man's boots on the pavement close behind, so much heavier than the light slap of her own sneakers. They swung around the side of the building, skidding in the process. A small crowd was emptying out of a side door. They ran through the blur of people and kept moving toward the front of the movie house. When the sounds of the man disappeared, Mia checked over her shoulder. He was nowhere to be seen.

"Get in the truck," Triana gasped. They moved to the beige truck, slamming up against it. Mia scanned the crowd as Triana grappled with the keys. Climbing in, they immediately locked the doors. "Let's get out of here," Triana panted, out of breath from running. She turned the ignition and floored it. As they pulled out of the lot, Mia looked back. She spotted the man standing in front of the theater, watching them leave. "What in the Goddess' name was that?" Triana kept looking at her wildly and then back to the road. The distance from the assailant wasn't calming her down.

"I don't know. I was waiting for the movie, and then I was in her head. Luce… Lucy? I could feel him. It was like I was her, seeing through her eyes, knowing everything she knew. It was like my dreams," Mia put her head back against the vinyl seats. "We have to help her. Her father… he… the man implied her dad wouldn't try to protect her from him." Triana eyed Mia for a second. Fear gripped her. "It was real… it was so real," Mia murmured. The shakes were back. She ran her hands through her hair, trying to hide the tremors. Her world was spinning out of control again. After the last few months of peace, it hit her harder than ever before.

"Let's drive around. Try to find her." Triana turned onto a side street only a couple blocks from the theater. The neighborhood wasn't a good one. Trash was sitting in front of old industrial buildings. Brick and cement had fallen into disrepair. Graffiti covered whole sections of the walls. It wasn't late, but buildings blocked the sun, creating a gloomy feel.

Mia desperately searched for blonde hair. All the buildings were familiar in a hazy way. She placed herself back in the girl's head… her last thoughts. She wouldn't go home, not tonight, but would it be more dangerous on the streets?

"Mia…" Triana started, but then fell silent. Mia peered down alleyways and waited. "When we met, you read me," Triana prompted. "You didn't tell me everything you saw." Again, a statement. Mia focused in on her. Triana took in a deep breath and plunged ahead. "Can you tell me the rest?"

Mia's stomach dropped. The images were still vibrant in her memory. She pulled her hoodie tight around her. "I saw the man in the other images…"

"He died," Triana confirmed with a sad smile. "Was there anything else?"

Mia thought back; the despair of that image had almost obscured the last things she had witnessed. "Yes," she confirmed. "I saw a man talking. He said the term 'lanamnas eicne no sleithe'." She struggled, trying to capture the pronunciation from her memory. "Then I saw a woman- she looked like you but older, with white hair. She was holding out her hand, and you were grasping it." Mia closed her eyes as the emotions attached to the final image returned. It was like relief, joy, and sorrow all wrapped into one.

But the final moment of pain- that she couldn't say out loud. If anyone had that kind of pain in their future, it was best they didn't know about it. All of her visions came true— she had never avoided any of them.

Triana turned even paler than normal. She sat back in her seat, her mind in turmoil. Triana drove silently. They continued through the back streets. Mia turned back to searching and was lost in thoughts of the girl's predicament when Triana mentally rejoined her.

The streets were coming to life as the sun set. New people were moving to the street corners and hanging out on stoops. Mia knew the girl would be nowhere near this crowd. She nodded dejectedly to Triana's silent question. Triana turned towards home.

"Mia, I think it's time you met your family."

CHAPTER THREE

Mia tumbled out of the old and dusty truck into the middle of the Appalachian Mountains. The sun was setting, turning the sky a warm rose. The trees sported a variety of colors: golds, reds, yellows. The farther the sun sank on the horizon, the darker the forest became, losing life and turning into dark hulking shadows. They seemed to be in the middle of nowhere. They had been driving for the last two days; the tension growing each hour. The last day had been completely quiet.

Mia looked around at the dense forest in front of them. They had entered the woods through a small service road that looked abandoned, yet before them stood trucks and cars sporting plates from all across the United States. As Mia reached back into the truck to grab her knapsack, Triana whispered the first words she had said in hours.

"Leave it." Then she started towards the woods, almost in a trance. Triana began to talk in a low voice. "Once a year on Samhain, the council convenes. All the clans meet to talk about the challenges facing them and ask for help from each other. If anyone can answer who or what you are, it is the members of the council." Mia winced on the 'what.'

"Wait," Mia grabbed her arm. "You said I was like you." The touch let Triana's fear move up Mia's hand from the point of contact. Triana flinched, pulling her arm away, then reluctantly met Mia's gaze.

"You are... more than I am." Triana frowned and walked into the woods.

Mia pulled her hoodie across her body, hugging herself. She could feel Triana pushing her away mentally and physically. The cold sank in past her skin. Singing voices and noise came from ahead of her, but Mia felt like she should turn away. Anyone that caused Triana so much fear couldn't be good. But Triana had come here for her, was facing her fears for Mia. She couldn't desert Triana now.

The crunch of dead leaves sounded like firecrackers to Mia's ears as she followed Triana. Mia had always lived in the burbs, and the darkness of the surrounding forest was intimidating. There was a warm glow ahead, and she headed towards it. Right before she stumbled into the clearing, she noticed Triana standing half in the light and half in the shadows, watching the scene in front of them. A look of pain transformed her features as she watched.

The clearing full of people was actually larger than Mia had expected. Tents were up around the periphery with a huge bonfire in the center. At the far end of the clearing was a log cabin. Everyone was in groups, drinking and laughing, but then looking suspiciously over at the other people around. Mia couldn't tell if it was the fire or the large group of people, but a warmth beckoned her forward.

Mia and Triana stood there a long time. Eventually, a young red-haired girl in her early teens noticed them. The girl froze in her tracks for a minute, then yelled, "Gaels!" Around the camp, others picked up the cry. People converged on them, stopping around ten feet away.

"Mia, what was the first thing I taught you as an Elemental?" Slowly, with her head held high, Triana stepped into the clearing without waiting for an answer. The crowd shifted as she walked, giving her a wide berth. *The first thing?* Mia stepped after her, knowing she did not look nearly as proud or beautiful. To prove the point, she tripped over her own sneakers. She stayed as close to

Triana's back as she could, her heart pounding in her ears. The crowd ceased calling and was eerily quiet in order to hear everything.

Triana arrived in front of the cabin at the far end of the clearing. What was the first thing? Was this going to be some kind of test?? A line of older people stood waiting for them. Each person looked wildly different, but the lady in the middle drew Mia's gaze. Streaks of snow white weaved through her hair. A variety of braids graced her head and traveled down her back. She was wearing a soft lavender tunic over loose-fitting pants. Silver chains and necklaces dripped from her neck, and rings covered her fingers. In one hand, she held a tall wooden staff with a carved decorative top. She was the woman from the vision, the older version of Triana. The woman focused on Triana. As Triana met her gaze, Mia could hear the quickening of Triana's breath.

"You are not welcome here, daughter. You made your choice long ago." The woman's voice was rich and deep.

"This is your MOM!?" Mia hissed, looking back and forth between them. They both had the same regal bearing, the same heart-shaped face. Triana ignored Mia.

"I am not here for myself, Mother." Mia shot Triana another look. "I bring a child of our people who was abandoned in the human world."

"I was not abandoned," Mia muttered under her breath. Triana finally spared her a glance. Mia widened her eyes to say, *Well I wasn't*. Mia moved her annoyed gaze back to the old lady and found herself under the scrutiny of everyone on the porch.

"Show us your arms, girl," a voice commanded.

"She has no marks," Triana offered.

"Then she is not one of us." The old woman turned away. The crowd began to whisper and talk.

"Take her hand," Triana challenged, raising her voice over the crowd. Mia pulled her hands into her hoodie. Silence reigned once more. Everyone was staring at Mia.

"No!" Mia exclaimed to anyone who would listen. "No, I don't want to."

Triana turned her full attention to Mia. "You have to trust me on this," she said confidently, but her aura said the opposite. The old lady glided toward them, eyeing Mia disdainfully.

"Give me your hand, child."

Mia hesitated, inspecting the old woman. Deep lines surrounded the woman's eyes. Her face was paler than Mia's own. The woman held out her hand, palm up. She waited without moving, but her blue eyes held a challenge. Mia raised her hand over the woman's and let it descend, keeping their eyes locked with one another. Immediately, strong images flooded Mia.

> An older man unwilling to touch a small girl as she asked for a hug. Two identical children, one in a casket. Being stopped in the mountains by a man wearing a swastika. A ship on the ocean, claustrophobia. A laurel crown placed on a young woman's head. Teaching children too young to be afraid. Facing Triana and having to turn her back.

The images kept coming, swirling, buzzing incessantly. The rapid pace made Mia nauseous, but the lady's grip was tight. She still stared at Mia; her eyes seeming to pierce into her soul.

Mia's knees buckled. As she fell, the woman let go of her hand. Desperately, Mia tried to find her equilibrium. The old lady just stood before her. Triana was still staring ahead. The crowd surrounding them watched Mia curiously. The woods were quiet except for the occasional crack from the bonfire.

"How old are you?" Mia gasped out. Nazis? Mia focused on the older lady's loafers until her head cleared. Everyone was still staring, but no one moved to help her up. Mia seemed to be on trial, and everyone thought she was guilty.

"She is Aether," the old woman eventually announced. "I need the four priestesses."

Four women worked their way through the crowd, each dressed in a different color. They were of different ages but possessed a gravity that made them stand out from their people. A soft murmur went through the crowd. Mia could hear the word 'Cailleach' repeated over and over. The women formed a diamond around Triana's mother and the bonfire. From a belt on her waist, Triana's mother untied a bag and weighed it in her hand. Then, she walked in a circle, making eye contact and nodding to each of the four other women. The women sang softly in a language Mia didn't understand. Triana's mother walked back up to her and looked into Mia's eyes. Then Triana's mother chanted softly. Energy flowed between them. Mia felt the hairs on her arm stand up. The air filled with static electricity. Mia wanted to see how the four women created this kind of energy flow, but Triana's mother held Mia in her sway.

Finally, Mia was released. Triana's mother bowed her head to the bag in her hands as she continued to speak. Then she knelt and allowed the contents of the bag to flow onto the ground. The woman throwing runes surprised Mia. One of the many books Triana had given Mia was on runes. The jet-black stones had familiar carved symbols on top. Frustrated, Mia didn't remember what each one meant. Triana's mother stared at the runes. She swayed, then fell to the ground. The four women around her fell silent. The energy around the women dissipated. With the other ladies' help, Triana's mother stood.

"The Goddess and the Moirae have spoken. The council must meet," Triana's mother announced, then shuffled towards the cabin. The people on the porch held a quick meeting. As they conversed, some looked at Mia periodically. Mia's heart wouldn't stop racing. Eventually, Triana's mother turned back to Mia and Triana.

"Triana, join us in the council chamber. The girl shall wait here." Triana's mother's gaze returned to the individuals on the porch. "Check with your people and then return to the council chamber." With that, she disappeared into the cabin. Triana turned to Mia.

"Sit on the porch," Triana said. "I promise to let you know what happens."

"Why are we here? Triana, who are these people?" Mia looked around. Everyone had dispersed into groups.

"It is hard to explain quickly. These are our people." Triana's gaze around the clearing was tinged with wistfulness. "They have the answers you seek. They will figure out who your parents are, why you are so gifted, why you have no marks."

"Why is everyone so obsessed with my arms?" Mia asked defensively.

"Traditionally, Aether have at least a clan mark on them by their sixteenth birthday. You are well past that, but you have no markings." Pausing, Triana shook her head. "I do not understand it; you are definitely one of us, but... I must go. Stay here, I will tell you everything that I can."

With Triana gone, Mia was alone. The people who once stood on the porch returned to the cabin, leaving packs of people speaking and gesturing wildly behind them. Mia slowly moved up onto the porch, walking to an old wicker chair. It was difficult to keep her head up and not show fear as she sensed people watching her from all over the camp. She wanted to find a mirror to make sure she hadn't grown a third eye, or worse - a huge zit, acting like a beacon. She focused on looking calm.

Mia started to list out questions she would pummel Triana with at the next opportunity. And then she waited, long enough for people to settle back into their groups. Every so often an older person would mount the porch and enter the small cabin without looking in her direction. She wanted to return to the truck to get her books but was afraid to leave the porch.

The tension slowly evaporated. The only sign of the upset that had occurred when Mia arrived was the eyes of a random person staring at her periodically. If Mia stared back, they would avert their gaze, moving on.

The noise and music returned. From the old cabin's porch, Mia watched people of all ages celebrating around the bonfire in the middle of the square. A chain of female dancers moved around the fire, including ladies that had to be in their eighties to girls her own age. Long, full orange skirts swished as lithe arms moved gracefully over their heads. As the dancers finished their round, they moved back to their own region with rousing cheers emanating from the people surrounding them.

After about an hour of observation, Mia recognized the dividing lines of five different camps. The tents had a bit of ground separating each distinct area, and the colors marked them too. The women in the old-fashioned dress came from the yellow camp. Their tents had yellow and orange ribbons circling the poles holding them up. There were also blue, black, purple, and green camps.

There were people of all ages. The majority were older, but quite a few teenagers were interspersed in the crowd. Everyone had marks up their very muscular arms. The younger had one or two, while the older sported full sleeves. The design of their clothes left their arms, and shoulders exposed. Despite the night chill, a few had openings in the back of their shirts, letting tattoos peek through.

It was mainly the young who were brazen enough to stare openly at her. Mia shifted in her seat, wishing she could move. There was something different about the teenagers here than at home. They laughed and talked, but they had a gravity and a confidence she wasn't used to. They all appeared athletic and muscular. Something else was odd too, though she couldn't put her finger on it. She walked to the far end of the porch, stretching her legs. The cool night air made her grateful for the warmth of her hoodie. Another person stared at her, this time a lanky teen about Mia's age with dark red hair.

"Is there something in my teeth?" Mia asked, sure he would scurry away like all the others.

"No," he answered, hopping up on the porch. "My name is Colin." He held out his hand in greeting, but Mia didn't take it. She may be able to control her visions with normal people, but she knew no one here was normal. "Of the family Nuelle?" After a beat, he let his hand drop. "And you are?"

"Mia. Mia Keen."

Colin looked her up and down, but not in a threatening way. He wore an off-white shirt with a pencil behind his ear and carried a leather notebook. Her skin broke out in goosebumps as she nervously looked at the boy out of the corner of her eye. Was she supposed to talk to anyone?

"So… do you know what's going on?" he ventured. The absurdity of the question unlocked something in Mia. She started to laugh. And laugh. She couldn't control it, and the harder she tried to stop, the more it poured out. Tears ran down her face. "Are you okay?"

The laughter turned into the giggles.

"I'm sorry," Mia gasped. "I'm sorry… I.. I just…." she slowly sobered. "I have no idea," she choked out. Then knowing she hadn't quite explained her own special brand of crazy… "I'm exhausted."

"Well, sitting in a chair for hours can do that to you," Colin shrugged. He moved over to one of the wicker chairs and sat down. His long limbs stretched out in front of him. Mia moved toward him warily, some of her tension gone with the laughing fit.

"I don't even know what this is," she gestured at the camp in front of the cabin.

"How about I make you a deal? You answer my questions and I'll answer yours?"

"I don't know if I know anything worth knowing," Mia said. "But I'll try."

"Deal!" He sat up in his chair. "This," he mimicked her gesture, "is the Samhain council meeting. Once a year, the clans get together to bring our problems to the council and ask for help. Nothing happens. Each clan has so many of its own problems, they cannot help anyone else. Mainly, we meet because it is tradition." He shrugged his shoulder again. "Your turn, where did you grow up so that the Aether didn't know you existed?"

"Connecticut," Mia answered reflexively. She watched disbelief cross his face. "What? My mom and I lived in Connecticut. I didn't even know 'Aether' existed until about six months ago when I met Triana." Mia looked out at the camp. She shifted through the thousands of questions she had been storing for Triana as she sat down in her own chair, hugging her legs in front of her as an extra barrier to the bizarre world off of the porch. Better to start simple.

"Everyone here is Aether?"

"No." He leaned forward. "They represent all five of the European clans." Mia gave him a blank look. "You don't know about the clans?" She shook her head. "Man, you really are from Connecticut," he laughed softly.

Mia couldn't bring herself to answer, feeling as stupid as he implied. She hugged her legs tighter, looking away so he didn't see the hurt on her face.

"Hey, no offense intended. It is just hard to imagine anyone not knowing... well... one of us not knowing." He paused. When she didn't respond, he sat up straight and tried a new tactic. "You know we are Elementals, right?"

"Yeah... no... I know we are Aether but I don't exactly understand what that means..." When she had searched on the Internet, she couldn't make sense of the conflicting information. Apparently, Aether referred to air? Or a chemical? All the philosophies from the ancient world didn't make sense as a people.

Colin shook his head. "It's hard to explain. We are all Elementals. Basically, each of the clans represent one Element of nature: Water, Wind, Fire, Earth and Essence. Each of the clans have their Element at their core." He walked to the edge of the porch like a teacher giving a lecture. "There are five clans. The Aether... which you and I are a part of. We represent the quintessence or the essence." He pointed to the purple camp.

"The Water Clan," he gestured toward the camp with the blue ribbons around their tents. Most of the people in that section wore at least one piece of dark blue clothing. "The Gnomes: The Earth Clan." The green camp.

"Wait... Gnomes?" She puzzled. "Like the things that people put in gardens?"

"No, and I would not reference those around a Gnome," he laughed. "Or if you do, make sure I am there to see it." He motioned to the yellow camp. "Those are the Sylph: The Wind Clan. And then there are the Salamanders: The Fire Clan." The black camp. "The people in the cabin are the representatives of each clan. They make up the council. The clans only get together this one time each year. Other than that, the clans avoid each other."

"I guess that's why Triana never mentioned them." Mia examined each camp again. They looked normal, only... exceptionally... well, large compared to everyone she had ever met. "Do you live among non-Elemental people? Or do all of you live at the gym? I mean, how have I never heard of you?"

"Okay… too many questions at once," he considered. "Each clan lives in communities of their own. We have some contact with the humans, but not a lot. You grew up in the human world… I have so many questions-"

"My father met my mother… However briefly," she finished under her breath. "If Elementals don't interact with the human world…"

"Well, I should say most Aether do not, but even we have people who trade and work in the human world. Most of us prefer to be where we don't have to pretend we are something we're not. As for the gym thing, well, I think we are a bit bigger than humans… barely. This is not a real representation of the Elementals. Mostly the clans send their warriors to Samhain, to show off. I am a bit of a runt, but I would say I am closer to normal for Aether."

Her eyes widened slightly. For a runt, he still towered several inches taller than her. True, he wasn't a walking steroid advertisement like most of the teens she had seen, but that wasn't exactly a bad thing to her mind. There was no way to say that to someone she barely knew, so she let her gaze wander back to the camps.

Other than the ribbons, there were other things that marked each group of people. Besides the general muscle-bound physique, the members of each group had roughly the same hair and skin coloring. The Fire clan were dark; black hair, dark clothes. Their skin was darker than the others, an olive tone that held a rich tan cut through by black tattoos. The Sylph were petite, thinner, with pale blonde hair. Unlike the Fire clan, they sported yellow tattoos, a range of pale yellow to dark burnt sienna and every shade in between. The Gnomes had an earthy look, dark brown hair with warm sun-browned skin. The brown tattoos made their skin appear darker. The Undine had light brown hair, many with blonde highlights. They looked straight off a beach somewhere. Their tattoos had a range of colors again, from the palest blue that barely showed on the skin to dark navy.

Mia looked back to Colin. He had dark red hair, distinctly different from Mia's vibrant red. "Do all the Aether have red hair and pale skin?" As she surveyed the crowd, she realized there were more red heads than she had ever seen in one place before. Each of the red heads had tattoos, but unlike Triana's pure white, they went from a soft lavender to a deep purple.

"Well, that is another question, and I never finished with the last set... but pretty much." He met her eyes. "Can you really read other Aether? Did you read Cailleach Malta?" Mia recoiled slightly. She swallowed and looked away. "You did, didn't you?" Slowly, she nodded, bracing herself for the look of horror.

"I don't mean to," she whispered, then turned away.

"That is amazing." Her head shot back. Colin was grinning. "The Moirae only give a few the ability to read other Aether. Malta... and... well... she is the only one I know," he laughed. "Well, until now."

"That old woman is Malta?" Mia asked.

"Yes. She is on the council. She is also my clan's Cailleach."

"What's a Cailleach?" Mia inquired.

"A priestess. Usually the strongest Aether and a leader in the clan. But, I have never known anyone who could read Malta. So what you can do... is rare." Mia tried to match his grin. It turned out as more of a grimace. She forced her muscles to relax.

"It doesn't freak you out?" she asked.

"Not really." Again, the automatic shrug. He stopped and watched the bonfire for a couple of minutes. "Not that I want you in my head, mind you, but... that kind of ability... it is... incredible."

"I'm not so sure about that." That reminded her. "What is the mor-some-thing?"

"The Moirae? Those are the three fates. The Aether believe they are three spirits who control a person's destiny. Some of the other clans believe they are the three faces of the Goddess: Maiden, Mother, and Crone, and the Goddess leads you to your destiny instead of controlling it."

As Mia mulled over the new information, she watched the people around the bonfire. People were disappearing, going somewhere to sleep probably. A few teens stayed out, exchanging barbs around the fire. They had been drinking. Mia stifled a yawn. Pulling her hoodie closer, she huddled up in the wicker chair. Colin stared at the people out near the campfire, making notes in his notebook periodically. Colin and Mia sat like that for a long while.

"Do you know where they sent everyone?" Colin asked. Mia had started to doze off, but she snapped to attention.

"Huh?"

"Right after you arrived, the Air, Fire, and Water clans sent someone away. I couldn't figure out why," he glanced at her, "But I guess they are keeping you in the dark as much as everyone else."

The voices around the fire began hitting higher notes. A black female moved aggressively towards a boy, a large brown-haired teen. Little could be seen of their faces, but their postures spoke of a fight. The boy was getting in her face now. Mia and Colin stood up and moved to the edge of the porch.

"Prove it, dirt boy."

"Shut up, Lizard," the boy spat.

"They do say, Gnomes know no honor," she taunted. With a roar, he picked the girl up and threw her at the bonfire. Her landing sent logs flying. The other teens moved out of the way.

"Oh my God, she's going to be hurt!" Mia ran down the stairs but Colin grabbed her hand and held her still. Her eyes darted to his hands, but no images came. She looked up at him in shock.

"Wait for it." His eyes never left the scene in front of them. His body was tense and at attention. She turned back, ready to struggle free to help the girl in the bonfire. She would have third-degree burns. It might kill her. The girl only laughed as her shirt caught fire. Slowly she came to her feet and removed the jean shirt covering her tank top.

"Did I hit a nerve?" the Fire girl jeered. Before the boy responded, several of his compatriots grabbed him and pulled him away from the ruckus. A slender Gnome girl took his arm. Over her shoulder, the female Gnome sent the Fire teen a condescending dismissal. The Fire girl picked up a burning log in response and tossed it. It landed in a shower of sparks at the Gnomes' feet. The boy turned slowly, spit at the ground, then walked away. The Fire girl didn't move, not even when her friends tried to pull her back towards the tents. Wait... up against her friends it became more obvious... she had darker skin than everyone else's, a light brown to their olive tones, her hair wiry to their smooth locks. Who was this woman? Only when the brown-headed boy entered a tent and vanished from sight did the fierce warrior storm out of the clearing.

"What in the hell?" Mia turned on Colin. The tension had already left his body, however, Mia's adrenaline still rushed through her veins. These people were crazy, lunatics. Why was she here? "He could have killed her, but the fire didn't touch her, and what is wrong with you people?!?" Too many questions. Right then, she realized Colin still held on to her, so she shrugged him off.

"She is a Salamander. The fire cannot hurt her." He picked up his notebook. "I have never seen it before.. only heard..." He trailed off, making notes.

"Lizard," she repeated the earlier taunt with greater understanding. "Fire can't hurt them?!" Colin nodded. "Is this normal?" She followed Colin. Maybe she should leave. Take the truck and keep driving until she could find a hotel... a faraway hotel with normal people. But then what?

"Tensions can get high by the final nights," Colin remarked absently. "My brother says more people hook up than fight."

"Hook up?" Mia squeaked. *What kind of sick cult am I in the middle of??* Her skin crawled and the light hoodie no longer kept her warm. Colin's face turned dark red. Full body blushes appeared to be an Aether characteristic as well. Colin shuffled his feet, looking anywhere but at her.

"I wouldn't, or don't, I mean.. it isn't..." Colin stammered.

"Stop!" Mia ordered, trying to end the uncomfortable explanation. She tried to gather her thoughts but failed. Too many things she needed to take in, too many world altering revelations for a few hours. Fire… Water… Earth… Air… and Aether. Neither of the fighters had been Aether. And here there may be someone to help her control her gift. The image of the black woman kept floating back into Mia's head. Perhaps because the Salamander differed from the others around her, Mia felt a connection with her. She took one wistful glance at the path to the truck, then settled in. As much as she hated crowds, Mia would willingly stay if it meant controlling her visions.

Mia and Colin stayed silent, the awkwardness slowly fading into the night. Eventually the comfortableness that had marked their earlier conversations returned. It surprised Mia. Other people never made her comfortable. But unlike everyone else in this camp, Colin seemed open and honest with her. He didn't seem to judge or threaten. He just accepted. Acceptance hadn't been a large part of her life.

"Thank you," she whispered. He looked up from his notebook, surprised. "For…" she floundered, "for talking to me." She mimicked his shrug, and he laughed softly.

"Thank you for letting me." His face contorted as if he was about to say something more, just as the door to the cabin opened. The council members came out. Most of the council members glanced over at Mia as they returned to their camps. The older lady that Colin had called Malta, Triana's mother, came out last. The woman paused in the doorway.

"You can go in… Mia." Malta looked past her to Colin. "Go back to your camp, boy." Colin nodded, immediately darting away. Mia didn't move until Malta walked down the stairs. When she reached the bottom, Malta turned back. "And Mia…." She considered her words. "Welcome home."

CHAPTER FOUR

The next day passed slowly. Mia's whole body ached from holding so much tension yesterday. Her dreams had been fiery, with smoke so thick in her mind that she woke up coughing.

Mia watched from the windows of the cabin as people moved back and forth. A group of Fire teens built up the wood for the coming night's bonfire. Eyes would inevitably move towards the cabin. Triana stayed in the bedroom all morning. Triana was shell-shocked. As much as Mia wanted to question her, she waited. After grabbing her books from the truck, Mia found that though they had allowed her an escape from reality all her life, they couldn't help her now. The words blurred under her gaze. Sentences made little sense since she forgot the beginning before she made it to the end. The waiting seemed endless. Books only chronicled the important moments. The pauses and waits disappeared in the chapter breaks. *What character would she be... not the heroine... the comic relief? Or because of her 'gift', the villain?*

Tensions mounted as the sun set. Triana found the bedroom too small for her pacing, so she invaded the living room as well. Eventually, Triana stopped and took a breath. "You are to be presented to all the clans tonight, Mia," she confessed.

Mia's heart leaped into her chest. "Presented?" she yelped.

"Malta has had a vision," Triana sat down on the armchair across from Mia's spot at the window. "She thinks there are others like you. Without the marks. But the other Council members do not believe it. We will find out tonight if each clan has a…. teen… like you. If they do, they will present them tonight."

Mia looked back out the window. Her skin was alive with goose pimples. Triana waited for Mia to ask questions, but Mia's voice left her. This was it, when they realize she's a freak and kick her out. The rejection before her felt keen, even though only moments before she had contemplated running. As weird as these people were, they accepted her. Mia had a hope of being just another kid, but even in this world she'd be a misfit. Her chest was at war, trying to figure out what she wanted. She came up empty.

"I thought maybe we should get ready?"

"Ready?" Mia turned.

"When I am about to face something… unknown," Triana smiled. "I am always more confident if I look my best."

Mia laughed. With all that is about to happen, did it really matter what she looked like? However, on inspection, she realized she was a crumpled mess. Oil had built up in her hair and on her face. It has been over forty-eight hours since her last shower.

"Subtle," Mia mocked. With a final glance out the window, she began to freshen up.

An hour later, Mia sat back, refreshed, her red locks still damp. She wore the best clothes she had in her bag, a nice dark pair of jeans and a white tank. Triana lent her a lavender button up. Malta had joined them to give Mia a once over. As night fell, people gathered around the roaring bonfire. Instead of the lively conversations from the night before, everyone spoke in hushed tones. They knew something huge was about to happen, but no one was sure what.

Once Malta decided Mia would pass inspection, she turned to her daughter and reached out her hands. "Triana, I am glad you are home," she pronounced, attempting to pull Triana into a hug. Triana moved across the room.

"I didn't think I would be welcome," Triana confronted her mother.

"You are my daughter… I am happy you have returned," her mother declared. "Please, I have missed you. We cannot erase the past, but I hope our future has not been written." Malta approached her daughter again. Triana watched her warily but stayed still. Malta brushed Triana's hair out of her face. Triana smiled at the maternal gesture.

"Thank you, mother." Despair and pain radiated off both of them. But also a sliver of hope. The last image she had seen when she first read Triana. Then Mia's body tensed. Pain was how the image had left her. Her eyes darted around the room wildly. What would happen now? "But the other Aether…"

"Even if things have not worked out as I hoped, you have still achieved a great deal. This will catapult you to the highest ranks of the Aether," Malta smiled with pride.

"I do not understand," Triana looked at her mother warily. "The council banished me…"

"You rejected our people. You had to do so," her mother conceded. "But the Aether only saw the rejection. You destroyed a treaty with the Salamanders…"

"I was not going to marry my brother," Triana scoffed.

"Brother?" Mia whispered.

"Brother-in-law," Malta corrected them both. "It was a brilliant alliance." Malta frowned. "Even if you decided against it, you should not have run away. I would have found a way-"

"They were not going to give me a choice," Triana bit out.

"The law is clear. The woman has a say. You could have broken the hand-fasting. You acted like a child. Do you realize what we had to do to smooth it over with the Salamanders?" she clucked.

"Mia," Triana addressed her without looking her way, "tell my Mother what you saw in your vision. What did the man on the council say to my betrothed?"

"Lanamnas eicne no sleithe," Mia stumbled over the unfamiliar words. The older woman paused. Triana expected shock, but the pause took her by surprise.

"You knew?" Instead of yelling, Triana's voice had moved down an octave. "Marriage by trickery, Mother. The council advised him to do whatever necessary to secure the marriage and you KNEW?!" Tears were running down her face. "I trusted in the council and they advised someone... to do whatever needed to create the political alliance they wanted."

Mia stared. Trickery? What had been in the bottle the older man carried in the vision? Mia took a step forward, ready to stand between the two women. The need to protect Triana from her... mother... was overwhelming.

"An Aether who is not an Aether," the woman answered calmly. Triana looked like someone had punched her in the stomach. "I had hoped you were the one."

Mia looked back and forth between them. She was missing something but didn't dare ask what. A tense silence fell. Noise increased outside the windows, accentuating the lack of sound inside.

Eventually, Malta crossed to Triana and softly said, "I am sorry." Triana moved away. Someone pounded on the door, causing Mia to jump.

"Everything will be better now. This is all part of the prophecy. The council may have appeared to betray you, but actually they sent you to your destiny. I thought you would be... Your running away brought us Mia. She will fulfill the prophecy." Malta's voice sounded disappointed. Mia wasn't sure if she should feel insulted or inadequate. "And once the Aether see the purpose in all of this, they will accept you. Our family will rise to prominence again." Triana recoiled.

"This is not about the prophecy," Triana cried in a panic.

"Of course it is." Triana stood in a daze, trying to grasp what her mother meant. "Mia is our future. Your work is done. Now you can just be my daughter again." Then Malta turned her gaze on Mia with a look so intense the young girl took a step back. Mia waited for Triana to yell, argue, or lash out, but she just stood there stunned.

"I will go with her," Triana finally whispered. Her mother took her measure, then nodded.

"I agree. The people should see how important your role is."

"Wait!" Triana woke up from her trance. Running to her bag of crystals, she pulled out a pendant with a dull orange stone. "Wear this."

"Carnelian?" her mother scoffed. "That is an air stone. She cannot wear that!"

In a lower voice, Triana continued. "They say carnelian helps you find your true destiny, not the one that others have planned for you. I have worn this pendant for so many years, I cannot count them. I hope it will guide you tonight." Triana's intensity implied a greater meaning than she could vocally convey. Mia allowed Triana to put the pendant on her, and in the process faced Malta. The older woman wanted to argue but thought better of it.

"Wear it under your tunic." Malta gave a disapproving look to Triana. "Remain on the porch, Triana," she ordered, then turned to Mia. "Stay with me child and do as I say." Malta headed toward the front door, then stopped. "All will be well," she finished in a soft voice. Then, before Mia's eyes, Malta grew in height and presence. It was as if the woman had pulled all the surrounding energy into her own orbit, radiating power.

As Malta opened the door to the cabin, her name echoed in whispered form, moving through the crowd. Mia followed in her footsteps, trying to appear confident, or at least not like a frightened kid. Triana stood behind her, attempting to lend Mia the strength she needed, but Triana radiated panic and fear. It didn't help, and Mia couldn't understand it. As soon as this was over, they would have a long conversation about Elementals and prophecies and non-burning fire people. If she thought there was even a chance of avoiding her this time, Triana underestimated just how pissed Mia was.

CHAPTER FIVE

"Good people, brethren, children of the universe, of nature in all its miracles, I greet you." Malta swept into a small bow, and the people in the crowd matched her. "Today will be the beginning of a new era. This will be the most important Samhain our people have had in over four hundred years. For today is the day all will change." She allowed the import of her words to work its way through the crowd. "Each of our clans has one who has not been marked, yet they will be the markers of a new age. From the Aether, I present to you Mia, daughter of Alain, of the family Thesek."

Mia's eyes went wide. *The family Thesek? What is she talking about?* Mia wanted to ask Triana. However, Malta gestured her forward. "Guess the questions can wait," Mia muttered under her breath. She moved down the stairs, leaving Triana and her support behind on the porch. A man with black hair moved forward from the black camp. Mia vaguely recognized him from the porch yesterday. Her eyes narrowed. He looked a lot like an older version of Triana's husband.

"The Salamander Clan presents McKenna, daughter of Aiden, of the family Ognyan. She is one of our fiercest warriors." The girl from the fight yesterday moved forward. From her combat boots to the fitted tank top that revealed muscled arms, she dressed all in black. Mia watched the aura around her in wonder. Pride and joy were mixed with anger and defiance. McKenna seemed to shake with the intensity of her emotion.

From the brown camp, another of the council moved forward. "The Gnome clan presents Damek, son of Delphi, of the family Delphin. He is one of our most skilled and learned engineers!" The Gnome from the fight yesterday moved forward. Unlike McKenna's pride, Damek appeared cautious. Distrust of the proceedings, yet a palpable curiosity surrounded him. Damek and McKenna eyed each other warily.

Then from the blue camp came a woman in a sweeping blue gown. "The Undines presents Calder, son of Maris of the family Kallan. He is faster than the waves." A Greek god moved forward, muscled with curling gold brown hair that had captured the sun's rays. The only thing around him was confidence so strong that Mia could feel herself being pulled into his orbit.

Finally, a man moved forward from the yellow camp. An air of menace surrounded him, making Mia shuffle backwards. Though he had the same white blond hair and blue eyes as the rest of the yellow camp, he seemed darker. Shadows dominated his face, filling his sunken eyes and cheekbones. "We have only been able to track one who has not been marked by their seventeenth birthday, but she is not worthy to be presented here in front of this esteemed council."

Malta's voice rang above the crowd. "Why?"

"As many of you are aware, several of our children have become addicted to a human drug called Coro. This girl," he snarled the word, "has used the drug. She is not a fit representative of the Sylph."

"Is she here?" Malta returned.

"Yes, but I beg you…"

"You will present her," Malta demanded. The man flinched at her tone, and then retreated to a tent in the yellow camp. Coro, why did that sound familiar? Within a minute, he returned, dragging one of the most petite girls Mia had ever seen. Blonde hair hung limply around her shoulders, falling almost to her waist. A simple dark yellow shift with matching pants hung off of her. Her aura was black and blue like a bruise, full of pain, fear, and desperation. The man pulled her forward and pushed her in Malta's direction. The girl crumpled to the ground in the center of the circle. Bones protruded from what little parts of her body could be seen past her robes. Gasps went up from every camp as they looked at the girl. She stayed on the floor, her eyes moving desperately around, trying to take in the world around her. Her eyes locked with Mia's. Mia fell to her knees as a rush of pain hit her. The necklace Triana gave her pulsed, and the image of the orange carnelian flashed in front of her.

Her entire body started to ache, the tenderness of bruises all along her sides. As she inhales a breath, a stab of pain pulsates in her chest. Blonde hair falls into her face as she attempts to lift her head.

"Stupid bitch," a voice mutters above her. "Is it a man you are trying to run away to, Brisa?" There is no point in answering. In the beginning, she had attempted to explain, but it has been such a long time since he has listened to any word she said. Instead, even trying to use her voice angered him. Unbidden flashes of laughing teens, gyrating to a pulsing beat flooded through her mind. The images cause more pain than her father's hand as it slaps her, trying to force her to respond. He can't understand. It isn't a boy. It's the freedom, the joy those teens possessed. That is what she wants. She allows her head to roll back. She can barely see her father through the fog in her mind. The image of him from what must have been weeks ago is easier to focus on than the actual man before her. But that was before an act of rage left her waking up in a small room, chained to the wall.

"I've tried to take care of you, and this is what I get," he mutters, pacing the room again. The large man crouches to her eye level and pulls back her head by the hair. Though they have the same sky-blue eyes, his are full of fury. She knew her own eyes only hold fear. "What do you have to say?" He pulls harder on her hair, overextending her neck. When she refuses to respond, he continues. "No one will come for you. No one else cares about you. You are mine," he whispers in her ear, revulsion causing a tremor to move down her spine. He throws her head to the floor. Her forehead bounces against the hard-packed dirt, causing the world to darken. She can't raise her head to watch the man, but she can hear him walking away. "I'm sorry, but you have to learn," he hisses. The door closes behind him.

She stays still, afraid to move in case he will return. When the sound of his boots recedes, her eyes dart to the wood slats of the wall. With every ounce of strength she has left, she pulls herself forward. Her hand crawls up the wall to the top of the first slat. A crack in the plaster allows air from the outside into the room. The tantalizing breeze touches her fingertips. Her lungs seem to expand, taking in the Element's power. Her body may be broken but as long as she can find some wind, she will not let him take her soul.

"Wind," Mia croaked as she realized she was still staring into the blonde girl's eyes. Mia reached out to the girl. The brute who had pushed the girl into the circle grabbed Mia's arm, jerking her away. Mia fell backward. She looked up to the man from the vision.

"Stay away from her," he growled, putting himself between Mia and the girl.

Shakily, Mia faced the man looking down at the girl in disgust. Mia could see him through the girl's eyes and her own.

"You tortured her," she rasped. "You locked her up in chains." Anger pulsed through her, helping her to stand again. It wasn't just her own anger at the villain, but the anger that filled the poor girl in front of her.

"She is a drug addict. I locked her up to keep her away from…"

"You beat her into submission!" Mia roared. "I… she has never touched a drug." The certainty of her statement reverberated through her without knowing where it came from. "You know that."

"You question me?!" He moved towards Mia, raising an arm as if to cuff her. Suddenly, he found a sword at his neck. "How dare you?" He paused, afraid to move any further. "I am Camden. I am the brother of Boreas, King of our clan. I am royalty!" At Mia's side, the warrior McKenna held the sword to his throat. Behind her, Mia felt the presence of the two boys that had already been presented.

"It seems *we* question you," Calder smiled wickedly. Then deferred to Mia.

"She is an embarrassment. She is not a Sylph… she is….."

"You're right. She's not a Sylph. This girl is one of us now. You will never touch her again," McKenna announced.

"She is mine," he sputtered. The girl flinched, withdrawing into herself.

"Not anymore," Mia rejoined. She turned, but anger and frustration pulled her back to face him. "What did she do? She tried to explain but you wouldn't listen… what did I… what did she do that made you hate her so much… from childhood…" The words weren't her own, but they came pouring out of her mouth.

"It is not true… I saved her from herself," he retorted, appealing to his clan. "No one believes her." He gestured towards Mia condescendingly. "I am one of you. You know me. "

"She is Aether," came a voice from the crowd.

He gestured down at the blonde girl. "Brisa has always been willful and trouble. Ever since her mother died, I have taken care of her."

"It is true. She was always a spirited girl." The King of the Sylph clan, Boreas, stepped forward. Mia recognized him, even though she didn't know how. "But this girl in front of us is not the child I remember."

"These allegations are not true."

45

"Prove it," Damek's voice came over Mia's shoulder. "Take off your shirt." That silenced the crowd for a moment, then furious whispering broke out.

"I will not give power to these children," Camden snarled.

"Take off your shirt," Boreas ordered.

"You cannot believe…"

"Take off your shirt," Boreas' face was hard.

"No," Camden whispered. He began backing up, his head swiveling, looking for a way out.

"Then we will remove it for you," Boreas replied. Two warriors from the Sylph clan seized Camden.

"No," Camden protested, struggling wildly. Mia looked down at Brisa. Brisa sat, watching the display, horror on her face. But no protest issued from her lips. Mia wobbled as the attention focused on the spectacle before them. Mia's chest hurt, raw from the visions. Her body felt bruised from the beatings Brisa had received.

Calder immediately supported Mia's elbow. Desperate to remain standing, she leaned into his strength. Her eyes riveted to the struggling Camden as the two warriors pinned him down. King Boreas stepped up and used a knife to rip open the back of Camden's shirt.

"I don't understand, what's happening?" Mia whispered to her left.

"They are exposing his spine." Calder's gaze did not move off the struggle.

"Why?" Calder eyes flicked to her confused face.

"The marks of a person's soul form on their spines. The essence of who they are. If he has hurt others, if he is a man who would hurt his own child, it will show on his spine."

"No way," Mia muttered.

The warriors held Camden up, exposing his back to the assembled Elementals. Shock rippled through the crowd. Angry cries began. When they turned him towards Mia, she could see a series of dark russet symbols down the center of his back.

"What does his back say?" Mia whispered.

"I do not know the symbols for the Sylph well but they look similar to Undines… I think they are controlling, power hungry," Calder whispered. "The symbols, they can mean a variety of things, good or bad, so they will ask the Aether leader to read them. Each clan has members who can read the symbols but never as detailed as the Aether. Since all clans are here, only an Aether will be believed." The men carried Camden to the porch and held him in front of Malta. She moved forward and the entire crowd fell into a reverent silence. Malta's hand hovered above the symbols on his back. Her eyes closed, and the crowd waited.

"Mia speaks the truth," Malta called out after a few moments. "Camden only wanted to control his child. He knew the girl was not a victim of the Coro." She held for dramatic effect. "He has denied her the wind." Angry voices issued from the crowd.

"For how long?" Boreas stepped up.

"Almost a full cycle of the moon," Malta replied. The angry voices turned to yells.

"What does it mean, he denied her the wind?" Mia asked.

"Elementals must commune with their Element. If you do not, you sicken, and eventually die," Damek furiously replied from her right.

The girl caught Mia's eye again, and Mia instantly moved to her. Without thinking, Mia helped pull her up in a sitting position and hugged her. She felt Brisa's tears through her shirt. Mia just held her until they quieted. "Thank you." Mia heard Brisa whisper. When the girl pulled away, Brisa and Mia looked up to see everyone watching them. Boreas moved towards them, but the girl flinched and moved closer to Mia.

"Take him away," the Sylph leader commanded over his shoulder, keeping his gaze on the girl.

"Do the Sylph not question locked up children?" Malta questioned.

"I am devastated by these revelations. I beg you to consider, he is my brother. Can anyone ever believe their sibling is a monster?" He turned to the crowd. "I will live with the torment of this for the rest of my life. She is my blood. No Sylph should be denied the wind. There is no greater crime." He knelt in front of the girl. "Brisa, I am in your debt. The entire Sylph people are in your debt. There are no words to describe our sorrow for what you have suffered." A Sylph in the front of the crowd knelt like Boreas. Slowly, one by one, each of the Sylph dropped down on their knees. Mia examined the faces that now surrounded her. Brisa's body pushed upward, but very little movement resulted.

"Help her," Mia stated without thinking. Instantly, the brown headed Damek stooped down on the other side of Brisa and offered his hand. After quick consideration, Brisa placed her hand in his. Between Mia and Damek, they helped Brisa get to her feet, though she had to lean on Damek heavily.

Mia braced herself so she could stay by Brisa. Brisa looked at Boreas and met his gaze. At that moment, Boreas moved his hand to his mouth, then guided it towards her, releasing a breath. All the Sylph repeated the gesture.

A fierce wind worked its way around the crowd, circling Brisa at the center, pushing Damek and Mia back. Brisa's face arched toward the sky with a look of rapture. She reached for the heavens. The wind picked her up and lifted her a few feet. Brisa hovered in the air, the wind enveloping her. Then the gusts died out, leaving tears of joy in their wake. Brisa slowly returned to the ground. Everyone in the crowd looked on in wonder. She put out her hands to Mia. This time Brisa did not place her weight on Mia but requested support instead.

Brisa looked to Boreas. The entire crowd remained silent, waiting to hear what the girl would say. Finally, Brisa held out her hand. A shaky smile crossed her face. Boreas stood before her and carefully took the hand offered to him.

"Brisa, you are always Sylph. You are our kin. We will do anything for you. If you do not wish to join the other unmarked, you do not have to. I will create a home for you with my family, where you will never suffer again if I can prevent it." Brisa fell into his arms, accepting his proffered hug. After a minute or two, she pulled back. Her eyes took in the four teens standing in the center of the crowd.

"I will join them. If the Goddess has decreed it, it must be," Brisa announced, her voice tentative. She let go of Boreas' hand and moved towards them, stumbling slightly. Immediately, Mia and Damek moved to her, grasping her arms.

Suddenly, Mia felt a tingling. She looked down and found a silver tattoo on the inside of her wrist. It matched the one Triana had; two triangles on top of each other, almost like a Star of David. The mark looked white until the light from the fire hit it. It gleamed. She looked up to see the other teens staring at their own arms.

"We are marked," came the rich deep voice of Damek. He looked up and met Mia's eyes in wonder. He held up his own hand to show a down facing triangle with a line through it in the same spot as Mia's star. Damek's triangle was silver as well, but the contrast with his dark skin was strong.

"We are marked!" McKenna cried, lifting her arm to show the crowd a silver triangle. Hesitantly, Calder raised his arm, sporting a silver upside down triangle.

Voices raised from the crowd. "Show us!" "A silver mark!" Damek raised his arm higher in response to the requests. Brisa hid slightly behind Damek and moved up her arm, revealing a triangle and line matching Damek's, only facing the opposite direction. Mia turned, watching the awed faces of the crowd. The voices became a chant.

All eyes fastened on Mia now. She tried to meet the stares with poise, but she quaked in her boots. Mystified, she slowly lifted her arm like the others around her. Only the force of Mia's will kept it from shaking while the clans stared at the prominent silver mark.

"I present to you the new conclave," Malta's voice pulled their attention. "For years, we have met here to share our troubles. For years, we have been unable to help each other. The Goddess and the Moirae have now answered our prayers. They will be the ones to solve our problems. They will be the ones that usher in this new age. They will be our newest leaders. I have seen our future, and it rests in their hands." With that proclamation, each person in the clearing slowly bowed. The last to bow were the old council members. Some looked defiant but bowed to the will of the assembled throng and showed deference to the teens before them. Mia's shock was mirrored on the faces of the teens standing alongside her.

"The new council will meet. Tomorrow, we will not only celebrate Samhain, we will celebrate this momentous occasion!" Malta announced. A cheer went up amongst the crowd. Malta caught Mia's eye and gestured toward the cabin.

Mia whispered, "Follow me," to the surrounding people. Mia moved as quickly as she was able, but it took all of her concentration to place one foot in front of the other. Damek followed close on her heels, picking Brisa up to move quickly. Calder followed, enjoying the approbation of the crowd. McKenna stayed in the crowd the longest, leaving her arm in the air as an act of defiance.

As Mia reached the door, she looked to the porch where Triana had been standing. It was empty. Mia searched for her in the crowd, but Malta walked up, blocking her view.

"Where is Triana?"

Malta gestured vaguely at the crowd. "There is no time to search for her now. Mia, it is time to begin."

CHAPTER SIX

E lementals crowded the cabin. Mia waited for McKenna before entering. Damek carried Brisa to an overstuffed chair. He lowered her delicately onto the seat. Concern dominated his features. As Damek stood up, his gaze met Mia's. She smiled a thank you for his support. His eyes immediately darted to the floor with an endearing blush on his cheeks. How different he seemed from the boy in the fight last night.

The gentle giant moved quickly behind the armchair and stood guard over the blonde waif. Brisa closed her eyes, as if after a long battle she finally had found a safe place to rest. Mia moved to another armchair, resting her head against its side. Too much had happened. She felt battered inside and out. Calder moved to one side, then stopped, taking in each of them.

McKenna had started pacing behind the couch, a triumphant grin on her face. For a long time, no one spoke as they absorbed their new companions and tried to make sense of what had happened.

After an exceptionally long time, Mia finally ventured, "So how often is there a new council?" No one responded. Instead, a strong voice came from the doorway.

"This will be the first." They all turned and faced Malta. She appraised them as she moved forward. The other veteran council members came slowly in behind her. "Usually the royalty or government of each clan send their representative. We are assigned diplomats, if you will. We are not sure what to do, frankly. I have seen the vision. I know you are all needed. You will become a new council, one that will focus on our problems and work to save us all."

"Well, that's rather dramatic don't you think?" another man who had followed her sneered. His muscles bulged, straining his black tunic. Casually, he sauntered to a seat, sizing up the occupants of the room. "The leaders of each faction usually make up the council. These are not even our best warriors. I see little good that can come from this."

"Brand is right." A lady in a chocolate dress stood right inside the doorway. Her eyes took in Damek, standing guard over the little Sylph. The lady nodded in acceptance, and then turned to the rest. "You are not warriors. Damek is fair, but more of an engineer. The Fire child is still in training. The Sylph is…. not ready for a battle, nor do I think she could be. The same for our new Aether child. That leaves you, Undine… are you a fighter?"

"I can hold my own," Calder hesitated, looking around. A woman in blue snorted.

"Are you planning on becoming one of the Undine's hunters or fighters?" Calder looked down. The lady in brown turned to the woman in blue. "Well is he, Sarila?" The blue lady, with the delicate features, frowned and shook her head. She looked at Calder as if taking his measure had found him wanting.

"We are all surprised by who the Goddess and the Moirae have chosen, Delphine." Malta swept to the center of the room, grabbing everyone's attention again. "They are to represent us, to solve our problems. Yet, traditionally only our strongest Elementals are allowed on the council, and these are… well… not." She gave a smile to the teens. Their faces had all taken on a grim cast. "However, this is a new age. One that requires more than physical strength. And this council is for this next generation, with our new problems. Our council is not up to the task. We are too busy with our own difficulties to help each other. Since they are not leaders in their own right, they can focus on what must be done for all of us."

"They will be a tool of our council?" Mia looked sharply to the man in black, who jeered menacingly. "They will do as we say?"

"No," Malta frowned. "They will be independent of us, on their own, to do as they need to help each faction with their greatest problems. We have not been able to mount a joint effort. But they will."

"They will create a greater mess," the silk fabric of the Sarila's blue dress fluttered as she waved her arm. "This is a ridiculous notion. They are not royalty. They are not even from the aristocracy."

"Malta has never been wrong in her visions before," Delphine admitted.

"They are five children," Brand spat out. "What can five children do?"

"There will be six new council members," Malta corrected without addressing his derision.

"Six?" Delphine queried.

"Mia cannot represent the Aether since she has not grown up with the Aether." Mia's face became scarlet. "There must be an additional Aether representative." All the old council members protested at once. With so many voices, it was impossible to make anyone out. After a few moments, Malta raised her arm. Attention returned to her. "If any other faction was to have an outsider, you would insist as well. But regardless, I know it will be true. There is one additional council member."

"Who?" Brand demanded.

Malta's brow furrowed. "I did not see their face. I just know it to be true. Mia will pick the person she wants as her supporter and guide while she leads the new council." There was a visible reaction from all the adults. *I'm supposed to lead what now?* Mia thought as her eyes widened. "We will assemble all the Aether's youth and she will make her selection tomorrow."

"No-" Mia tried to interrupt, but Brand cut her off.

"This girl is not a leader," Brand stated. "I cannot ask one of my warriors to follow such a weak thing. McKenna should lead." McKenna looked at Mia with the challenge.

"Damek is older and wiser than any of the others. He should lead…" Delphine began.

"What assurance do we have you aren't making this up to benefit the Aether?" Sarila raised one eyebrow. Malta gained strength and height from her indignation.

"An Aether who is not an Aether. The prophecy has begun," Malta started. That quieted the adults, but the teens looked confused. "I have been on the council for decades." Malta slowly moved her eyes from one council member to the next, fixing them with her gaze. "In that time, I have helped every faction who has asked me and I would hope that has earned me your respect. I am the head of this council and I give you my word."

Though they didn't say anything, Mia watched each council member back down. Mia wasn't a leader. She was definitely in the follower category. In the silence, she considered each of the other teens. Brisa had folded into herself. Damek stoically looked on. Calder's face appeared mildly amused. McKenna wanted to punch someone, probably Mia.

The door to the cabin slammed open, and Boreas entered the room. He took in the tension and assumed he was the cause.

"We have locked Camden up. I apologize for my delay." Boreas walked toward Brisa, but Damek took a step forward, warning him away. Boreas hesitated, trying to decide if it was worth the battle.

"What do we do now?" Delphine sighed as she smoothed the wrinkles in her brown dress.

"We give them our support and endorsement," Malta looked around.

"Our endorsement?" Brand roared.

"It doesn't matter what we say, Brand. Our people witnessed their marking. We can try to deny them and the Moirae's choice. But the damage is done. Better we support this than divide our people." Sarila moved to the couch and sat down. Now Sarila had moved closer, Mia noticed she was considerably older than Mia had originally taken her for. "Besides, I sincerely doubt they can make things worse." Mia wasn't sure how to take that.

"If you have doubts about their abilities, the only thing to do is to put them to the test," Boreas spoke up. "The Sylph will support the new council and place our problems at their feet. We will pledge as much assistance as we can. If they can face what we see as an invasive problem, it should give them the credibility for the rest of the council to support them."

"I can agree to that," Delphine smiled. "I have faith in Damek. He is one of our brightest young men. If that is the caliber of the others on the council, they may move mountains." She smiled fondly at Damek. He blushed slightly. "In addition, I will support the addition of a sixth member chosen by the lost Aether. The girl will need guidance as she knows nothing of our people."

The blue-clad Sarila nodded slowly, "I will agree." She sent a look of distaste at Calder as she stood. "The new council can keep Calder. If they can help the Sylph, the Undines will support them." Everyone turned to Brand.

"Fine," Brand snorted. "I will agree on both counts… for now. We will need to reconvene."

"At the winter solstice, or should we give them until Beltane?" Sarila queried.

"We will have them send word when they finish their first task," Boreas announced. "I have a hard time believing they will finish by the solstice. But since my clan will support them, I accept that they may need our support through Beltane… but no longer. That gives them six months."

"It is the last day of our Samhain council meeting. Tomorrow is Samhain. Will you all disperse tomorrow? Or stay until the day after Samhain, as is tradition?" Sarila asked.

"My people will leave after Samhain. After I have had time to meet with my people's new representative on this council," Brand eyed McKenna. "I would also like to be there when the Aether picks her 'mentor.' Perhaps she will choose a warrior, so the Fire clan will not be solely responsible for the group's protection." He sniffed and sauntered towards the door. Sarila and Delphine nodded in agreement and followed.

"I will talk to the new council about the challenge we are placing before them tomorrow, after Mia chooses the sixth member," Boreas confirmed.

"We will have the selection first thing in the morning," Malta agreed. The older council members exited, talking quietly amongst themselves.

Soon only the motley group of teens were left, eyeing each other warily. No one was willing to break the silence until a small voice came from the little blonde, Brisa. "Thank you."

"Don't thank us, it was the right thing to do," McKenna huffed and threw herself onto the sofa.

Calder grabbed another armchair. "She's right," he threw a winning smile Brisa's way. "Besides, you're one of us now, and we have to look after our own." He glanced over at the others. "Especially since the old council won't."

"Bunch of children… make things worse… ringing endorsement all right," McKenna muttered.

"Look on the bright side. Expectations are so low we can only rise in their esteem," Damek peered through the window, his hand clenched into fists.

"Well, at least your council member likes you," Calder teased and Damek turned red again. Mia looked around at her disheartened and scared peers. She had never really belonged to anyone or anything before. Her mother was her only connection until Triana. Thinking of how each of their council members insulted them, Mia felt oddly protective of the teens.

"Just because they have low expectations of us, doesn't mean we need to have low expectations of ourselves. They've failed already. We haven't even tried yet," Mia insisted.

McKenna snickered, "So our fearless leader speaks."

"Trying to take her place?" Damek interjected.

"You just like to be led around by weak women, don't you Gnome?" McKenna scoffed. In a flash, the two assumed fighting postures.

"That is twice you have insulted me, Lizard," Damek snarled.

"Truth hurts." McKenna kicked a coffee table out of the way. They stood within inches of each other.

"Stop it!" Mia shouted, thrusting herself between them. Her head pounded. She didn't want to be the stupid leader. She just wanted all of them to leave. "If you want to beat each other up, do it outside." McKenna and Damek took a step back, but the tension between them didn't falter. "You don't have to like each other, but if we are going to work together, we all have to stay in the same room without attacking each other!" No one moved.

"I have nothing to go back to," Brisa said softly, "I would rather have a purpose than none." A respectful silence fell. What would any of them be doing if not this? Mia didn't have a plan for the future. Everyone contemplated Brisa's remark.

"Perhaps we should tell each other about ourselves," Calder suggested, breaking the silence.

"Good idea. We need to know what we have to work with," McKenna threw herself back onto the couch. "My strengths are with sword and dagger and hand to hand. Decent at strategy- warrior class. You, Gnome?"

"As Delphine stated, I am an engineer. I like to see how things go together. However, I have trained in combat." Damek observed McKenna warily, then retreated to his position behind Brisa. Mia was thrown for a loop… *What strengths did she have??*

"I'm a strong Undine, I don't know how else I'm special. Though I must admit, the ladies like my smile," Calder boasted, flashing his rakish grin at the rest of the group. Mia and McKenna rolled their eyes in unison. "And apparently that power won't work here."

"I'm a standard Sylph," Brisa whispered. "There is nothing special about me."

"You're strong," Mia interrupted with confidence. "You're strong and resilient." Brisa smiled and looked down.

"What about you?" McKenna ventured.

"I'm not sure what to say," Mia frowned. She didn't understand her powers, didn't want her powers. She didn't understand what the clan names meant. What did it mean to be a strong Undine?

"Can you see inside our heads?" Calder gaze had riveted on Mia.

"No…" she answered, startled like a deer in headlights.

"You saw what my father did to me?" Brisa voice was shaking.

"I…" Mia stuttered, trying to find the words.

"Hey, calm down…" Calder raised his hand as if a slowdown gesture would work on her mind and thoughts. "It's okay," he smiled reassuringly. "Regardless, you are one of us, but I've never heard of Aether being able to see inside the heads of other Elementals without touching them. But you seemed to do that with Brisa." Mia's chest was still tight. There was nowhere to run, nothing to do but face the music.

"I don't know," she swallowed. "I've only ever seen through someone else's eyes twice. Once with a girl being attacked at a movie theater, and once tonight." As Mia spoke, they watched her warily. Better to get it all out. "I can see images from the past and future of a person…"

"Even Elementals?" Damek interrupted. Mia turned to his pensive face.

"Yes, apparently…" Mia admitted. "I can usually tell what people are feeling… in a vague way. I can see their auras… even Elementals." She turned back to the group. "Is that unusual?"

"Yes," McKenna stated bluntly. She took Mia's measure. "You read Brisa's thoughts?"

"No… it's like… I'm them… with their memories… with their feelings…" She turned to Brisa as she spoke. "I could feel the pain you were in, and I knew you needed wind, even though I have never had that sort of need… It was as if I needed it… if that makes sense?" Brisa nodded slowly and blushed. "But I would never tell… I wouldn't share unless you asked me to… You seemed to want help and I…"

"You were right," Brisa met her eyes. "I knew you could help me… I don't know how… I knew you could be my voice… that you were with me." Her voice was still soft but you could hear a pin drop everyone was so silent.

"Tactically, that would give us a great advantage," McKenna mulled.

"No," Damek responded immediately. McKenna turned on him.

"If she can see what we see, even if we're separated. To contact each other…. And people would never know? Have you ever heard of someone able to do that?"

As he considered this, Damek's face remained stony. "No," he replied.

"Exactly," said McKenna, regarding Mia again.

"But that isn't how it works… I can't turn it on and off at will," Mia started. Whatever grandiose plan McKenna was hatching, there was no way Mia could make it work.

Apparently, McKenna wasn't listening, "The real question is how much we can trust you… to see inside our heads." Everyone in the room shifted slightly.

"I don't willingly use my… abilities. I don't want to… Sometimes I just can't stop it," Mia confessed, holding back tears. "I can't help what I see." She focused on the floor. Between the pain of the visions and the barrage of questions, she just needed this to end. So much for being a part of something. Then she felt pressure on her arm. She looked up quickly and Brisa stood in front of her. She had moved so silently; Mia hadn't heard her coming.

"I trust you," Brisa smiled slightly, "The words you spoke, how you defended me…" Mia shook her head.

"They were your words," Mia responded honestly. "I remember talking, but don't even remember what I said."

"I trust you," Brisa repeated.

"Well, that's one of us." McKenna's whole body was tense. "I, for one, would prefer it if you stayed out of my head for now," she remarked.

"You can take my hand," Calder offered it willingly to Mia. Mia automatically backed away. "Or not…"

"I… I'm sorry… I… I can't see anything else today. I just…" Mia stammered.

"Perhaps, we should call it a night. We can meet again in the morning, when everyone has rested," Calder suggested.

"'Til morning," McKenna agreed, walking to the door. Calder nodded and followed. Damek bowed his head to Mia and Brisa, then exited on Calder's heels. Brisa was all that was left.

"Trust is earned. Give them time. Until tomorrow… my friend." Brisa gave an attempt at a smile, then followed the others out. Mia's tears began to flow freely. What did each of them think of her? Did they see her as the weak link she felt like? They didn't trust her, but then no one else ever had either. But Brisa had called her a friend. Mia had never had a friend before. She tried to focus on that as the adrenaline left her and exhaustion set in.

CHAPTER SEVEN

The next morning came a little too soon. Mia passed out in the chair as soon as the others left. But sleep hadn't made her feel any less raw than she had been at the end of yesterday. She sat by the window, watching as the different factions took down some of their tents and packed up their belongings. Some of the oldest and youngest Elementals appeared to be leaving early.

Most of the morning passed with Mia lost in thought. Triana had never returned to the cabin. Periodically Mia saw a strawberry blonde woman, but it never ended up being Triana. Was Triana being kept from her? Triana and her mother seemed to find a truce last night. Was she busy visiting family and friends she had been denied for the last few years? Or was she afraid to tell Mia about the prophecy? There had to be more to it than what she could piece together from Malta's words to the Elementals last night.

From her perch at the window, Mia noticed a rather tall beefy man trailing Malta. Malta's aura sparked with uncomfortable frustration. They talked with broad gestures, but since no one stopped to listen, Mia figured their voices couldn't be that high. After a few minutes, the man said something distinct to Malta and stormed off. Malta turned, a plethora of emotions flowing in waves across her face: anger, frustration, angst. But when Malta's eyes met Mia's from across the clearing, her face immediately fell to a placid smile.

Briefly, Mia wondered about the tension between Triana and her mother. Did the Aether still create arranged marriages? Would she be expected to marry someone she didn't even know or want? Would the clan try to force her? If there was even a chance, the time to leave was now. Could she even leave the council? Where did Triana go? The questions went around and round.

At that moment, Mia made herself a promise. If she is ever put in the same position as Triana, she would leave. She traced the tattoo on her arm with her finger and wondered what would happen.

Eventually, the Aether converged on the center of the square. A line of Aether warriors, sporting muscles and red hair gathered in the middle. They looked like an army, carrying swords and wearing leather armor. The other clans wandered over. They formed a loose circle around the warriors, vying and preening for everyone's attention. Mia took a deep breath. They would be coming for her soon. She tried to see if there was anything that would stand out about the warriors. The Fire guy had argued for another fighter on the team. Admittedly, Mia didn't know how to fight, and after the incident at the movie theater she was hyper aware of how important being able to protect herself was. Maybe McKenna would help her. How did their swords deal with guns? Mia wondered, watching the parade outside. On these missions the clans have set before them, how much danger would they be in?

Mia spied Colin in the crowd. Despite his height, the warriors dwarfed him. Mia fingered the white tunic Malta had given her that morning. She felt like a sacrificial offering. The tunic was long enough to work as a dress, but Mia had decided to wear her dark blue denim under it. Her hair hung loose, a riotous mass at her shoulder; the hair tie she habitually wore on her left wrist had broken the night before. Mia's only adornment was her father's necklace. All too soon Malta arrived at the door.

"It is time," Malta announced, looking content. "I have brought you a proper stone to wear as an Aether representative." She held out a necklace with an amethyst in the center of an ornate silver piece. It resembled a huge collar from Egyptian times. Mia couldn't bring herself to touch it.

"Thank you but… I have a … problem with things tight around my neck." A strained expression came across Malta's face. "But if you want me to wear an amethyst I do have one." From her backpack, Mia took out the simple amethyst pendant Triana had given her so many months ago to help control and focus her gift. Malta was not happy, but she gave Mia a tight smile.

"Remember you are responsible for finishing the new council. Think of the things that this group needs. You need a warrior, since you are unable to fight. You need a strong Elemental, someone connected to others in our clan…"

Mia took the obvious cue, "How would I know that?" The feigned expression of surprise almost made Mia laugh. Obviously, Malta thought Mia was a fool.

"You have a point. Perhaps I should tell you about each of the warriors assembled? Give you some advice on who to choose?" Malta moved in, reaching out a hand to Mia.

"I thought I'm supposed to choose someone?" Mia countered.

"Yes… but you are right, you do not have knowledge of our people." Malta gave a gracious smile. "I do not believe I can refuse to give assistance if you would like it." *What was going on? Malta knows I can read people- doesn't she?* Tentatively, Mia reached out to read Malta but she didn't get anything. Triana had said there was a way for Aether to block other Aether. Malta must be a master.

"Where is Triana?" asked Mia. Malta's eyes met hers straight on.

"She left."

"Why?"

"Her work with the council is done. Officially, she is still banished. I will work to correct the misunderstanding that has kept her from us for the last few decades. It is better if she returns to her life instead of staying here for now. Hopefully, that will eventually change." A ripple appeared in Malta's calm façade. "Regardless, Triana cannot help you. She does not know our people well anymore. Do you want advice on your selection?" Triana had promised to stay with her. Mia's stomach heaved. A huge boulder settled on her chest, restricting her breathing.

"I'm alone." Mia wheezed.

"Mia?" Malta's voice was closer now.

"No!" Mia struggled to breath normally. Mia attempted to act confident. "I'm supposed to do this on instinct alone." The excuse was the best she could come up with. Her gut twisted. Triana had left her. She really was alone. Facing a crowd of people was hard enough when Triana stood beside her but on her own? No way. How could she get out of this?

"If you change your mind, I will tell you anything you want to know," Malta offered.

"No," Mia responded absently. "You won't."

"You do not trust me," Malta bristled. Mia didn't respond. What was she supposed to say? She had no reason to trust her. Not only because Triana obviously didn't, but Malta was clearly trying to manipulate her. Brisa was right… trust is earned. Mia's panic swelled. Words…. Words aren't as important as the intention behind them… that was the first lesson Triana taught her. Malta intended to manipulate and Mia wasn't going to play that game. Malta took a second to breathe in an effort to keep her temper from snapping. Her aura pulsed with rage. Then, it slowly changed from a sickening mustard yellow to a soft green.

"You do not know the Aether well," she glared. "It is very hard for us to lie."

"And yet it can be done… or the truth can be obscured or hidden," Mia replied, remembering another of her earliest lessons with Triana. Mia watched Malta's aura falter between colors as warring emotions fought for precedence. Suddenly, a new red of shock emerged as Malta realized she was being read.

"Yes," Malta ground out as the two came to an impasse. "The point of this gathering is to pick someone you can trust to help you. Someone who will be beneficial to the new council, a warrior perhaps," she paused. "If you don't trust me, perhaps you will see someone you can trust in the selection. However, they are waiting." She moved quickly, pushing open the door and stepping outside. Slowly, Mia crossed the room. She couldn't stay inside the cabin forever. Faking a bravado she didn't feel, she walked out the door and to the edge of the cabin's porch. The warriors had lined up in the square.

"Welcome, warriors," Malta strolled into the square. Mia stayed at the top of the three short steps. As Malta began talking to the crowd, the teens from the night before walked up the stairs and stood in a line behind Mia. Malta threw an irritated glance their way. Mia continued to smile. If Malta didn't want them with her, then it was probably a good thing they were. Mia stepped back so she fell into line with them.

"Any thought, guys?" Mia whispered, keeping her eyes on Malta. The woman continued to pontificate on the importance of the new council and the honor that would fall on one of the brutes assembled. The teens took Mia's cue to face forward.

"No idea," Brisa returned, gawking at all the people in front of them. "They all look huge." Mia stifled a laugh. Anyone would seem huge compared to Brisa.

"Malta says we need a warrior," she tilted her head to McKenna. "Do we?" McKenna remained silent for a long time.

"Yes, we do," McKenna admitted. "But just because someone is big, doesn't mean they are brave. A warrior is someone with *strength*." Mia's eyes darted to McKenna as McKenna continued, responding to the doubt on Mia's face. "My mentor would say 'Strength is a measure of the soul, not the body.' I never completely understood, until this moment. Standing up to the Sylph on Brisa's behalf; that is the mark of a warrior. I'd say you have more 'warrior' in you than most of the people before us. So yes, we need a warrior, a fighter, but don't mistake what that truly means." Mia nodded. Malta was winding down.

"Anything else?" Mia whispered quickly. "What else do we need?"

"Heart," Brisa responded.

"Intelligence," Damek muttered.

"Adaptability," Calder finished. Mia looked his way. "The Moirae created a new council for a reason. The old ways aren't going to work this time." Malta finished her rant. As Mia watched, Malta nodded to someone in the crowd. It looked like …*Colin?* His gaze went from Malta to Mia. When their eyes met, he smiled and gave a little wave. *What was that about?*

"These are the candidates put forth by the Aether people," announced Malta, moving toward the cabin again. "Alma, daughter of Valda, of the family Wana-geeska." A female stepped forward. Everything about her was severe, her face, her hair, her expression. Like McKenna, she wore a shirt that bared her arms, showing off her muscles. As Malta started talking of Alma's accomplishments, Mia didn't listen. Alma was wrong. Adaptability was not going to be in this woman's play book.

"Lerato, son…." Malta droned onward. This time a large brick wall moved forward. Mia's eyes widened. She was afraid to go near this one. Mia noticed Colin shaking his head "No." So that's the game. Malta wanted Colin to help her choose. Interesting. Did Colin think she was an idiot too? But then, if she hadn't noticed the exchange between him and Malta, she probably would have taken his help. He was Aether after all, and she didn't know what she was doing. She purposefully looked away.

Malta introduced another warrior. "Valdis…" Where did they get these names? This one was like the last, a little less intimidating. Mia let her eyes wander to the next person in line, and then the next. No one felt right. Each person had a serious expression on their face as they stood in as strong a pose as possible. In total there were two women and five men. "Enid…" How do you tell if someone has heart? Her new companions had stood up for Brisa without knowing her- that was heart. Without that, would she have known? What stood out about the teens beside her? There was a spark in their eyes, a natural easiness. None of the warriors created the same feeling. Malta moved down the line, but Mia knew this was wrong. None of the people here were meant for the council. Mia swallowed. What was she supposed to do?

She couldn't pick any of the candidates. Maybe she should listen to Malta and Colin. She looked back at Colin as the last two names were called out. For both of them, he shook his head "no." Who did he want her to pick? She let her brow furrow in question as she met his gaze. He held up three fingers. Number three. Well, there were two number threes based on which side of the clearing she started from. Three from the right, well, that was an older man, approximately twenty-one-ish with a scar on his right cheek. Very intimidating. Three from the left, definitely a more likely scenario since Malta had started on that side, another hulking behemoth. Only this one looked arrogant, as if this was just a game for his amusement. Mia caught Colin's eyes again. She leaned to the right and raised an eyebrow, immediately he shook his head "no." She leaned to the left and he started to raise his head up and down as surreptitiously as possible. Damek frowned. He had obviously noticed the exchange. Had anyone else? No one else looked her way.

Mia examined Colin's suggestion; the arrogant one. No, he wouldn't work well with the team. Why would Colin recommend him? Colin was facing Malta now, nodding. *Ahhh… it wasn't his idea at all.* Malta had advised him. Colin had implied yesterday that he admired her. He probably believed he was helping Mia because Malta told him so. That had to be it. The kind boy who had taken the time to explain things to her yesterday seemed too honest to purposefully mislead her. And it was a misdirection. The boy Colin recommended was obviously wrong. She stared at his choice for a second. He looked familiar…. He looked a lot like the man who had argued with Malta earlier that day.

"Who do you choose, Mia?" Malta walked to the bottom of the stairs as Mia took a step forward. Mia's gaze wandered along the line of candidates, desperation setting in. This is wrong. What had Malta said… candidates put forth by the Aether people? The Aether thought Mia should choose one of these people. Yesterday, however, Malta stated Mia could choose any Aether. And with the advice of her new council, Mia needed someone brave, adaptable, kind, and smart. Mia had only seen one Aether that fit that description. She took a deep breath, knowing that she was about to cause a lot of problems.

With a smile on her face, Mia announced, "I choose Colin, from the Family Nuelle."

CHAPTER EIGHT

A wave of shock rolled through the crowd. The people surrounding Colin moved aside, leaving a clear view. His face was slack with surprise. He glanced from Malta to Mia and then to everyone around him.

"I'm not supposed to be on the council," Colin stammered, dropping the formal cadence he had used last night. His eyes darted back to Malta. "She's supposed to pi---"

"Colin!" Malta sharply interrupted. The fury on Malta's face faded as the Elementals focused on her. "What Colin means to say is he was not selected as a candidate by the Aether." The teens on the porch remained very still. Mia sensed the nervousness wafting off of them, but to their credit, they appeared completely calm.

"I am Aether," Mia stated boldly. "I select Colin." She willed herself not to twitch. Her entire body wanted to move; her breath wanted to quicken. Somehow, she found the strength to fight her impulses. "I have seen the council and Colin is the sixth member," she lied, meeting Malta's gaze and daring the woman to contradict her. Which she probably could. Mia hadn't seen anything about the council, but Malta had. After a moment, Malta bowed her head. The people around Colin started pushing him forward until he joined the council on the porch.

"You weren't supposed to pick me," Colin whispered urgently as they moved inside.

"Yes, I was," asserted Mia, giving him the most confident smile she could muster. At that moment, he stared down at his arm. His light lavender mark faded to silver in front of them. They exchanged a wide-eyed look. A myriad of emotions crossed his face: relief, wonder, and even fear. Mia put a hand on his arm, "You're going to be fine." In a daze, he fell in step behind her.

While the group assembled in similar positions to yesterday, Colin sat next to Mia. This time, the teens were seated and the council remained standing near their representative. Everyone in the room sized up Colin. They took Mia's choice in stride, save for Malta. Despite the obvious effort to calm herself, Malta was still livid. Her aura throbbed. A brief silence reigned, then Boreas made his way to the center of the room.

"I have brought the Air clan's problems to other clans multiple times in the last month unwilling to wait until Samhain. Unfortunately, they have been unable to help. I bring this problem to the new council for assistance," he nodded to Brisa. "Several of our teens have gone missing." As Boreas spoke, Brisa didn't flinch already aware of the problem. McKenna moved forward itching to begin. Calder and Damek looked to their elders who didn't meet their gaze. Mia looked to Colin who returned her worried gaze and took her hand, looking for support as much as giving it. "It took us a while to realize that they were not just wandering…." Boreas stopped, overcome with emotion. Mia looked to Colin.

The Sylph are travelers. They are constantly in motion. Generally, they are artists, poets, adventurers, always searching for a new horizon. It makes sense that it would be hard to keep track of everyone. Mia's eyebrow raised in understanding and Colin's face mirrored her own shock.

You can hear me? Colin asked silently.

Yes! Mia response had enough force to jolt Colin back. The connection severed as their hands parted. Boreas started talking again, but it took a moment for them to pull their focus back.

"We may have still believed that they were wandering except two months ago one of them returned. Her mind was addled, her body was gaunt… She was unable….." Boreas' pain at the memory radiated off of him.

"Unable to what?" Brand said sharply. Boreas halted to regain his composure.

"She was unable to tell us anything. Her arms were covered in needle marks… she kept saying the word "Coro" and repeating the names of her brother and a friend of hers- Kenneth and Nephele. All in their late teens, all of whom we had not seen since Imbolc."

"Coro?" Mia questioned aloud without thinking. "There's a drug on the news called Coro. It's highly addictive. They're calling it an epidemic."

"Yes," Boreas confirmed. He continued, "She managed to get to a small Sylph group at the base of the Calhutta mountains. Her feet were bloody. She was wearing rags. We think she had walked to the mountains from somewhere near Atlanta. The Sylph elders were devastated that we had lost one of our children. We began a hunt for the other two. We insisted that all wind communities across the continent check on their youth and do a search for all members of their clan. We worked together to find those who were wandering. After two weeks, our poll was completed. Twenty-four other young adults were missing. Two or three from different areas of the country," Boreas paused. "We believe they have succumbed to this drug, Coro. We have sent Sylph into every major city searching for the missing in slums and shelters, in suburbs and city streets. We can find no sign of them." Boreas directed his attention to each of the new council members. "We want to bring our children home. We want to help them if we can. Brisa, Camden said he found needle marks on your arm. Camden swore you were addled and he was trying to help you defeat the addiction. We believed him since he had been so protective after his wife… after your mother died… he claimed he would stay with you until the worst was over and then let us know what you could remember. We continued the search… That was…"

"How long?" Brisa forced out.

"Three weeks ago," Boreas swallowed. "We focused on finding the others and in so doing, failed you. Our people wish… I wish to apologize for everything you have been through." He stopped, unable to meet Brisa's eyes. A hush filled the cabin as everyone digested the new information. Brisa hugged her legs to her chest.

"The Sylph are asking the new council to find the missing teens?" Mia's voice faltered slightly as she pulled the collective attention away from Brisa.

"Yes," Boreas hesitated as if he had more to say but stopped himself.

"We should head to Atlanta," McKenna declared, pushing the conversation forward. No one responded. She looked to Mia, who frowned. The older council appeared unmoved by the story. They had obviously heard it before. However, underneath each person's facade roiled deep emotion. Brand was full of malice, while Delphine evidenced true concern for the lost youth. The focus on someone else's problems annoyed Sarila. Malta still seethed from her early loss. Something was wrong with the old council, and Mia instinctively knew they should not discuss this openly in front of them. Colin was clearly asking Malta for guidance so Mia took his hand.

It is time to make a decision. Colin turned to her, surprised. *You are a puppet of Malta's or you are a member of the new council. You can't be both.*

But they know more than us. They are the elders. Colin disagreed.

No. There is a reason there is a new council. If we only do what the elders tell us, we are pawns. I know you're joining us late. However, we've all agreed to take these steps away from the elders. Colin looked to Malta, who stared at him with a quizzical expression on her face.

"McKenna is right. Atlanta is the best place to start," Mia agreed quickly in an effort to fill the silence. She dropped Colin's hand. "Perhaps we can discuss and strategize on the road... if we only have until -- "

"Beltane," Boreas supplied. Mia glanced to Calder, who mouthed May. "The Sylph will support you to the best of our ability until then. I will give funds to Brisa to help pay for your expenses, but there is not an unlimited amount of money."

"The Undine have a deserted house near Atlanta. The new council can use it as a base of operations," Sarila supplied.

"The Aether will supply a van for their travel," Malta offered placidly.

"The Salamanders will outfit the group with swords, daggers, and other technology that may help in their quest," Brand sneered. "Perhaps McKenna can teach your children something."

"The Gnomes will assist with food and supplies," Delphine added.

"I think we should listen to the plans of this new council and perhaps guide them on this first mission," Brand offered a little too nonchalantly. All the teens watched Mia, even McKenna.

"Thank you," Mia said, after a moment of hesitation. "However, we have to prove ourselves. This is how we start. How soon can we leave?"

"Well, you can't leave until after Samhain. It's the last night when we celebrate together," Brand cajoled.

Why is he smiling at me like I'm a mouse caught in a trap? Mia wondered. Brand was trying to intimidate her and turning away would be a sign of deference. His mouth twisted into a wicked grin.

"I believe all of our business is concluded. Come everyone! Tonight is a time to celebrate," Brand winked at Mia, then headed out of the door. Mia shot a worried glance to McKenna, but McKenna was watching Brand's back, filled with anger.

CHAPTER NINE

"Mia, come out and play!" someone shouted, pounding on the door. Mia's heart leapt into her throat. The fires had been lit even before the fall of darkness. The noise around the camp grew louder as the sun set. Different strains of music came from the various camps. Despite their differences, each type of music blended harmoniously together. More and more people moved into the square. No one returned to the cabin, leaving Mia alone for most of the afternoon. The solitude suited her. She had been around more people in the last two days then she had been in the last two years. And people kept touching her. She put on her hoodie as a shield.

"Mia! Open up!" came the voice again. It was a woman's voice. On the second yell, she sounded like McKenna. Mia moved closer to the door. The pounding started again, causing Mia to jump. Even if McKenna stopped, everyone knew Mia was in here. She couldn't stay inside forever. Worse, Brand could come back and she didn't want to be alone with him.... in a small cabin... oh, God. Plastering a smile on her face, Mia opened the door to find McKenna grinning wildly.

"My new sister," she exclaimed, swinging an arm around Mia and pulling her out of the cabin. McKenna's voice dropped lower so only Mia could hear, "You can't stay inside. You represent our council now, and they will judge all of us on how brave and confident you are. So if nothing else... pretend." McKenna let out a laugh as if she had told a hysterical joke. Mia managed a tight smile. "You don't trust the old council?" McKenna asked, pulling the hoodie off of Mia and throwing it back into the cabin. "Wear this," she ordered, handing Mia a fitted jacket.

"There were a ton of emotions in there, but none were supportive. I just had a feeling they wanted to manipulate us," stressed Mia, putting on the warm black jacket. It wasn't as cozy as her hoodie, but she had to admit it looked better. Mia met McKenna's gaze and uttered the words she had been thinking all day. "I don't want to be the leader or anything. I just want to be a part of the group!"

"Yeah, well, we'll see," McKenna seemed to take her measure. "That's better. You don't resemble a turtle anymore. And don't worry, we'll watch out for you just in case you're right about the old council. Fortunately for you, I dislike them more than I dislike you." Mia blinked. Was she serious? At that moment Calder approached, and McKenna subtly handed Mia off. "I'll get you a drink!" McKenna laughed, joining the celebratory crowd.

"It's baby-sit the newbie night..." Mia observed as she cringed and leaned against the railing.

"You aren't so bad," Calder flashed a devastating smile as he joined her on the porch.

"Tell that to McKenna," Mia sighed. Calder jumped up, straddling the railing and leaning against a post.

"I have to admit this isn't how I planned on spending Samhain."

"Sorry," Mia whispered, watching the crowd. The flickering light from the bonfire was reflected on the crowd's faces.

"Oh, it isn't you… I wasn't originally invited here. Even then, usually I'm just another handsome face," he grinned, "but tonight, this council thing…. it changes everything. Some people regard me with more awe than my perfect physique can usually inspire. The question is whether to take advantage…" Mia eyed him suspiciously, then hopped up on the railing.

"Are you really this full of yourself or is it an act for my benefit?"

"Probably a little of both," he admitted. Calder settled back to watch a group of earth-toned ladies from the Gnome contingent. They walked slowly by, ogling Calder. When he winked, they giggled.

"Good Lord," Mia laughed, "that was kinda pathetic." He joined in and gave a relaxed smile. That grin was… well, gorgeous. But Mia refused to resemble the giggling twits. She took a deep breath, "What about the others?"

"Hmmm….." he shifted his focus to her again, after smiling at another group of females, this time from the Fire clan. "What others?"

"The ones who do not look on you with awe?" she countered. It was strange, he was so intense when he was flirting with everyone passing by. But every time he focused back on Mia, he relaxed and the intensity disappeared.

"Well, with the Undines… I'm getting a lot of disdain…"

"Disdain?"

He shrugged. "They don't like the fact that a male is representing them. Traditionally, the Undines only have female representatives. Plus, I'm not even a member of the aristocracy. There isn't a drop of royalty in me, so obviously I am unworthy," he snorted. Mia's brow furrowed as she listened. "Then some seem to fear me. And others seem to have decided that they, suddenly, want to be my friend." He flashed that wicked grin again. "Regardless, it's making for a very interesting night."

"Well, at least with you up here, no one is paying much attention to me." Mia's eyes roamed the camp. Most of the attention was definitely focused Calder's way.

"Don't worry. McKenna talked to all of us this afternoon. That woman doesn't trust anyone, not even her own kind." He leaned in as if they were having an intimate conversation. Mia matched his posture. "One of us will be with you all night." His eyebrows raised seductively.

"I'm the weak link?"

"No… We're keeping an eye out for each other. Probably better not to be on your own for your first Samhain anyway. Now smile as if I have said something exceptionally clever!" he whispered intensely. Instead, she laughed, realizing he was trying to fake a seduction in front of the whole camp.

"Don't think I'll fall prey to your charms for somebody else's amusement," she smiled pulling her jacket tighter across her chest.

"And there goes my ego." He returned the smile, then pushed himself off the railing. "I do have a reputation to protect."

"I am sure there are tons of ladies ready to swoon for you at a moment's notice, but…. I don't think I want to be known as one of them." Her eyes went back to the camp and landed on Damek. He was on the far side of the bonfire near the Earth camp. A woman his age with long brown hair and a slender figure kept touching his arm and moving in close. When the girl turned, Mia could see it was the girl with Damek at the fight two nights ago. Mia sensed Damek's confusion across the entire campground. At that moment, he noticed her watching. He gestured to the female and then started slowly moving through the revelers towards the cabin.

"I wonder what that's about." Calder had followed her gaze. "Looks like Damek will join you next," he winked. "Don't worry, I'll be back at the end…" he assured her as he started to move away. "Be careful," Calder turned back. Pure concern replaced his flirty persona.

"I will," Mia nodded. She turned back to watch Damek's progress towards her. He was three quarters of the way to the cabin. Mia jumped down from the porch railing and moved towards the wicker couch. On arrival, Damek flopped down on the couch next to her. The amount of emotion pouring off of him was nauseating. Unthinking, she reached out and touched his arm to comfort him. He jumped.

"I'm so sorry," Mia withdrew. He knows what I can do, she berated herself. Of course, he didn't want her to touch him. She looked away as tears welled up automatically.

"No, I'm sorry. I wasn't afraid of you. I just… I think I was lost inside of myself for a second and forgot you were there. I'm sorry, really it isn't--"

"It's okay," she smiled through the tears. "I'm sensitive… I'll get over it." After a significant pause, she asked, "Do you want to talk about it?"

"No," he blurted. *Well, that felt like a slap.* Mia moved farther away from him. They watched the party in silence. This was the guy that threw McKenna into the fire. Maybe it was better if they didn't become friendly. Focusing on the people off the porch was amusing. Unlike the other days when people stayed with their own, the people were mixing. They were wary, but curious about the other clans around them.

Slowly, Damek's emotions calmed. The tension in his body released. Suddenly, Mia realized he had stopped watching the revelers and had started staring at her. With a deep breath, she faced him.

"Can't you tell what I'm thinking?" Damek asked.

"No. I'm not a mind reader. I can tell you are tense and confused, but that's it."

"You saw the girl… woman… well… her?" he leaned forward, studying his hands.

"Yes, she wanted to know you better," Mia joked.

"Yeah, well… she knows me…. She….. She was my intended." His face turned red. "We were going to get engaged at this Samhain."

"But you're only seventeen?!" Mia exclaimed.

"Yeah, well, in the Earth clan…. A good number are promised between sixteen and twenty." She cringed, "It's normal, I swear." At Mia's dubious expression, he laughed again. "Well, it is, ask … Colin." This time he frowned.

"Okay," Mia looked out again. That was so wrong. She would never consider being married at seventeen. My God, she had never even gone out on a date. At seventeen, he was already willing to commit his life to someone.

"Marriage in the Gnome clan is very political. Alliances form early, especially in political families. Our parents planned our marriage before we were born. Normal Gnomes wait until their thirties or forties."

"Seventeen is young but forty?"

He frowned, "Don't humans usually marry in their twenties?"

"Yes."

"Well, that's the Elemental equivalent." His brow furrowed as he watched her confusion. "Mia, most Elementals live upward of a hundred and fifty years. Some longer than two hundred." Her entire face went slack. She would live over a century? There were Elementals still living born in the 1800s??? Suddenly, the view of the Nazis she had witnessed through Malta's eyes made more sense. Mia felt like the ground had fallen from beneath her… again. "Are you okay?"

"Two hundred years? We live two hundred years??" she whispered.

"We can live that long. Just like humans, we die from war, famine, disease. You never know how long you will live. You can't depend on a possibility," he explained.

"Right," she nodded and took a deep breath in. It was just a possibility. It was scary, but at the same time, exciting. What might happen in the next two hundred years? She finally met Damek's eyes. "That will take some time to process." She smiled to relieve his obvious worry. "What happened with… Gnome girl?"

"Well, when I didn't get my marks at sixteen, she hesitated. Said she couldn't trust me." He took in Mia's frown. "Elementals who marry are marked together, with matching bands on their fingers. If you are a bad match, the marks will not show. If you are a good match, you will be permanently linked. There is a ceremony and …." He blushed again. "Well … long story short… she decided without the marks she wouldn't know if we were …. a good match… She wasn't willing to take the chance and her family agreed." He swallowed. "I embarrassed her. She made the break very… public." The silence quickly became awkward.

"She was holding your arm the other night?" They hadn't appeared very broken up.

"McKenna was getting in her face, and I stepped in. She was… grateful." Damek looked off in Gnome girl's direction. "Anyway… now that I'm 'marked' she wants me to go through with the ceremony. Evidently, we would make a 'powerful couple,'" he finished confused.

Mia laughed, trying to ease the tension. "You're having the same problem as Calder! Inspiring more awe than should come from just your handsome face." He looked up in shock and Mia realized what she had implied… Hell, what she had said. She thought he was handsome… not that that was a shock… *Sorry, but he is handsome.* Mia rolled her eyes. Anyone would think he was handsome. She was sitting in the middle of a super model convention. Damek was studying his hands again, but a small smile lifted the edges of his mouth. The dancers from two nights ago were back, only their numbers had swelled. She attempted to laugh. "Well… did you say yes to…???"

He grimaced, "Solange… I haven't answered her yet." Mia saw the forlorn expression on his face. She glanced away, trying to give him his privacy while he was working things out in his head. A group of girls were clearly looking Damek over, trying to catch his attention. It was kinda sad to watch. Finally, Mia nudged Damek with her foot and nodded to his groupies. His face went red as he deliberately turned away.

"What was McKenna's plan?" She laughed, trying to change the topic.

"Colin's supposed to join you next," Calder focused in on her. "But look over to the right, at the heart of the Fire camp. Brand has been staring this way. I'm not sure that Colin would be much of a deterrent."

Mia swallowed and smiled. "Well, as much as I would love to save you from your fan girls, I think we better do what McKenna planned. Apparently she created it because of my concerns, I should at least…" Her eyes met Damek's. "Though I would appreciate your keeping an eye out for me?"

"Of course," he replied seriously. "Should I wait for Colin?" When she found Colin, females surrounded him: his face bright red and panicked. At that moment, a random woman bumped into him, spilling her drink down his back. He jumped. Then his wet shirt inspired a whole new set of comments and women trying to touch him.

"Maybe you should go save Colin?" she gestured.

"May the Goddess protect us….I'll be back." He walked purposefully towards the encircled Colin.

"I don't think he could be more awkward," she whispered to herself.

"It's true," a deep voice whispered back. The voice came from right over her shoulder. Her entire body tensed immediately. She took a step away and turned, expecting to see Brand behind her. Instead, it was the muscle-bound marvel from the selection that morning. He smiled winningly at her. "I just wanted to introduce myself. I didn't have time to talk to you this morning." She took another step back but found herself up against the porch post. "My name is Valdis…" His arms moved to the railing on either side of her.

"I'm sorry the selection didn't work out for you..." Her mind jumped a thousand directions.

"The only reason I am disappointed… is because it means I won't be spending as much time with you."

Mia's brow furrowed. "With me?"

"Are you fishing for compliments?"

"No. I honestly don't understand what you're talking about." As he attempted to size her up, she ducked under his arm and moved away from him.

"Then maybe I should tell you what everyone is saying?" He leered again, "You're new… and powerful…" As he moved towards her, his voice became deeper, "and very attractive. Before all the other men try to capture your interest, I would like to get to know you better." He moved to place an arm around her. Mia's hand automatically shot up, slapping his away.

"Are you trying to be seductive? Because frankly, you're just coming off as really creepy," Mia asserted. At creepy, he took a step back confused. Seizing the opportunity, she slid to the right towards the stairs. She kept backing up until she met with something solid. Mia released a deep breath. It was Damek.

"Apparently, the boys aren't the only ones with unwanted attention," Damek commented, fixing Valdis with a pointed look.

"Unwanted?" Valdis repeated. "I think you are just trying to keep her for yourself," he took a step forward, reaching for Mia's arm. "Perhaps you should leave the lady with her own kind. She's too strong an Aether to breed with the likes of you." He spat out the final word.

"Breed?" Mia squeaked. "Oh, Hell no!" She sidelined both and headed down the stairs. Her mind was racing… she wasn't an animal… What in the world were they talking about?… Suddenly, a tidal wave of emotion hit her entire body. She collapsed to her knees, keeling over. A vision knocked the air out of her lungs. Her amethyst pendant pulsed. Images flash.

The sounds of hollering echoing through the camp. Colin being grabbed by a tall man wearing the blue of the Water camp. The man is overly friendly, buffeting Colin's lanky form and pushing him purposely toward the center of the camp-ground. As he releases him, a determined Earth teen bumps into him, forcefully sending Colin sprawling backwards. Then a lady from Air smiles at him, propelling herself towards the sky and sending a gust of wind in Colin's direction, roughly pushing him into the bonfire. His shirt bursts into flames. Mia screams as Colin becomes a human torch.

CHAPTER TEN

Mia reeled, disoriented from the vision. Damek was at her side, kneeling. The rebel yell sounded from the Fire camp. She scrambled to her feet.

"Colin... grab Colin before he ends up in the fire." Mia ran toward the bonfire, weaving through people, forcing her way forward. She could sense Damek moving beside her, his frame barreling through the crowd. People jumped out of his way, making their movement faster. Mia looked up to see the blue guy release Colin. Time slowed down as Mia watched the Gnome move determinedly forward. Mia wasn't going to make it. Damek was pulling ahead, making straight for Colin. Mia veered toward the Air lady who was watching Colin, a slight smile on her face. Colin was falling backwards as the Air lady pushed up. She never saw Mia careening into her. The two landed in a pile. The woman growled but Mia's vision was riveted on Damek pulling Colin away from the flames. Mia turned on the woman who she had pinned. "Who told you to push him into the fire?" Mia hissed.

"I don't know what you are talking about..." The lady attempted to push backwards.

"You were going to take off and shove him in the process. Why do you want him dead??" Mia tried to get a read on the woman.

"Let go of me!" The woman demanded as she stood. Mia had a firm grip on her opponent's left arm. The lady moved closer, then slammed a fist into Mia's stomach. Mia's breath left her as she doubled over. "See ya," the woman whispered, melting into the crowd. A second later, Damek was at her side.

"Are you okay?" Damek asked. She managed a nod as Colin walked up.

"Thanks for lending a hand," Colin laughed. "That could have been bad!"

"What was that about?" Damek whispered. Mia watched the crowd. It seemed full of menace now. She tried to get a deep breath of air.

"Someone tried to kill Colin," she replied in a sotto voice.

"What?" Colin yelped.

"Get him to the cabin. And get him another shirt. They poured alcohol or something flammable on his back." Damek grabbed Colin by the arm and guided him slowly through the crowd. Mia followed, attempting to find McKenna, Calder, and Brisa. Damek and Colin went inside as Mia remained on the porch. She sat down stretching out her sore stomach and grimacing.

"Your friend should be careful," Brand warned, walking up to the railing. "Apparently, he is very… ahhh… klutzy."

"Or someone doesn't like him," Mia admonished, trying to take in Brand's aura. His aura was dark but lacked the frustration caused by a plan of his not working out.

"That is more likely," he smiled. "And no… your friend doesn't affect me in any way. So it wasn't me." He watched the people around the fire. "Everyone here has alliances, across all Elements. Some people have known others for decades, and people owe favors. You have to see past the surface. Trust me, I do not just see the surface when I look at you." He took her hand and kissed it, slipping a piece of paper in her palm at the same time. He grinned again, then walked away as McKenna hurried up. McKenna bowed her head to Brand in deference.

"What happened?"

"Someone tried to take out Colin," Mia swallowed as she watched Brand look back. She couldn't believe she had just used the term "take out" for something other than food. Mia shook her head, trying to get a grasp on what had almost happened. She placed the slip of paper from Brand in her pocket for later.

"Colin?" McKenna asked, glancing around, "What happened?" McKenna leaned against the porch rail in a relaxed posture. "You probably want to tell me like it is an interesting story." McKenna chuckled, but her eyes were intense and bored into Mia.

"Four different people, all from different clans, worked together to knock Colin into the bonfire."

"I only saw three," Damek commented, joining them on the porch. "Water, Earth and Air."

"There was a fourth from Fire that poured her drink down his back. Whatever it is, it's highly flammable." Mia smiled in Damek's direction, willing him to catch on to the upbeat tone and join in.

"Straight alcohol from the smell," Damek noted, struggling to grin. Calder arrived, carrying a bottle and five cups

"It looks like you could all use a drink," he announced loudly and handed out the cups.

"Please tell me this isn't anything that will muddle my mind," Mia tried to joke.

"Well, not too badly," Calder flirted back then finished in a lower voice, "it's only water." He poured the drinks, prompting them to try it. "Now relax guys. Your fake fun conversation isn't even close to believable." He watched as each one forced themselves to relax. "I saw you close to the bonfire, grabbing Colin."

"Group of four tried to push him in and make it look like an accident," McKenna commented. She took a swig from her glass. Her face contorted as if she had taken too much of something strong, then laughed. McKenna was quite the actress.

"Who would want to hurt Colin?" Mia asked. Would that same person try to kill Mia?

"We wouldn't know," Brisa responded from behind her. The group made room for the addition. "We aren't Aether."

"But the people who attacked him weren't Aether," Mia responded, looking out at the masses. Mia was the Aether. She should be able to tell who it was. But there were too many people, all with pulsing auras. Drama was everywhere. Even anger and pain. But there was no way to tell from where it originated.

"Who would benefit the most from him being gone?" Calder posed.

"Malta was pretty upset her guy didn't make it on the team," Brisa commented thoughtfully.

"And that would explain why that... Aether was coming on to you," Damek added. He jerked back when he saw Mia cringe. "Not that he wouldn't... it isn't... I need to keep my mouth shut." He sighed as the others laughed.

"No, he was really aggressive," Mia frowned.

"Malta is my family," Colin stated from the cabin's open doorway. There stood Colin, wearing Mia's hoodie.

"Is that my hoodie?" Mia questioned, taking in the ill-fitting jacket.

"Uh... well... none of your shirts would fit. And I didn't want to walk around half naked," Colin blushed.

"I don't know. Some ladies here apparently like the scrawny look," McKenna snorted. Colin turned an even deeper shade of red.

"Why don't we sit down?" Mia moved to the right side of the couch. The rest joined, filling in the sofa and the two armchairs. McKenna lounged on the porch railing, leaning against a post. Though her posture was slouched, her body radiated awareness. She kept one eye on the people who ventured past the cabin.

"Let me repeat. Malta is my family. I know she doesn't want me on the council, but I don't think she would be okay with me getting hurt. Maybe maimed..." he joked, trying to lighten the mood.

"If not Malta, who?" Calder looked around.

"Well, who is the Neanderthal who bugged me earlier attached to? Does anyone know who he is?" Mia questioned.

"Right now, he's talking to an older man by the purple tents," McKenna commented. As one, they turned before McKenna made a tutting sound. Calder refilled McKenna's glass, taking a look in the Aether direction. Mia jumped up, holding out her cup.

"That's the guy who was arguing with Malta this morning," Mia whispered.

"He's an Aether?" Colin asked. "Around Valdis? Older man, grey hair, rather round belly." McKenna nodded. "That's Valdis' dad. He is on the Aether high council. He and Malta have been vying for power from each other for years."

"He tries to get rid of Colin and put his own son on the new council?" Brisa wondered. McKenna lifted her hand in warning and laughed. They all stopped talking at once.

"Who knows how to drive?" Mia jumped in. McKenna, Colin, Calder, and Damek raised their hands. "I call shotgun," she exclaimed with a smile at Brisa. A group of younger Elementals were drifting towards the deck. They were trying to overhear something or learn more about the new council members. More and more of the other partiers disappeared into the woods or into their tents.

"Perhaps we should continue this on the road tomorrow?" McKenna asked. She received slight nods from all over the porch. "However, as nice as our theory is about this 'accident', we don't know if it is only Colin that someone was after. Return to your camps but be careful. Take note of anything and anyone strange. And stay away from fire." McKenna chuckled. "Can't believe I just said that." She started heading for the Fire camp, grabbing arms with another warrior. The two stumbled their way back to the Fire tents.

"'Til morning then," Calder grinned at the crew, taking his bottle with him. He sauntered to the blue tents, swinging his arm over the shoulder of a simpering blonde as he went. Brisa and Mia exchanged a look and laughed.

"I'm not sure I want to head back to my tent. Not after earlier," Colin whispered.

"Sleep on the couch," Mia offered. He suddenly turned into a tomato.

"That wouldn't be… I mean… I couldn't… people would think…" Mia's face quickly became the same red.

Brisa laughed, "I'll stay too. I just have to go get my stuff." She frowned at the Air camp. "Actually, I might get more sleep this way." She started to move.

"Wait, how about we both go together?" Colin offered. Brisa nodded, and the two headed off.

"She can't sleep?" Damek questioned Mia with concern.

"She is feeling a little smothered," Mia confessed.

"You're still connected to her?"

"No, it… it's her aura. The discomfort increases any time there is anyone from the Air clan near her."

"About earlier, that cross breeding comment…. I never… I wouldn't-"

"I know," Mia cut him off. She was going to be permanently red. Mia sighed. "I just don't… I could tell he was implying…. something… but I didn't… I just didn't get it."

Damek turned red too. "Some Aether marry into other Elements. Those unions usually produce an Elemental priestess." The bonfire had almost been deserted. "He was implying I would try and … use … you to help the Earth clan." He turned back to her, "I would never do that… I…"

"I know," Mia replied again, pulling her legs up against her chest. She placed her arms around them as if she was hugging herself. As she looked around the trashed campsite, Mia felt a little lost. "Marrying an Aether is something other clans try to do. That's why they wanted Triana to marry the Fire guy."

"Triana?" he frowned. Mia shook her head and leaned it back on the couch. It had only been three days since she was warm in her own bed. Triana's awful folk music coming down the hall. Mia's head jerked up as she listened to the music still coming from the different camps. The music reminds Triana of home, Mia realized. Damek was studying her with his dark green eyes.

"I could stay too… if you needed… or if it would make you feel safer," Damek shrugged.

"It also means you could avoid making a decision about what's her face?"

"There is that too," he grinned sheepishly.

"You are more than welcome, but I think we'll be okay."

"Will you?" he inquired. "This is a lot to take in, and don't get me wrong, you seem to be taking everything well. But I can't imagine being thrown into the middle of so much so quickly. I'm overwhelmed going from 'non-marked poor Damek' to 'special marked powerful Damek.' Forget finding out about a whole world changing thing."

Mia's eyes welled slightly. "It is a little overwhelming." She faced him. "Growing up, I kept thinking I was a freak. It was hard being so isolated. So I'm trying to focus on the fact that I'm no longer alone." She hugged her legs a little tighter.

"You aren't alone," Damek pronounced. "And you're stuck with us, so you'll never be alone again." He smiled. "I promise." Colin and Brisa were returning. "I guess I'll go back to my camp. I have some goodbyes to say."

"Not worried about…."

"Solange," he supplied, then shrugged. "I'll see you in the morning." He acknowledged Colin and Brisa, then left for the green tents. Mia watched him leave until Colin came up to her side.

"Okay, let's find somewhere for you guys to sleep," Mia jumped up and headed back into the cabin. She would never be alone again, she repeated in her mind. He promised. Mia felt her heart catch slightly, even though she knew it probably wasn't true. With a sigh, she focused on the task at hand.

CHAPTER ELEVEN

The new council were on the road early the next morning. When Mia prepared to leave, she found several pieces of Triana's clothes and jewelry left behind after she disappeared. Did someone else pack Triana's things, so they didn't know what belonged to who? Mia placed Triana's belongings with her own worried about where Triana had gone. After a final inspection, Mia closed the door to the cabin for the last time.

Different clan members loaded a beat-up van that could seat seven with supplies and handed the keys to Colin. At some point all of the new council, except Mia, were pulled aside by their elder for a brief meeting. As each of the teens arrived with their elder counterpart, the relationships between them became obvious. Brisa was uncomfortable around Boreas but cared for him. Brisa's arms encircled herself as he hovered only a few steps away. There were dark circles under her eyes from the tossing and turning Mia had witnessed last night. The poor man was guilt stricken by what he felt was his neglect of a beloved niece.

McKenna trailed after Brand. The girl was angry again, but since Mia met her, McKenna had shifted back and forth between anger and hyper-alertness. When Mia finally read the note from Brand, she found Triana's handwriting. All it said was 'Trust no one and do what YOU know is right'. It made Mia tense. Could she really join this council without giving them her trust? If they were going to be a team, it would be necessary. Wouldn't it? And why was Brand giving her a message from Triana?

Damek and Delphine were close. Their features were so similar, Mia could see the relation. Their facial expressions were almost the same when they were thinking. They sported the same half smile when talking to each other. It was hard to believe Damek was the one that threw McKenna in the fire only three days ago. He came across as calm but was the most worried about what Mia would see if they touched. Even though he claimed he was willing to distance himself from the old council, there was little distance between him and Delphine. And the ex, Solange, kept creeping around the perimeter with a constant eye on Damek.

Calder followed Sarila at a distance. The woman looked down upon him. He had mentioned royal blood last night. The old council had mentioned the general lack of it when referring to the new council as well. If he wasn't royal, was he... like... a peasant? How did that work? Especially in modern society? Sarila treated him like dirt on the bottom of her shoe. There was definitely no love lost there. He clearly felt no loyalty to her.

Finally, Colin arrived with Malta. The conflicted woman worried about Colin, and, from what she could tell, about Mia as well. Colin looked to Malta with affection, but also with a bit of confusion. Evidently, their warning to distance himself was being taken seriously. His ties to Malta were strong. Perhaps he was the one Triana was warning Mia about.

As the others loaded and piled in the van, Malta came to stand next to Mia. "Triana said you needed help to control your gift. That is why she brought you here. It has been a few generations since we have had someone as connected to the spirit as you seem to be. However, based on the stories we have passed down from Cailleach to Cailleach, no one can control their gift. Because of your gift, you are a vessel of the Goddess and the Moirae… the fates. You can learn to channel that gift, study and learn to become a Banduri… but the gift itself…" Mia stomach dropped a little. So much for stopping her visions. "When you could see with the girl's eyes, your hand clutched the carnelian at your neck,"

Malta continued. Mia tried to think back. Had she? She remembered seeing the rock, but not any of her movements. "An attempt was made on my nephew's life," Malta stated. "I watched you fall and have the vision before it happened. Again, you grabbed at your neck. Were you wearing the amethyst?"

"Yes. I was representing the Aether so I thought it was appropriate." Malta stayed silent for a moment.

"I owe you a debt," Malta started. "Colin is very… precious to me. You saved his life." She finally turned and looked Mia in the face. "I know my… style is not yours. Though you would not accept my last gift, I believe this one will assist you with the task ahead of you." Malta held out a simple silver necklace with a pendant containing five colorful stones, all set around a white moonstone. "These stones represent the five Elements. Carnelian for Air, as you have already discovered. Amethyst for the Aether. Obsidian for Fire. Lapis for Water. Agate for Earth. Finally, a moonstone for yourself in this new world."

Mia took the necklace and turned it around in her hand. It was simple but beautiful. Immediately, she felt connected with each of the stones and put it on. "Thank you."

"I know you do not trust me… but I do wish you well. Be careful in this new world. May the Goddess be with you." Malta bowed her head slightly, then moved away.

The tension in the van was thick. The newly formed group headed south into the Appalachian Mountains on the Blue Ridge Parkway. No one talked as the van wound its way through the mountains. The tangled roads doubled back on themselves. Mia lost herself in the beautiful vistas, forgetting the others in the car. This was so different from Connecticut. Most of the trees were bare except the evergreens, leaving little to block her view. No one can control their gift. Malta's words haunted her. But everyone was so determined to help the 'Morey' thing, had anyone actually tried? It may be an honor, but it was one Mia didn't want.

As the mountains began to tower above them, limiting their view, she returned her attention to the people in the van. The tension wasn't as intense as it had been a few hours before. Colin focused on the road. Damek and Brisa were in the far back, sitting next to each other. They both had a wistful look on their faces as they watched the mountains around them. McKenna and Calder were in the middle. They had moved themselves as far apart as possible. Guess it made sense; Fire and Water probably didn't mix well. Her fingers kept moving up to touch the necklace from Malta. She took out her book and tried to read, but her eyes would unwittingly move upwards to watch the road. She wondered where it may lead.

Hours passed, but still no one really talked. It was an unspoken agreement to allow each person to sort their thoughts before sharing. When they arrived in Atlanta, they would probably talk for hours, but for now the silence acted like a healing balm. Eventually, they settled in on 75 South for the final stretch. The monotony of the highway lulled Mia to sleep. The bumps of a coble stone driveway woke her with a start. They pulled into a ranch-style house with green shutters. It was made out of a painted brick. The architecture was dated, but it was a place to stay.

"Welcome home," Calder exited the van. He moved up towards the front door, pulling out the keys.

"Looks like close quarters," Mia guessed.

"Who's gonna be roomies?" asked McKenna, grabbing a couple of bags as she headed to the door.

"It's bigger than it looks," Calder said, opening the door.

As they moved through, the group stopped, overwhelmed. As soon as the light was flipped on, they realized the outside did not match what was inside. They immediately stepped down four stairs into a large living space with vaulted ceilings. Near the front, there were doors on the left and the right that led, on inspection, to two small guest rooms. Hardwood floors led to a far wall comprised entirely of glass, save for a huge stone fireplace at its center. Beyond the glass wall, the lake offered a stunning view.

"This is insane," Mia muttered. It felt like they were in one of those TV shows that featured the lifestyles of the rich and famous. Most of the apartments that Mia had lived in would fit into the living room of this place. Large dust cloths covered all the furniture. On the left was a staircase that spiraled downwards. On the right was an open huge modern kitchen and dining area. The front left had a door to a master suite that had a wall of glass open to the lake as well.

The group split up; Calder and Brisa headed out to the porch while Mia, McKenna, Colin and Damek made their way down the inside stairs. Below was another central living space with a huge screen television on the wall in the middle of another set of glass walls. Doors led to the left and the right with two additional bedroom suites.

"How about the ladies take one floor and the gentlemen the other?" Damek suggested. "The guys should probably take the lower floor. Brisa will get more wind upstairs." McKenna agreed and headed back up. As Mia and McKenna reached the top floor, Calder and Brisa entered.

"Bri, ladies are taking top level. Which room do you want?" McKenna asked.

"Actually," said Brisa, walking over, "I think I'd rather be out on the porch. There is a couch out there and I… I'd rather feel the breeze for now."

"It's November. I know it isn't as cold down here as up north, but I'm sure it gets cold during the night," Mia glanced at McKenna.

"I'll move in if I need to. I just… Why don't you two pick your rooms and I'll just come in if I need to …." Flashes of the confined cabin Brisa had been held in went through Mia's mind.

"Right now you need the space?" Mia prompted.

"Well, why don't you take the master then Brisa- It has access onto the porch, so you can stay out as late as you want," McKenna suggested. Brisa agreed. "All right, I'll take the left." McKenna moved toward her room, leaving Brisa and

Mia in the middle of the living room. "Let's get everyone together on the patio in a half hour." McKenna disappeared.

"I'll take the right then," Mia confirmed. She watched as Brisa went back to the patio, settling on a green couch.

Mia picked up her bag and moved to a spare bedroom decorated in a blue motif. Pictures of the lake in different seasons adorned the wall. She flopped back on the bed, and a cloud of dust flew up around her. *Yuck*, Mia thought as she pulled the comforter off the bed. The sheets underneath appeared clean, so she laid down and stared at the ceiling. The expanse of white was comforting. Almost every ceiling, in every home she had ever lived in, had plain white ceilings. Silly, the things that make you feel stable. Soon Mia heard McKenna heading back through the living room, calling to Brisa. Rifling through her bag, Mia checked to see if she had enough power to turn on her phone. As soon as it lit up, she called Triana. There was no answer. She heard McKenna yell her name. *Guess it's time to see what's up.*

The entire gang gathered around a fire pit behind the house. There were houses on both sides, but dense trees gave the illusion of privacy. Mia watched the group regard each other warily.

"How is this house deserted?" Mia ventured. "I mean it's incredible." Calder relocated to the wrought-iron bench beside her. He positioned his arm behind her and leaned in.

"In 2010, they had to drain the lake to fix a dam. They piped the water back in, but until all the water recirculates through nature, the water isn't pure enough to be an Undine's main water source. Atlanta… well… it's totally land locked. But lots of business goes through here… So they kept the property but won't move back for a couple more years. They didn't mind loaning it too much."

Calder's eyes were a fascinating blue green. His lazy half grin was contagious, instantly making Mia smile. Colin had tried to take the seat next to her before Calder slipped in. Colin settled on a log a couple of feet away, still carrying his leather notebook. Damek was sitting protectively next to Brisa on an opposing bench, and McKenna was working on bringing the fire to life in the middle.

"Pipes taint the water?" Colin asked as he opened his notebook.

"Human processing does. Being held in man-made tanks, all of it taints the water."

"Is there a chance they could monitor us in the house?" McKenna didn't look up from the growing embers of the fire. The cozy atmosphere immediately dropped away. Calder leaned back.

"Monitoring?" Brisa looked around.

"Listening devices, microphones," McKenna focused on Calder.

"You think the Undines are spying on us," Calder stood, tension thick in his voice.

"Undines are known to be manipulative," McKenna faced him head on.

"Excuse me!" Calder snapped.

"Okay, calm down!" Damek barked.

"Who put you in charge, Gnome?" McKenna sneered.

"A Lizard was the one who soaked Colin's shirt," Damek snapped.

"Earth and Water pushed him towards the fire!" McKenna's voice raised.

"And a Sylph tried to push him in," Brisa concluded quietly, but with enough gravity that everyone stopped.

"Four different clans conspired to kill Colin. Right now, I think it is best if we assume the only people we can trust are sitting in this circle," Mia cautioned. There was a pause as Mia's attention darted from one figure to the next. Each seemed to take in the idea.

"Okay," Calder acquiesced. The tension didn't leave him as he sat down. "Our meetings stay in the open where it is less likely we can be heard?"

"Couldn't someone still be listening? They use long range listening devices on TV," Mia commented.

"In a wooded area, it would be hard to hear, even with a device," McKenna scoffed. "But we need to be aware. We will need to be vigilant," she added grudgingly, taking a seat. Damek followed her lead.

"And Sylph would have to have a clear path between us and them to hear us," Brisa noted.

"Sylph?" Damek asked.

"Sylph can hear long distances, as long as there is nothing to impede the sound wave."

"Cool," Mia responded. What else could you say? Brisa remained silent. Colin was writing furiously in his notebook again.

"Did anyone have anything weird happen before we left?" McKenna changed the subject.

"I stuck with Mia and Brisa. No one really came near me again," Colin remarked.

"Nothing here," Calder chimed in. Damek shook his head.

"Then the question remains. Was it just Colin they were after, or was it an attack against all of us?" McKenna's brow furrowed. They sat contemplating for a time, but no one had an answer.

"Why would anyone want to kill us?" Mia whispered, a shiver traveling down her spine. Calder put his arm around her shoulders. Without thinking, she flinched. Immediately, his arm jumped back. He gave her a reassuring smile. Mia wanted to kick herself for the reaction but going from no one touching her to constant human contact was leaving her raw.

"We're a threat to the ways things have always been. Some people don't want change. It scares them. And because of that, they lash out. Fear can undermine the best of people." As Calder spoke, his voice comforted more than the words did. "But change is inevitable, just like the changing of the tides. You either ride the waves or you're destroyed by them."

"I didn't know the Undines were such philosophers," Colin quipped.

"Well, one of the clans has to be," Calder volleyed back.

"I am not sure that it was about the creation of the new council but an effort to control the new council," Damek mused.

"How so?" McKenna turned to him.

"Malta and her ilk were obviously trying to get a specific person on the council. Someone who would answer to them. They had no say about the rest of us. Mia's choice was the only one they could influence. Frankly, Mia threw them for a loop. Then that choice is immediately attacked?" Damek dismissed his own thought. "But it seems a little too obvious. They must have known it would be suspect if Colin died."

"Unless they said it was a sign, or a powerful Aether sanctioned it," Calder filled in.

"Still, Damek's right. It is a little obvious," Mia agreed.

"With us leaving so quickly, they may have felt backed into a corner," Colin added.

"For now, I would say Colin is safe," McKenna pointed out, "but if someone thought they could get rid of and replace one of us, that person probably thinks they can do that to any of us. We need to be careful."

"And look out for each other," Damek agreed.

"The Sylph elders talked to me before we left," Brisa said softly. "They didn't tell the entire story at the council meeting. They didn't trust the council with the truth." Everyone focused in on the small blonde waif. Brisa battled with the information they had given her. "They want me to ask for your blood oath that the information I am about to impart does not go back to your clans." It was the first true test of trust. Each of the teens wrestled with their decision.

"Can the information be used against any of our clans?" Calder asked. All heads turned towards Brisa as she considered her answer.

"No, it only affects whether your clans could hurt us. That is their fear. That this information could be used against us."

"We were told the Moirae created this council to help all Elementals. By accepting their charge, we are choosing to side with all instead of just one,"

Damek reasoned aloud. Damek's gaze was on a faraway point as he thought it through. "If it doesn't hurt any other Elementals, then I think our council should keep quiet anything that could hurt an Element. It is part of the trust we have been given."

"At the same time, we're responsible for all. If, in the end, this information is needed to protect another clan, it would be our responsibility to share it," Calder responded. "Is that a fair stipulation? If in the mission's course it becomes a threat to another, we will have to inform them. We will not keep information that could help or harm another clan by this oath."

"I believe that is fair and true to the task we have been given," Brisa agreed. "I realize that even though we are trying to assist my clan, my greater allegiance from this point onward must be to the new council."

"This is the moment. By accepting this oath, we are all swearing our allegiance to the council over our clans," McKenna ran her hand into her hair.

"Didn't that happen when our marks came in silver?" Damek offered. "We are of our clan, but not the same as our clan." *An Aether who is not an Aether.* The words from the prophecy floated through Mia's head. With the words reverberating through her mind, she regarded her fellow council members. They were pensive, evaluating the other teens. Mia tried to comprehend what they were being asked. If she had to choose the new council over her mom… or Triana… would she do it? But was that even the same? They were being asked to not only put their parents second but also their friends, neighbors, and everyone they had ever known.

"Then let it be our oath," Brisa stood, breaking the silence. Brisa reached out her hand to McKenna, who pulled out a knife. McKenna carefully put it in Brisa's palm. "I, Brisa, daughter of Camden, of the family Boreas, swear my allegiance to the new council." Brisa made a cut in her palm, then placed a finger in the blood and traced it over the silver Sylph mark on her wrist.

Damek released a long breath, then stood.

"I, Damek, son of Delphi, of the family Delphin swear my allegiance to the new council." Accepting the knife from Brisa, he cut his palm. One by one they stood and followed suit.

"I, Colin…"

"I, Calder…"

"I, McKenna…"

"I, Mia… Well… I really don't have a clan other than the council. So, I swear all my allegiance to it." Mia finished sheepishly. She cut her palm, trying not to wince from the pain. Then she copied the other teens and traced her mark.

"Well, that was intense," McKenna let out a huge breath. The others laughed while taking their seats.

"Well, new council," Brisa's face contorted as she struggled to convey her thoughts, "there is a rather horrible twist to this story. Apparently, the drug, Coro… it takes away a Sylph's ability to fly. It severs our connection to the wind." The reactions of every person around the circle was powerful. McKenna swore, Damek stood, and Calder and Colin tensed.

"I don't get it," Mia puzzled, wishing Colin was next to her so she could ask him silently.

"Being cut off from your Element… that's a death sentence," Colin murmured.

"Worse than a death sentence," Damek followed. The sound of fear that tinged Damek's usually strong voice made Mia shiver.

"And information that could be used against the Sylph," McKenna supplemented. "I understand why they didn't want to share that information."

"I told them they could trust you," Brisa declared, "and that you needed the information."

"You were right," McKenna asserted. Murmurs of agreement came from around the circle. "I agree. We should tell no one else about it, not unless this drug, Coro, can sever any Elemental from their Element. If that's the case, this drug is a threat to all; not just the one." Brisa nodded. "However, that changes things. If she couldn't ride the winds north, the girl was on foot the entire time. That decreases the distance she could have traveled."

"We need a map to see where they were in relation to the city," Damek stated.

"We can go to the spots that traveling Sylph would frequent in the area," Brisa offered.

"We can talk to the Sylph that found her," Calder said from over Mia's head.

"Are there any other Sylph clans in the area?" Colin chimed in.

"There are no other European Sylph. There is an African community around Stone Mountain," Brisa said slowly, "but my understanding is they do not separate by Element." Colin immediately started writing again.

"Were they contacted? Were any of the non-European Sylph contacted?" Calder asked.

"No," Brisa shook her head. "I don't think so. The Sylph have better relationships with the others than most Elementals, but we barely contact each other. Forget our distant relations." Mia tried to question Colin, but he shook his head slightly. She held on to the inquiry for now. Then Mia noticed McKenna staring at her.

"What is it with you two?" McKenna demanded.

"What do you m..mean?" Mia stuttered.

"You and Colin? I know he's supposed to be your guide but…" McKenna's gaze flicked back and forth between them. "You keep staring at each other. Didn't you just meet? Or is that a lie? In the last council meeting, you seemed to be talking." Colin coughed.

"That's because we were," Mia confessed. "When I hold Colin's hand, he and I can talk to each other."

"You read his mind?" Damek jumped in.

"NO!" Mia and Colin yelped at the same time.

Colin turned to Mia in a panic, "You can't, can you??"

"No!" Mia looked around the circle. "I only hear what he wants to say, like he's saying it out loud. We found we could do it when we were meeting with the old council. He answered some of my questions, so I could follow what was going on."

"Can you do that with any of us?" McKenna asked.

"No... rather I don't think so." Mia said. Calder's face had a huge grin.

"Here, try me," Calder insisted, holding out his hand. Mia regarded the hand warily. "I've offered it to you before... this time... take it." Calder coaxed. Mia placed her hand in his. No images flooded her. Tentatively she said, *Hello?* "That is sooo cool!" he exclaimed.

"You're supposed to say that silently," Mia teased. He laughed in return.

Can you hear me? Calder's voice whispered in her head.

Yes! Mia beamed.

Okay, we will have to think of super-secret conversations to have, otherwise this will be totally wasted! Mia chuckled at Calder's excitement.

"It works, I take it?" Colin commented sarcastically.

"Yes," Mia confirmed.

"Well, that could be really useful," McKenna mused. "Can all Aether do this? Or just the powerful?"

"I have never heard of it before," Colin admitted. "So it must be rare. Though our most powerful Aether do not speak of their gifts so I do not know everything they can do."

"Then it's a great secret weapon," McKenna sat back. "We need to work on everyone's skills. Brisa, we need to build up your strength again. Mia, have you had any kind of training?"

"No," Mia confessed, thinking of the punch the Air girl had landed at Samhain.

"Then we will start tomorrow." McKenna stood up confidently. "Tomorrow at dawn, we will start running. Everyone think about your strengths. And recognize your weaknesses."

Damek bristled, then added, "We have several leads. I think we start with the Sylph who found the teen before she died. Maybe they can give us some clues to help backtrack to where she was." Each member of the group nodded their agreement.

"Let the games begin…" McKenna muttered to herself, the fire flaring as McKenna walked away.

CHAPTER TWELVE

She feels the adrenaline course through her body, lighting her veins on fire. All the training, all the practice, it comes back to her effortlessly. Her staff swings, and she can feel it cutting through the air. Stupid humans and their belief in guns. She wants to laugh, but then a bullet hits her from behind. What feels like a sucker punch pounds into her left shoulder. Her vision goes red.

"Mia… wake up… MIA!" The room was dark as Mia woke up with a start. McKenna stood over Mia; her face completely freaked out. "Damn, Mia…" McKenna sat down on the side of the bed when she realized Mia was awake. Mia's mind tried to recapture the images from her dream… It was night… in the middle of a fight? She was shot. Someone fired a gun at her, and it hit! That one fact stayed vivid as the rest of the dream faded away. "What kind of nightmare was that?" McKenna asked.

"I don't know. I… it was like a vision, but…" Mia blinked.

"You were yelling," McKenna stated. She took in Mia's terrified expression.

"I was… There was a battle… I was fighting… I was shot." Mia tried to free herself from the nightmare, but fear gripped her.

"Well then… get up!" McKenna threw Mia's blankets off her. "We need to get you battle ready." Mia just sat, paralyzed. "Mia, move… Shake it off. Use the fear to motivate you. Mia!" Mia made herself focus on McKenna. "There you are. You are back in the here and now… and now… we run." McKenna pulled her out of bed. "Get dressed, we leave in five."

When they arrived at the small suburb of Alpharetta, Mia still hurt. Her sides and legs were sore from the early morning "run" McKenna had dragged her on that morning. Run being a positive way of describing the stuttering jogging that broke down to walking by the end. Mia's lungs were still in pain from the burning cold of the morning air. McKenna had pushed Mia as hard as she could. The dream haunted them both, pushing Mia to do more than she probably should have. The only satisfaction Mia had was that McKenna was in pain too. Apparently, the hills around Berkeley Lake had taken a toll, even on their resident warrior. As soon as she finished her session, Mia turned on her phone. Immediately, she entered Triana's number. After the tenth ring, Mia gave up.

Each of the new council had decided on how to best present themselves to the Sylph that day. Everyone, except Mia, was wearing their clan colors, since those were the clothes they had brought to Samhain. For McKenna, the black tank and black leather jacket enhanced her role as the muscle. Calder was joining her in the role, but his blue wasn't as intimidating. He wore a shirt that exposed his muscular arms. Brisa didn't have many clothes with her, only a few donations from the other Sylph at Samhain. So Brisa had washed and was wearing the yellow tunic she had been in at her presentation. The official looking style fit her role as the Sylph representative and therefore the main contact. Damek was wearing a dark green sweater and dark blue jeans. Since the Gnomes were the opposite of the Sylph, he was a front man, showing support in the Sylph time of need. From the first moment, they wanted to present the new council as being different and connected to all the Elements. Colin wore white to represent Aether. Colin's only job was to stand back and observe. Which left Mia. She didn't have any white clothing, so she settled for a soft green sweater, which brought out the same green in her eyes. It was the nicest shirt she had with her and the sleeves were long, allowing her to tuck her hands inside of them. Damek insisted Mia was one of the main ambassadors to the Sylph since the story of her defense of Brisa had undoubtedly spread quickly and would earn their respect.

The suburbs were the same as every other suburb in the country. The van entered a small gated community which had its entry thrown open. The houses were all similar in build and frame, but the similarities ended there. Each house had its own unique hue. There were sculptures in some front lawns, others were bursting with color from patterned vegetation. Kids ran around outside from one house to the other. It was a warm and welcoming community of artisans. Mia gaped at the variety and vibrancy of the small community.

"Wow," she marveled, waving at a small kid who had stopped at a corner to stare at them.

"Air," Colin quipped from beside her. "Lots of artists, poets, storytellers." Brisa didn't say a word as they moved farther inside the neighborhood.

"Remember, Brisa is our spokesperson with this group. We default to Mia, they are more likely to trust you, then Damek," McKenna repeated trying to cover up her own nervousness. The van pulled up in front of a large house at the end of a cul-de-sac. It was painted a vibrant green with yellow shutters. A large white-haired man came out of the front door. He wore painter's overalls and a Henley underneath. The teens jumped out of the van easily. McKenna was watching Brisa but Brisa wouldn't acknowledge her. Mia came up behind Brisa and put her hand on Brisa's elbow.

Are you okay?

It looks so much like home. Brisa was studying the ground. *It… it just reminds me…*

I get it. Really, I do. But these people will look to you. Brisa's head came up sharply. With a deep breath, Brisa pushed back her shoulders and nodded to McKenna's concerned stare. Brisa moved toward the man on the porch. Mia quickly fell in right behind her, next to Damek who gave a concerned glance. McKenna, Calder, and Colin followed in the rear.

"You kids are the new council," the older man said with one eyebrow raised.

"Yes," Brisa proclaimed. The entire group pulled themselves up, trying to exude as much authority as possible. Mia was sure they resembled a ragtag group of children. "We need to speak to the people who met and took care of the girl." He stood for a moment, scrutinizing them. Doubt radiated from him, but with a shrug, he released it.

"Okay." Then he was quickly off. Brisa followed him slowly. Mia's mouth twisted with amusement at the determined pace set to contradict the man who walked off. Mia reached for Brisa's elbow again.

He is doubtful but willing to give us a shot. Mia projected. Brisa nodded without looking back. Immediately, upon entering the house, their already slow pace came to a halt. Stained glass pictures, floor lamps, and sculptures surrounded them. The early afternoon sun reflected through the glass, painting the walls with rainbow hues. They moved into a large living room, then settled down on two couches. The older man collapsed into a large lazy boy recliner.

"The girl is upstairs," he offered, "but she isn't exactly capable of giving us any information. Her mind... it's... muddled." His face turned up as if he could look through the floor. Sympathy poured off of him.

"She's alive?" McKenna interjected. The man slowly turned to study McKenna. She blushed, which made her angry.

"Yes," the man stated. "Did you hear otherwise?" The teens waited for Brisa to step up. Mia signaled Damek. Just as he started to reply, Brisa's soft voice broke the silence.

"Boreas referred to her in the past tense. We assumed from there," Brisa answered. Her head stayed up, but it was obvious she was fighting to portray confidence. It may have been a mistake to push her into the forward position. Mia gestured to Damek. It was time to help her.

"That is probably because of her lost..." the old man interrupted himself.

"Connection?" Damek supplied. "King Boreas informed us that was the case." As the older man stuttered and turn red, Damek added, "We will not tell this secret to our clans. But it was imperative we know to help the Air clan. You have our Oath." The old man considered the teens, his gaze lingering on McKenna. All the teens bowed their heads when he looked their way.

"I have to imagine it's a living Hell," he shook his head. "She murmurs things, but nothing that makes sense. Our Cailleach has been with her since she arrived. We've even had our doctor examine her. The doctor insisted on running some tests. She doesn't believe a drug caused this. There are apparently no foreign... things... in her blood. I've called the doctor and she should be here soon to answer your questions."

"Have you informed the king?" Calder asked. "He still thought it was drug related when we spoke with him yesterday."

"We haven't. We only received confirmation of the results yesterday. And not everyone believes them. King Boreas called to say you were coming. I figured it would be better to talk to you first since you're the ones charged with dealing with this mess."

"Thank you..." Mia prompted.

"Neil," he stated.

"I'm Mia." She quickly introduced the rest of the council.

"The girl being alive changes things. Mia may be able to communicate with her," Calder interjected.

"Tana," Neil supplied. "Her name is Tana." He leaned forward and rubbed the stubble on his chin. "How do you propose to do that?"

"I-" Mia started. She didn't want to use her gift.

"She's an Aether," McKenna cut her off.

"She's a strong Aether... so maybe she will see something," Calder finished. Mia tried to let her insecurities show. At least now, the doubts she had about herself can help them.

"I don't know if you should go in there by yourself," he grimaced. "It's hard... to see... to witness. Our doc sedates her and feeds her through a nose tube. Our Cailleach uses every method she knows to ease the pain. But the lack of wind makes her feverish. I don't know how much longer she can last. I thought she would have left us weeks ago."

"Perhaps we should go now?" Damek offered. Brisa spun toward Mia with a panicked expression.

"Why don't you guys wait here? Too many people may make it harder for me to connect with her," Mia suggested. Brisa relaxed slightly and stared out a window. Her hand trembled slightly. Calder moved in, taking her hand and sitting down. Mia moved around the couch, following Neil as he exited the room. Only Damek followed. They proceeded up a narrow set of wooden stairs. When they reached the top, Neil hesitated.

"She's the one denied wind," Neil stated more than questioned. "She's doing well then? I… watching the pain this young girl is in, I wouldn't wish it on anyone. Not even my worst enemy." He placed his hand on the doorknob. "It's … It's painful to see. I want to warn you. We've taken as much care of her as we can, but without the wind… no matter what we do, she's wasting away. I can't believe…. Well, I don't believe it will be long now." He opened the door.

Neil slowly entered through the door of a small bedchamber filled with light. It was a corner room with two large open windows. The center of the room contained a bed occupied by a young woman. She slowly rocked her head back and forth on a cream-colored pillow. The sheets were partially thrown off to expose a gaunt body. Most of her joints were tied with yellow string. Stones and crystals had been placed around her bedside. Inaudible whispers issued from her mouth. Her white hair was stringy. Beads of sweat covered her brow despite the cool air. The man walked over and covered her with the sheet. Then he placed a white embroidered cloth over the sheet. "This is our Cailleach, Cailleach Ilma," Neil gestured to an older woman. An old lady sat beside the emaciated girl, speaking to her in gentle tones. The woman didn't look up when she was introduced. Instead she untied old yellow string and put new ones on, muttering as she knotted them.

"Do you need to touch her? Will you be able to go in her head, like with Brisa? Or just see images?" Damek asked under his breath. They stood at the door, watching Neil use a wet cloth to wipe the girl's forehead as the old lady finished her knots.

"I have no idea," Mia admitted. "Damek, I've never tried to use my abilities… except for when we talk to each other, I have never chosen to see anything. Sometimes I just do." They would find out at some point. Every time Mia thought she had some control, the Moirae laughed at her and showed how out of control she was.

"No pressure here. If you don't see anything, we're just back where we thought we were anyway," he reassured her. "Does the wind through the windows help her?" Damek asked in a louder voice.

"No, she doesn't commune with it," Neil frowned. "But it calms her. You can come over. It doesn't seem like she has much fight in her today." Damek and Mia approached. Mia positioned herself in front of a chair next to the bed. Mia focused on Tana's face. Tentatively, Mia grasped Tana's hand. Pain rocketed through Mia's body. Her vision went white.

The next thing Mia knew, she was on the floor. She opened her eyes to the round, worried face of the old woman.

"Children…" the woman clucked as she waved a cloth around Mia's head. Mia could feel pressure dissipate with each swipe. At that moment, the door to the room came crashing open. Calder and McKenna barreled through.

"What in the world?" McKenna exclaimed; knife drawn.

"Are you okay?" worried Damek. Mia realized she was being held in his arms for the first time.

"What happened?" Calder demanded.

"I…" Mia frowned, "I touched her… and… the pain…." Tears started to fall.

"Don't know what you were thinkin'. No groundin'… no crystals… just went ahead and touched the girl," the old woman griped. She helped Mia into the bedside chair. Colin and Brisa entered. At the first view of Tana, Brisa's legs gave out from under her. Colin caught her, but Damek rushed over to assist.

Damek carried Brisa out of the room and back downstairs. "Poor child," the woman clucked again.

"We heard you scream and came as fast as we could." Calder rushed over to Mia, taking her hand.

"I didn't expect…. I've never felt that kind of pain. It felt like every nerve was on fire." Mia considered the girl in the bed. She really was little more than a skeleton. Neil was right, with that kind of pain it might be better if this ended soon.

"Well… I suppose in your defense.. how many times do you come upon a girl in this situation?" Cailleach Ilma was still clucking around. She was short and portly, fussing at them like a mother hen. She cleaned the air around Mia's friends. This time, Mia could see their auras lighten in the process. The lady opened a huge box full of glass bottles. "Ahh… here we are." She pulled green herbs from two different bottles. The smell of mint and rosemary drifted through the air. She wrapped the herbs in a small piece of cloth. "Now, go give this to the little Sylph. It'll help her recover. A little in her tea. The posy can be kept in her pocket." She handed it to Colin who headed out the door. The woman turned back to the teens. "Humph, you were trying to connect with the child," she gestured in the bed's direction.

"Yes, ma'am." Mia acknowledged. "But with the pain… I couldn't…"

"Then we can't see where she was, or anything about her past," Calder stated matter-of-factly. McKenna looked to Mia.

"I can try again," Mia cringed.

"No," Calder responded instantly. The old lady harrumphed again.

"If you only feel pain," McKenna added, "there really isn't any point. We know she's in pain."

"I didn't expect it. I didn't prepare myself," Mia confessed. "I should try one more time."

"No," Calder repeated.

"Do you want to?" McKenna looked her in the eye, taking her measure.

"No," Mia admitted. She regarded the gaunt girl. Who did this to her? Were there others in the same condition? Mia took a deep breath, trying to be brave. "It's the only lead we have."

"Perhaps I can help," came a new feminine voice from the doorway. A petite blonde entered. She was wearing scrubs and carrying a bag.

"Vi, we've been expecting you," Neil exclaimed. The blonde moved in and kissed Neil on the cheek. He turned to the others, "This is Doctor Vianca Kellen… my daughter," he added with pride.

Calder gave her one of his flirty smiles. "It's nice to meet you, Dr. Kellen."

"Call me Vi," she responded. She didn't seem impressed. Right then, Damek returned.

"Brisa is downstairs with Colin," Damek shook his head. "She isn't speaking."

"As I was saying, I think I can dull the pain. If I dull the pain for her, will you be able to see past it? To what happened to her?" The doctor placed a medical bag on the end of the bed.

"You aren't touching her again," Damek interjected.

"We have no other leads," Mia repeated, but Damek's look was skeptical.

"Stand down, Damek," McKenna stood her ground when he stared at her. "It isn't decided yet." McKenna turned back to the doctor. "You're proposing that you drug Tana enough that she can't feel the pain… so Mia can see past it."

"Basically, I…" Vi frowned, "I don't know what she is feeling. Being cut off from your Element, what kind of pain is that? I can try to cut out the pain in her body, but I don't know how much of the pain is in her mind or soul. There is little I can do to save you from that. Honestly, I thought she would have been gone weeks ago."

"She's holdin' on for somethin'," the old woman commented, startling everyone with her continued presence. "I try to help her, but… the pain is so much… it's hard to know if it helps."

"Everything helps," Vi tried to mollify the old woman. The elder gave a derisive snort and collected the old ties, wrapping them in a cloth. Vi explained.

115

"In the old religion, tying knots binds the pain and pulls it out of the body. Cailleach Ilma has been caring for the girl since the beginning." The old woman muttered something about doctors under her breath, then left the room, grabbing a tall staff just like Malta's along the way.

Mia surveyed the room. Calder and Damek were obviously against the idea, and McKenna was wavering. What Mia had felt was so overwhelming that she passed out after only a second or two. That she had no recollection of screaming scared her. The moaning woman's fingers were now reaching out, searching for something. Perhaps it was Mia she was seeking. Maybe the girl was holding on, still trying to help her friends despite the torture of her existence. It made no sense that she would hold on for any other reason. Not if she was constantly living with the pain Mia had only felt for a moment.

"Cailleach Ilma is right," Mia struggled with the name. "She needs to tell me something so she can let go." She sank down into the chair. "I have to try to help her." All three of her friends exchanged glances.

"Is it possible for us to help?" Calder postured. "Can we help you anchor? Hold your hand?"

"I don't know," Mia's eyes went wide. "People have been afraid to touch me until now."

"Well, we're over that fear now," Calder grinned. "If you are going to do this, I would feel better if one of us was attached, so we could tell what was going on."

"How could you tell?" Vi asked quizzically.

"Tension, shaking, fever," McKenna jumped in. "If one of us is in physical contact, we will feel and see any issues." Though lame, there really was no other excuse but the truth. Mia agreed.

"We can… rather you can hold my hand." Mia blushed, looking down at her hands. They were trembling. Quickly, she shoved them into her jean pockets.

"I'll do it," Damek volunteered, cutting off Calder and McKenna's protest. "I was here the last time. I saw what happened. If you think I can watch again without at least trying to help, you're wrong." The last was said fiercely. The other two acquiesced.

"Damek," Mia whispered. "I haven't taken your hand yet." He had avoided her; avoided touching her until this point. His surprised expression was proof he hadn't thought it through. "It's okay… you don't have to." Damek grabbed her hand and held it between them. No images appeared. "Nothing." Damek released a breath.

"Okay, do you need some time to regroup before we try this?" McKenna interrupted.

"I would rather get it over with," she divulged. "I don't want to have to sit waiting… that may be worse."

"This time do it right," came the old lady's voice from the door. "Where are your groundin' stones? Your amulets?" Triana had given Mia a collection of stones to assist with grounding. Mia had tried using them but didn't feel any connection. Grounding was for when someone wanted to use their powers. Mia only wanted to ignore them. She left all the grounding stones with Triana. Cailleach Ilma started tsking, "Well, I suppose I'll have to assist."

"Cailleach Ilma, I don't think…" Vi started.

"No, you don't think child, bless your heart." The woman patted Vi on the cheek. "You may have turned your back on the old ways, but this is beyond your medicine." Mia could tell there was a history there. They were opposites. Cailleach Ilma was balanced. Her energy swirled serenely around her. Vi's energy was more like a tempest. The Cailleach went back to her box and pulled out what appeared to be a small jewelry box. She opened the compartments and pulled out the familiar smoky quartz and obsidian.

"I've tried using the stones at home but I couldn't…."

"Well then, let's do this together." Ilma placed the stones around the bed. "Okay Gnome, I have never tried using a different Element for groundin', but it's worth a shot. When Mia is ready, take her hand." Damek nodded. Ilma placed her hand over Mia's other one. "Reach out to the stones… focus on the energy… the vibration coming from them." Mia closed her eyes and reached out with her mind to the stones surrounding them. Mia focused on their energy, making out a slight pulsing from each stone. That was all she could do. Next to her, Mia could hear Ilma's voice humming. The vibrations from each stone melded together, creating a soft and soothing melody that matched Ilma's song. Mia allowed the music to wash over her, feeling the rhythm in her body as if she was standing in front of a huge speaker.

Mia opened her eyes and met Ilma's. "I'm ready."

"Then, let's do it," McKenna shifted to the far side of the bed. "Doc, do what you can do."

The doctor approached the bed. They watched as she pulled out a vial, filled a syringe, and pushed up the sleeves of the patient. The girl's arms weren't much bigger than twigs. They had pock marks and white scars all down them. It was easy to understand why the elders had assumed drugs were the culprit. Quickly, the doctor found a vein. Vi injected the contents of the syringe into her system. It was only moments until all movement coming from the bed ceased. The doctor stepped out of Mia's way.

Damek held out his hand to Mia, and she grasped it. *Are you sure about this?* He asked silently. Mia nodded and turned to the bed. Her other hand reached out, still shaking slightly. Damek squeezed, *I'm here, I'll be with you.* Ilma's hand stayed over Mia's as she reached out.

I'm not alone, Mia repeated and touched the young girl. This time it felt like someone was shouting in Mia's ear. Instead of her skin on fire, Mia's head was throbbing. She tried to focus on the melody from the stones. It was still playing faintly in the background of her mind. Slowly, the music became louder, with words singing to the tune. It was drowning out the pounding from the girl. Mia could feel the pain through the girl's body. It was as if Mia was lying in a tanning bed, heat enveloping her. Throughout Mia's body, she could feel cool spots at each of her joints. Mia focused on the cool spot. The pain drained away, leaving Mia able to process a series of images in her mind.

A bright green lawn, her brother, a hospital room, stars in
the night sky, running and running until she collapsed.

The visions ended and Mia let go of the girl's hand. Mia was back in the
room at the Sylph house. Mia's other hand was losing circulation because of
the viselike grip Damek had on it. He was down on one knee, holding his head.

"Damek??" Mia crouched before him. "Are you okay?" His eyes were tightly
closed but at the sound of her voice, he opened them.

"Is it over?"

"Yes," she answered, bewildered. "Did it hurt you?"

"It was pounding in my skull," he grimaced.

Mia turned to Cailleach Ilma, who had collapsed in a chair. "Did you see
all of that?"

Ilma wearily lifted her head. "No," she smiled weakly, "I'm a Cailleach, but
I am not an Aether. I was only able to lend you my strength to enhance your
own." To Mia's amazement, Tana's eyes opened and focused on Mia.

"I heard you. We will find them," Mia promised. Tana's hand twitched.
Unconsciously, Mia reached out and grasped her hand. Instead of pain, Tana
flooded Mia with love. The faces of Tana's mother and father, grandmother,
her brother Kenneth, and a younger sister, Paige. Mia nodded, receiving the
message, then Tana's eyes slowly closed. The small amount of tension in the
girl's body left, and she sank further into the mattress. A ragged breath. Tana
was gone. Calder came up behind Mia and put a hand on her shoulder, his
other on Damek's.

"Are you both okay?"

"Yes," Mia replied, not looking away from Tana, "I think so. I could see some
clear images. That poor girl suffered so much." A tear went down Mia's cheek
and she felt McKenna's hand on her other shoulder. Vi confirmed what they
already knew. Neil said a prayer as he covered her body with a sheet.

"Come, Cailleach Ilma," Vi offered to escort the woman, who was showing her age. Neil went to Cailleach Ilma's other side to escort her, too.

"Let's go downstairs," McKenna urged softly. Mia didn't move. Calder accompanied Damek out, but McKenna and Mia stayed at the foot of the bed.

"She didn't do this to herself, McKenna. Someone did it to her," Mia whispered. McKenna's face darkened.

"We will find them," McKenna repeated Mia's earlier promise, "and we will end this." She added. Mia nodded again. With a deep breath, Mia's body began to shake. McKenna awkwardly put her arm around Mia, holding her until the tremors past.

CHAPTER THIRTEEN

When McKenna and Mia came downstairs, the number of people in the living room had doubled. Brisa had moved to a window seat with Colin beside her, while Damek and Calder stood guard on either side. Neil was in the middle of a conversation with Vi. A large number of older people milled around with a lot of young men. The attention of the room was focused on Brisa. As soon as the room realized McKenna and Mia had returned, everyone shifted their attention to Mia. It hit her like a punch to the gut. Instantly, Mia's entire body blushed.

"Oh no," McKenna whispered, taking the temperature of the room. "Go stand by Damek." McKenna gave Mia a nudge. Mia shot her a confused look but agreed and proceeded to Damek's side. Silent communication flowed between McKenna and Damek. Then Damek moved his arm possessively around Mia's waist.

Why is everyone staring at me and Brisa?

You two are the only single females in the room. Suddenly, Damek's possession made sense. He was trying to deflect the men's attention. As she glanced around the room, it wasn't making an impression. The men were assessing her, some subtly, some quite blatantly. After their perusal, they talked to one of the older individuals in the room and left.

Why aren't they staring at McKenna? Mia asked. Before he could reply, Neil ambled over when he noticed the council had grouped together.

"The elders are organizing a dinner to honor Tana. I hope you will join us."

"We want to talk to your doctor," McKenna responded.

"You will… at the dinner," he attempted to placate them. "Vi has some other tasks this afternoon. You are welcome to explore the community, or we can prepare a room for you. It is only two hours from now."

"Of course," Mia agreed, ignoring the waves of displeasure radiating from Calder and Damek.

"We would like a room, but perhaps a walk would help to clear our heads first," Calder requested. Colin assisted Brisa in standing. She allowed Colin to wrap her hand around his arm. Neil led them to the front door.

"There's a park about three blocks that way," he pointed. They quickly left, making their way down the sidewalk.

"What was that about?" Mia asked out loud.

"It's the same thing as Solange," Damek postured. "You're powerful, and therefore attractive."

"Oh," Mia frowned, a bit disappointed though it made sense. Self-confidence was hard enough around so many good-looking people. Just looking around intimidated Mia. On the other sidewalks walked gorgeous, pale, blonde women layered in vibrant colors. They smiled the smiles that made men drool. If all pure Elementals looked like this, Mia's life would be a constant fight against feelings of inadequacy.

"You are beautiful in your own right," Calder joined Damek and Mia. He flashed Mia a grin, while Damek appeared confused. Calder sighed. "That Mia is on the new council is not the only reason a guy would look at her." Damek turned red.

"I didn't mean, I…"

"No, it's okay." Mia blushed again. "Well… I… thanks for the compliment." Mia lowered her head and walked faster to catch up with McKenna.

"You really are an idiot sometimes," she heard Calder chastise Damek in a light-hearted voice.

"Shut up," Damek growled. McKenna smirked at Mia, who was watching the ground in front of them while they strolled.

"Uncomfortable with the attention?"

"I've spent my entire life avoiding attention. It's weird being at the center of it," Mia frowned.

"I hate to tell you, but… You will be the center of attention a lot." Mia head lifted, flabbergasted. "I know you don't know the clans well yet. But the story of you reading Malta, that will spread, and fast. Malta is powerful, all the clans know of her. And if you can read her, well… that's a legend in the making."

"I'm not a legend. I don't even really know how to do… well… what I do." Mia sighed. "Everyone is in for a rather big disappointment."

"Well, that depends," Calder shrugged as he joined the conversation. "I don't know why the Moirae chose us. I think we all feel a little out of our depths. I've been trying to think about what we have that others don't. But I… I don't have an answer. The best I have is Mia's ability to read people. Of all of us, you're the only one I completely get being on this council. The rest of us… we are unusual in a different way." McKenna glanced over, annoyed with his assessment. Colin was escorting a silent Brisa. Damek had shifted back to them when Calder had joined Mia and McKenna.

"There is actually a lot of animosity between the clans. The fact that we have come together so quickly is… strange," McKenna pondered.

"The work of the Moi- thingy?" Mia questioned.

"The Moirae, the fates, do work in subtle ways," Calder responded. "I think the fact that we weren't marked for so long is what eased the transition. We are all members of our clans. We love our clans and know our heritage. But as we had to wait to get marked, we were distanced. It disconnected us from our clan just enough that when we were asked to leave it, we were able to in a way that most couldn't comprehend. Colin is still struggling a bit with it."

"He had his clan mark. He was completely connected to his clan. I still worry his loyalty is to Malta and not to us." McKenna considered Calder's statement. She glanced over at Mia. "Did you really see Colin in a vision? Or were you just trying to piss Malta off?"

"I… I don't have visions like that. But, I can read people. No one she presented was right. But Colin, he approached me without fear when I first arrived. He was willing to explain things to me and didn't treat me like a freak… he didn't covet what I could do. He just thought it was cool, no strings attached. He was open, and that was what I felt we needed most," Mia answered as honestly as she could.

"But you saw the attempt on his life before it happened," Calder pointed out. Mia considered that. She had been so wrapped up at that moment, she had never realized it. Mia had seen the future without touching someone. What's more, she had changed her vision. The realization made her dizzy.

Right then, the council reached a small park with a few trees, some picnic tables, and a kid's playground. It was empty except for a little girl who ran away as soon as she saw them approach. Without hesitation, McKenna led them to a table. They just fit.

"What did you see?" McKenna prompted Mia impatiently. Mia took a deep breath and closed her eyes. She let the images filter in, just as Triana taught her.

"The first image… we are lounging on a large green lawn. There is a large white house at the end of it; one of those old-fashioned southern plantations with a huge veranda and rocking chairs. Other groups are hanging out all over the lawn. Some are sunbathing, others talking, reading… We're sitting on an old quilt. It has patterns of blue and green. It's… soothing. Ken and Nephele are holding hands, laughing…. I'm slowly splitting up an orange and giving them pieces. My hands are sticky… I… I feel safe... happy…" Mia tried to focus outside of herself at the world again. "The other people are teens… I think they're all Sylph. There are around twelve… maybe more… but… they aren't all like me… they aren't European. They are from different tribes… African… South American… there are all types of people." Mia blinked, trying to dispel the images grip on her consciousness.

"The other tribes," Calder said grimly. "We need to contact them immediately."

"We can check with Neil about their location and the best way to approach them," McKenna agreed.

"Sorry guys… I'm lost… tribes?" Mia directed the question at the group.

"Each of us are from the European tribe," Colin explained, darting a glance at McKenna.

"At least partially," McKenna gave Colin a withering look.

"Elementals are from all over the world," Colin continued. "There are clans on every continent. But in North America, mainly because of the United States, there are clans from almost every continent here. I think the most Europeans have relocated here, but who knows. The Europeans were looking for open places as Europe became crowded, running from poverty and depressions. Many left because of religious persecution… Also, during the world wars. There is a huge European Elemental network here."

"Traditions differ dramatically from continent to continent," Calder added. "Most clans are led by people born over a hundred years ago, many in a different country. Everyone holds their own traditions sacred. So the different tribes don't contact each other much."

"The Sylph are travelers," Brisa spoke for the first time since they left the house. "We contact the other tribes more than most. They should be more than willing to listen and talk with us." Her voice faded as she finished speaking.

"We will contact the other tribes," Damek granted. "The description of the house. Was there anything unusual? Was it a home? Or a hotel? A hospital?"

"I…" Mia thought back, "I think… it was… a resting spot? Maybe a hotel? They seemed rooted to the place. They weren't in a hurry to leave but had been there a while."

"We can research hotels then. I am not sure that's enough to help us find the actual house, but it will help us recognize it when we do," McKenna deliberated. "Was that all you saw?"

"That was all I saw in the first image," Mia confirmed.

"How many images did you see?" Colin piped up.

"Four, but I'm not sure there is much more information that will let us find them."

"What was the next?"

"A hospital room. I'm trapped in bed, not constrained but nauseous, feverish… I can't move because I'm ill. The vision is hazy because I think it is hazy for her. She can't see clearly. There's a nurse. She's putting something into an IV attached to my right arm, then she moves to the end of the bed to check my chart. She's wearing navy blue scrubs…."

"Can you see her arms?" Calder interrupted.

"No… she's wearing a long sleeve shirt under her scrubs. Her hair, brown… dark brown… and she's wearing glasses… In my left arm, there's a tube coming out… red… And something cold, very cold coming back in? There is talking but I can only make out some words, not even sentences. Experiment… faster… Coro… And then the drugs from the IV take effect and the world gets fuzzier…" Mia slid off the bench but Calder caught her as she tried to shake off the image. "I… think…"

"Hey, it's okay…" Calder's voice helped pull her from the vision. Mia turned crimson.

"Sorry." She pulled herself up.

"The nurse couldn't have been an Elemental," Colin stated.

"Why?" Mia turned to him.

"Glasses? Elementals don't wear glasses."

"Unless they weren't to help her eyesight. They were to hide who she is. She was wearing long sleeves. That would hide any marks," Calder contested.

"Brown hair... sounds Gnome," McKenna added as Damek bristled, "If it was an Elemental, that is where we need to search."

"It isn't common, but the clans do work together," Brisa contradicted.

"What was the next image?" McKenna prompted again.

"Running away. She's running down the lawn from the earlier vision, but it's late at night. Everything is doubled, hazy. There is blood trickling down my right arm where I pulled out the IV. My hand is covering it. No one seems to have noticed. No one is chasing me yet, but I'm scared... At the end of the lawn are manicured bushes, but beyond that... wilderness. I'm not as panicked once I reach the trees. I still run.. racing as fast as I can to get away. I'm wearing scrubs... like the ones the nurse was wearing earlier, but no shoes." Mia's mind switched to the last image. "Then the last image which is of the running. It feels like days later. My whole body is shaking from fever. Staying in the trees even at inhabited areas. I... need Sylph... can't fly... Can't hide myself... My feet hurt so badly... Can't catch the wind.... I can hear Sylph though... my grandmother, guiding me... I can hear or feel... I just know to keep going..." This time, Mia was shaking and Calder's arm was around her as she came out of the trance. Everyone stayed silent.

"She didn't understand her inability to feel the wind? She didn't know what had happened to her?" Damek finally asked.

"I only felt confusion. I was so feverish... it felt like I was hallucinating. The fire was there. I... She could feel it in her veins. She was disconnected, but she didn't realize it." They were silent again until Brisa finally whispered.

"When you start to lose your connection, it feels like a fever... like you're sick... headaches, body shivers. It isn't overwhelming. It comes on slowly. I think the first week or two was like that. But then, the fever gets worse. You sweat... The world seems to shift around you and you can't tell which way is up. Your body aches. You can't control the shaking. People talking to you... you don't know what is real and what isn't, after a while. You just get lost in the pain. Time moves so slowly..." Brisa's voice faded out. "And I could get a little wind, without any... it may have occurred faster," Brisa choked out. Damek instinctively embraced Brisa as her entire body stiffened. He moved to release her, but Brisa's hands were grasping the front of his shirt as tremors moved through her body. Damek held her tighter until the shaking passed. It froze everyone at the table. How do you help? How must it feel? Mia's perception of the pain the girl had been in was excruciating. To have felt it for any length of time… Mia couldn't imagine.

"Then it wasn't a hotel, it was more of a hospital. Tana could tell there was a problem… that they were doing something to her and she felt the need to escape. She wasn't let go willingly," McKenna redirected everyone's attention.

"I'm surprised there wasn't a wall or gates or something, if they were truly being held prisoner," Calder added.

"They're Sylph. What are walls or gates to them?" McKenna pointed out, but Mia frowned. Could Air go through walls?

"Sylph can ride the winds, over any kind of gate they would have. McKenna is right, though. I am not sure how much of what Mia saw helps us," Colin explained.

"She was walking in the woods for days. With very little civilization. Until she reached Sylph?" Calder jumped in. "Then at least we know she had to be outside the city by a bit. Where can we find that much untouched wilderness in north Georgia? Did she make it to this community? I find that hard to believe… we're surrounded by other burbs."

"No, they found her farther out, at a cabin at the base of the mountains," Brisa sat up, trying to focus on her companions instead of her memories. "They brought her here to see Cailleach Ilma and the doctor."

"Going to the cabin may prove useful. We can trace back as much as we can. There is only so far someone can walk, even in several days' time. It would give us a more manageable area to investigate," Damek offered.

"Especially with as far gone as she was. I do not know how she did it. The amount of strength it would take… Tana is remarkable… She… was… remarkable," Colin commented.

"True," McKenna agreed.

"She was focused on saving her little brother. That kept her going," Mia disclosed.

"Then we need to save him for her," McKenna declared fiercely.

"First, we need to go see the other tribes. Have them find out how many of their teens are missing. We may be searching for considerably more than twenty-four. We need to go to the cabin and scout the land, see where she could have come from. She definitely was not in Atlanta itself, nor could she have gone through it. We need to explore the north," Damek looked around.

"If this was a resting spot for Air teens on their travels, they would have had to get word on it," Brisa said. "There isn't a known spot like that in Atlanta so they would have to have heard about it while they were here visiting the... parks." She paused. "Sylph who are traveling are not supposed to go into the big cities much. We keep to the National Parks. Maybe a day trip, or two, to see the museums. It has only been in the last fifty years that young Sylph have been ignoring that edict. It's kept secret. Those of us about to go on a rata... a coming of age, inspirational journey, are told what cities to visit, but not much more. Perhaps we should travel to general tourist areas Sylph would be inclined to visit. See if we hear of a... resting place."

"Mia, you only saw Sylph in the vision, correct?" Damek asked.

"Except for maybe the nurse?" Mia verified.

"That means that they may tell Brisa, but none of us. Sylph don't travel with other clans, so we can't be with her. And frankly, Brisa shouldn't go by herself." Damek stated the last as a fact.

"He's right," McKenna acknowledged. "But you are too. Perhaps there are some Sylph here we can trust?" She turned to Mia.

"I can try to evaluate them tonight at the dinner."

"I don't like the way they are trapping us here so we can see the doctor," Calder said uneasily. "Why are they so insistent we stay? What do they want?"

"They seem most interested in Mia and Brisa," Damek observed, frowning.

"I noticed that, too," Colin added. "There was general curiosity about the new council, but more than that it centered on the two of you. Perhaps it is the rumors of Brisa imprisonment. As horrible as that is, they may just be curious out of sympathy or wanting to support her?" He asked Mia.

"I don't know, I didn't focus on their thoughts, I was just…"

"Trying to hide," McKenna smirked. "The focus on you could be due to your reading of Malta."

"They had most of their young men there," Damek's face twisted. "Maybe they're thinking wooing a strong Aether is an idea with merit." Mia turned crimson from head to toe.

"How am I supposed to face them if that is true?" she whispered, completely embarrassed.

McKenna broke the tension by laughing. "Mia, they're trying to impress you. You don't have to respond and knowing what they're up to should let you see through what they're doing. Besides, it can't be too horrible having tons of handsome men trying to win your favor." Mia had no response. Lanamnas eicne no sleithe. If she rejected the suitors, would they try to force a marriage? How would they try to trick her? Panic filled her chest. She repeated her promise to herself. If she was ever put in the same position as Triana, she would leave.

"We won't leave you alone," Calder added gently. Mia concentrated on Calder to quell her fear. "You're Aether, so any of the guys can hang around you without suspicion. Brisa… you probably need to stick with Colin. The closeness is something they would understand more." Brisa nodded. The conversation made little sense. If she couldn't get ahold of Triana, Mia would have to ask Colin later.

"If this is a funeral, are we dressed appropriately?" Mia asked, changing the subject. She looked down at her casual wear. Attention moved back to Brisa.

"Sylph dress up but with bright colors. We view death as an event to celebrate. It is the beginning of a new journey, a new adventure."

"Are other clans usually welcomed at a Sylph funeral?" Damek asked.

"No," Brisa frowned. "Which is why their insistence we stay is very unusual."

"What can they gain then?" Calder queried.

"Keep track of any unusual questions or conversations people try to raise with you," McKenna encouraged.

"And try to keep your temper," Calder added. "They may push to see how we react."

"I know that one's for me. I'll do my best," McKenna scowled.

"We've got your back," Mia offered.

"It's been at least an hour. Let's go get cleaned up and see what the Sylph have in store for us at this dinner." They stood and stretched their legs. Mia noticed on the far side of the park Cailleach Ilma in a rocking chair. She sat on the porch of an old wooden house that didn't match the others in the community.

"You guys go ahead, I want to check in with Cailleach Ilma." Mia jogged to the porch as the rest headed back down the street. "May I join you?" Mia asked. Cailleach Ilma nodded and Mia sat in a neighboring rocking chair. "We've been asked to stay for the funeral this evening."

"Asked?" the old woman gave her a sideways glance. "No... I don't think they asked... coerced, perhaps." She sighed. "My 'successor' is considerably more political than I ever was. It's not the way of the Cailleach to control clan business, instead to be a resource in times of need."

"Cailleach... that's a priestess?" Mia queried.

"A Cailleach is one who encompasses many roles in the clan. They are medicine women, priestesses, storytellers, leaders, philosophers. The Cailleach is all of those put together in one person. You must train from an early age and continue to learn until the moment they place you in your grave. Cailleach is the old-world term... though some call us teacher, others witch." She gestured at the community. "The young though, they don't want to train or learn. They want it given to them. They want power without the work," she sniffed. "Some don't believe in the old ways at all. They believe in their modern medicine and mock what I use. I've had to be tricky... No one ever refuses a cookie from an old lady… and they never ask what's in 'em," she chuckled, then looked back at the community. They sat in silence for some time.

"Thank you, Cailleach, for teaching me how to use the crystals for grounding."

"Of course, my dear," Ilma gave a weary smile. "You still have a lot to learn but keep your heart and mind open and the lessons'll come as you need them," she urged.

"The ties you used to bind Tana's pain, are they Sylph magic?"

"That's simple knot magic. You can do the same. Just visualize what you want 'em to do and ask the universe to assist you in the binding."

"But you used a different language."

"My mother's language. She was the Cailleach before me and taught me in her mother tongue. English'll do. It's the intention… not the word. However, I think the bigger challenge for you will be believing you can do it." Ilma appeared exhausted. Better to let her rest. Mia stood up.

"Will you be at the funeral tonight?" Mia asked.

"Yes, some will need me there. I think there will be mixed feelings about this funeral. I must comfort my people."

"Why would the feelings be mixed?"

"She lost her connection to her Element. Does that mean she'll be cut off in the afterlife? Is it a blessing because she'll be reconnected on her next journey? Is she trapped here like a spirit? I wish I had the answers for 'em. But this… well… there are no stories or legends to prepare us for this." She rose from her chair, "If you don't mind, I think I'll take a nap before the funeral," she shuffled towards her house, but added, "and perhaps do a little bakin'." With a wink, she was gone. Mia took her time as she walked back to meet the others, her head filled with a thousand thoughts.

CHAPTER FOURTEEN

The dinner was a potluck. The Sylph placed tables down the center of the street. A crazy assortment of chairs had been placed out as well. People poured out of every house in the neighborhood, bringing covered dishes and bottles of spirits. As the sun set, music played. Just like at Samhain, there were lines of dancers, only this time the ages of the participants spanned from four to eighty. The new council grabbed seats together at the center of the long table. They sampled the food and avoided the spirits. Despite tons of people coming by, the doctor wasn't one of them.

"Are you attached to the Gnome?" A blonde-haired man in his early twenties blatantly flirted with Mia. She startled, surprised he would ask in front of Damek, but then noticed a woman had pulled Damek away from the conversation.

"Damek," she emphasized, "is my friend and fellow council member."

"Ahhh," he winked. "Not taken. Everyone has been wondering, green sweater and all. We heard you were unattached but wanted to be sure the rumors were true." His eyes went over her shoulder. He gave a subtle nod to someone.

She swiveled to try to find who he had nodded to, but there was no one obvious. "There are rumors about my... Singledom?" Her voice went up an octave which must have alerted Damek. He was back at her side in a second.

"Hi, I'm Damek," he stood behind her, attempting to tower over the Sylph male. It only lasted a second until the man stood, proving he was a few inches taller. But then the weirdest thing occurred; Damek appeared to get even taller. Mia blinked, trying to take it in.

"Guthrie," the man's lips twisted in amusement as he introduced himself. "No need to be so protective, Gnome. The lady is allowed to talk, isn't she?"

"If she wants to..." Damek countered.

"I think she wants to," he confidently smirked.

"Actually," Mia waited for the man to look her in the eye, "I don't." Mia cocked her head. Then she sat and turned to Damek. "How was your conversation?" Her obvious dismissal of the Sylph made Damek grin as he joined her. The Sylph snarled and walked away.

"Sorry, I think the entire purpose of the conversation was to distract me long enough for that guy to get through." He watched the retreating man. "Did he bother you too much?"

"No," Mia surveyed the crowd. Another guy in his late teens was looking her over. "It's weird. I know McKenna said that all the guys would try to impress me, but they just seem to be sizing me up." After a slight jolt, Damek appraised the situation. She could count four other guys at that moment that were looking at her, but the auras were evaluative not interested.

"That is weird," Damek noted, but his aura was turning a mustard yellow, with anxiety and stress dominating.

"What do you know?" Mia asked, without thinking.

"Nothing... I just... don't trust the Sylph.... I... where is the doctor?" he tried to change the subject. Fine, but she wouldn't forget.

"There's Neil. I'll ask." Mia stood and strode over to Neil, who was talking to an older woman. As she approached, Neil flushed. Mia wondered what he had been talking about to cause such a reaction.

"Neil, we need to talk to the doctor. It is time for us to leave and we have not seen her," Mia bluntly stated.

"You can't leave now," he blustered. "We…" he gestured to the woman. "We want to spend more time with all of you… learn of the new council." His aura pulsed. Mia's heart started going a mile a minute. They were being played… somehow…

"You aren't an adept liar, Neil," she bluffed. "Lying to an Aether, not so bright."

"Surely, you understand our curiosity," he stammered. Mia remembered the presence Marta exuded. She took a deep breath, trying to emulate the intimidating Aether.

"And yet, you are keeping us from our mission, which is not acceptable." Mia forced her face to remain neutral. "We would like to talk to the doctor… Now." Neil looked to the older woman, who nodded. "Thank you." The woman was observing Mia's aura. Mia mentally pushed against the woman the way Triana had trained her, and the woman took a step back. Shocked, the lady lifted her chin as she walked away. Mia's attention returned to Neil, and he quickly went to find Vi.

"What was that all about?" Damek asked as Mia sat back down.

"Vi is coming." She slipped her hand in his. *That woman with Neil. She was trying to read me. Is she Aether?*

She's blonde, so no… maybe she's a priestess. Damek searched over Mia's shoulder, trying to find her.

A priestess?

Half Aether, half Sylph. Every clan has mixed blood members. They work within the clan to read symbols, run ceremonies. They are powerful forces within their clan.

She must be Cailleach Ilma's successor. They watched as the doctor from earlier made her way to the table.

"I heard you asked for me," the doctor said with a grin. "Sorry for the delay. The elders refused to let me see you until they sent for me. What did you do to make Dad so… nervous?"

"I called him out on his delaying tactics and informed him we would leave."

"Can't say that I blame you," Vi sat down. "I've been waiting to leave myself."

"You don't live here?" Damek asked.

"No, I live in Atlanta." She shrugged. "Neil is my father. There is such a thing as living too close to home."

"I thought most Sylph-" Damek started.

"Most Sylph have a home base with their family. They travel a lot. But as a doctor, I had to stay in one place for my schooling and residency. Not all Sylph are travelers. Those of us who aren't, prefer our space. I'm an easy phone call away and can come in an emergency, just like I did with the girl. I assume that's what you want to know about?"

"Neil said you insisted on running some tests," Mia started.

"I took a sample of her blood. I couldn't find anything that was added to her blood- no drugs, no foreign chemicals of any kind. What I found was weird. Her blood was very low in red blood cells. "

"Red blood cells? What does that mean?" Mia asked, moving closer.

"Well, it can mean several things. Most of the time it is a sign of disease, anything from leukemia to cancer. Or something simpler like anemia."

"Sylph don't get sick easily. Is this a new disease? Do we need to warn the other clans?" Damek cut in.

"I have never known a Sylph to suffer from any of those diseases. I checked her anyway, the best I could in the state she was in. I found no other signs of those illnesses. It is hard to tell if it is something new. She has fever, chills, aches and pains."

"We have been told those are the signs you are losing connection to your Element," Mia offered, glancing over toward Brisa.

"Which is why it is hard to tell if it is disease related. There are no outstanding symptoms that are unusual aside from the low blood cells."

"Is there anything else it could mean?" Damek questioned.

"Excessive bleeding. I examined her injuries. She was scraped up pretty badly. Her feet were especially bloody, but not enough to cause this kind of deficiency. The only thing I can think of that explains the low red blood cell count and the track marks on her arm, is over donating blood. I know that you can donate blood for cash in some locations, especially rare blood types. She was 0 negative. So maybe she was trying to make money. But… that doesn't make sense."

"Blood is sacred to Elementals… we don't… donate," Damek explained. "It would have to be an emergency."

"And that doesn't explain the visions," Mia whispered to Damek.

"Visions?" Damek and Mia both turned to the doctor abruptly, in response to her query. "What did you see?"

"I…" Mia hesitated.

"Let me guess… you don't trust me enough," Vi sat back. "No, I get it. Especially with this group staring at you all night, I'm sure you're on guard. Do you have any other questions for me?"

"Are there any known reasons that someone would lose the connection to their Element?" Mia asked. Damek shook his head at the same moment Vi did.

"Besides denying them the actual Element? No. Until now, it's unheard of. There are folk tales about people rejecting their Element, and in turn, it rejects them. But those are just fairy tales," Damek informed Mia.

"The reason the Sylph didn't tell the other clans about it was because of out and out fear. If an enemy could sever someone's connection with their Element, that would be a powerful weapon. A horrible torture. An incredible threat. When they thought it was a drug, something that could easily be used, the elders were in a panic. Now… I'm not sure what they think. If the other teens weren't missing, they would want to dismiss this and pretend it wasn't happening. But with so many gone…" The doctor trailed off.

"How many of the Sylph know what is going on? I mean, really know what happened to Tana?" Mia asked.

"Most know the teens are missing. Most still think it's drug related. No one wants to admit Tana was sick with something that we don't know how to combat. Whereas, everyone can teach their kids not to do drugs." Vi took in a deep breath. She looked at them for a moment, then decided. "Not all of us are tied to the old ways. We welcome the idea of a new council and hope you will succeed. I sat by that girl's side for weeks. If twenty-four others are missing, and they may be in this kind of condition, or may end up in this condition, I want to help. And frankly, you may need my medical expertise. I won't push you, but I do offer my services." She reached to her back pocket and pulled out a business card. "My cell is on here." Mia accepted it. "Call me. I live in the Poncey Highlands district in Atlanta. I can be almost anywhere pretty quickly. Just let me know. And if there is any way I can help, I would like to… on the record or off," she finished in a whisper.

"Thank you," Mia smiled. *I think we can trust her.*

"We will call you in the next day or two. We can definitely use your help," Damek smiled as he and Mia stood. From farther down the table, McKenna gestured to Colin, Calder, and Brisa.

"Absolutely." Vi sat back down. Damek and Mia joined their group, but at the last moment, Mia turned back around.

"Vi, how many local kids are missing?"

Vi thought about it for a moment. Then responded with a furrowed brow, "None."

As they headed towards their van, Mia spotted a familiar face. She stopped and recognized the mother from Tana's final message. Without thinking, Mia approached the woman, surrounded by a large group of Sylph. They had been telling stories and laughing even though it rang false. As soon as Mia approached, they went silent. Damek touched her elbow.

Mia? She raised a hand to acknowledge him. Mia had to pass on the message. How?

"I met your daughter before she… passed on…" Mia started. "I can see images of an Elemental's path, their past and future. The final image I received was of her giving me a message for you," Mia took a step and offered her hand. She gathered the image in her mind trying to find the words to describe the feeling. *It was more than love. It was a thousand little webs of connections, memories, heartache and joy all at once.* With it fresh in her mind, Mia opened her eyes. Tears were running down the faces of both parents.

"Thank you," the mother whispered back, grasping her husband.

"You could see?" Mia was shocked.

"We could feel… I do not know how you…," the father said haltingly. "You could not have given us a greater gift or…"

"Thank you," the mother interrupted, then wept.

"And please," the father said with a little more strength. "They told us you are searching for the others who are missing." He approached Damek warily, who nodded. "Please… Find our son." His voice cracked on the last word. Tears came unbidden to Mia.

"We promise, sir. We will do everything we can to bring him safely home."

"Gnome," the man hesitated. Damek tensed. "Lycka till." Damek bowed in deference to the family, and Mia copied him. Whispers filled the air as they quickly walked away.

CHAPTER FIFTEEN

Smoke is everywhere. One eye can't open completely, but she sees flames are licking the walls only feet from her. Her throat burns and her eyes water. She tries to push up but pain lances through her body, forcing her to collapse back to the ground. She looks at her arm, clad in the thick wool suit. No breaks are visible, but the agony is acute. At least the air is better down here. She tries to laugh. There is no water left in the air, and her skin can feel the lack. The heat and lack of moisture cause her to feel on fire.

"Mia!" McKenna shouted, shaking her roughly awake. Mia sat up quickly, gulping for air.

"Water..." she squeaked. McKenna disappeared out the door. Mia was covered in sweat, the blankets kicked to one side of the bed. McKenna quickly returned, holding out a glass of water. Mia drank it so quickly, water dribbled down her shirt.

"Another nightmare?" McKenna confirmed. "What this time?"

"Fire..." Mia trembled. McKenna was shocked.

"Guns, now fire…" McKenna pondered. "And these things were definitely happening to you?"

"It feels like me… It could be someone else nearby. The girl in the theater was in trouble and close enough that I connected with her."

"Then let's go for a jog. Make sure no nearby houses are on fire." Mia chugged down the rest of the water, then ran after McKenna. Whoever it was, they needed to save them.

The others were awake by the time Mia and McKenna returned. They didn't find a fire, smoke, or even light in any windows. The streets around Berkeley Lake were calm and serene. The dreams left Mia wondering if she was experiencing her own future every night. At breakfast, they set the plans for the day. Brisa called Boreas to gain an introduction to the local African community. He would send a message to the other tribes, warning them to check their traveling teens. She also gave him an update on Tana. They would spend the early afternoon at the local thrift store to find some extra clothes for Brisa and Mia. Also at a shop that would have the stones Mia needed to sleep. Hopefully, they would talk to the African community before the end of the day.

Because of her early morning run, McKenna spared Mia the groups daily jog. Then Mia watched with Brisa as Damek, Calder, Colin, and McKenna sparred in the backyard. It was amazing. McKenna was unstoppable, making Damek and Calder work hard to keep up. But through it all, McKenna prompted with advice and tips to improve their skills. Damek and McKenna put their animosity on hold as they focused on Tana's plight.

"Were you trained this way too?" Mia asked Brisa, observing the dance from the balcony above.

"Yes and no. Each clan has warriors who train like McKenna. The rest of us… we can choose. With Sylph, they teach us basic self-defense so we have safety when we travel. Almost all of us are given basic training. Since so many of us are smaller, our training is a bit different from what you see. More about defense and using weight leverage." Brisa's voice was soft. Her eyes were riveted to the view below. Mia scrutinized her for a second. It was hard to tell if Brisa was captivated by the fighting or the sight of the sweaty men below. Despite the light chill, Calder and Damek had stripped down to tanks. Colin was still in a t-shirt. He was so much smaller than the rest and didn't really understand what was going on. He learned the basics, and McKenna was careful to make sure he felt a part of the group.

"You were trained when you were a kid?"

"Yeah… that was… years before my mother died," Brisa swallowed. "Did you see all of it?"

"No, I saw only a few moments when you were stuck in the cabin," Mia said softly. "You don't have to talk about it unless you want to."

"There isn't much to say." Brisa pulled her knees to her chest. "He wasn't always… When my mom was alive, I didn't even see him much. He traveled. When she passed, he became possessive. He… hit me a few times. At seventeen, I was expected to travel…. All Sylph go on a rata. We travel the country, going to the natural wonders and famous museums; finding a wellspring of inspiration for our future work. I thought I could last. I stayed near the house like he wanted but stayed as far from him as I could. It was only a couple of weeks before my seventeenth birthday when the news came about Coro. He must have decided that was the way to keep me from leaving. One day, I went further from the house than usual. I heard this music coming from a campsite. I just went to look. There was this group of teens, dancing, partying. They seemed so… full of joy. I lost track of time watching them. When I went home, I was late. He hit me so hard I blacked out. When I came to… he had chained me to the wall in his hunting cabin. Honestly, since I was so feverish, I don't remember most of my… imprisonment. Now, it seems like a bad dream or nightmare. It's hard to tell what was real and what wasn't." Brisa's attention returned to the boys below. Mia knew the conversation was over.

"I'm surprised McKenna doesn't have me down there," Mia commented.

"I have a feeling she will train us later. You probably need training more like what I received." Brisa looked up to see Mia's gaze and blushed.

"I guess, it is fun to watch," Mia teased. And it was. Watching McKenna was like watching a cat. Her movements were lithe and graceful, yet powerful. The guys… well… it was a sight. Especially now that they were glistening. Mia was almost embarrassed to watch. Just as the thought entered Mia's mind, Calder looked up. He shoved Damek and pointed to the ladies. Calder gave them a wide smile. Damek turned pink. The distraction allowed Colin to take down Calder. Loud laughter erupted from everyone else.

"Okay, I'm calling it." McKenna wiped away tears from her laughter. "Good job, Colin." Damek quickly threw on his shirt. Calder accepted Colin's extended hand to help him stand up.

The shopping excursion was relatively successful. First, they found the stones, allowing Mia to look forward to that night's sleep. Afterwards, they bought extra clothes in the right colors and for the changeable Georgia weather. Cell phones were part of the supplies given to them by the Salamanders, but minutes and data had to be purchased to make them work. The phones fascinated Damek endlessly. Apparently, he had never played with a real smart phone. At one-point, Mia had to stop him from taking it apart. They downloaded an app so they could keep track of each other. Even though no one but Mia reacted negatively to the energy emanating from the devices, they kept the phones off while they were together, in deference.

Then they waited. It was one in the afternoon when Boreas called to inform them the African community did not want to meet. They did not believe Boreas that their children might be missing.

"I don't understand," Mia said as she watched Calder move around the kitchen. Brisa had taken her usual spot on the balcony. Damek, Colin, and McKenna were out trying to find maps and tourist info for the area. In the meantime, Calder had taken on preparing dinner with Mia's assistance. Not that she was much help. So far, he had only allowed her to skin potatoes and watch.

"What this time?" he asked, dicing the vegetables.

"Why do the 'tribes' not communicate?" Mia grabbed a piece of carrot and popped it in her mouth. "I mean- if they are all the same Element, wouldn't they have enough in common to foster some kind of relationship? I would think it would be cool to meet people from around the world."

"Well..." he thought it through. "It's hard to explain. The tribes. Well, the tribes didn't really have any communication between the continents. The Elementals of Europe... our numbers were small after all the witch hunts and inquisitions. There was a time around 400 years ago when we were afraid of extinction. We moved away from the humans and created communities of our own. Then at a Samhain council meeting the decision was made to further separate into clans to preserve the bloodlines. We largely lived in secret. But then the United States opened their borders. People relocated here as war, famine, or persecution devastated their own homes... it's the story of the U.S. really. We're no different from how everyone else got here. In the last hundred years, the other continents have moved this way. And a hundred years... isn't a lot of time. Most Elementals live longer than that. A good number of the elders and leaders in our communities grew up in Europe. Everyone is interested in preserving their own traditions. With how everyone in this country melds... I think the elders worried they would lose their culture."

"What about North America? Aren't there any native Elementals?"

"I'm sure you've learned American history. Those who weren't murdered, mainly succumbed to disease. There are some left, but not many. Some small communities are in the west, I believe. My understanding is many of them melded with the African tribe. I am pretty sure the first Elementals from Africa didn't come willingly... but honestly, I don't know their story." What about McKenna? Mia wanted to know but couldn't think of a way to ask delicately. Instead, she changed the subject.

"Disease? I thought Elementals didn't get sick?"

"What, you never had a cold?" Calder's lip twitched.

"Well, yeah," Mia rolled her eyes.

"We're susceptible to disease. We're a hardy lot. Very rare with cancers or inherited issues. But introduce a foreign disease to our systems, then we can catch it just like anyone else. We're stronger, have better recovery rates but... we still die." Calder stopped what he was doing for a moment. "We aren't immortal... as much as we may want to be."

"Where do you come from?"

"Okay, in light of the conversation, I'm not sure how to answer that," Calder grinned again as he added the vegetables to a sauté pan.

"Where do you live? I met you in the mountains. You don't have an accent. Where are you from?" Mia leaned forward. He expertly lifted the pans and let the vegetables flip as they cooked.

"I am actually from just north of Chicago. Right on the Great Lakes. I have to say – the South is fascinating... completely different from home." Reaching into the oven, he removed the trout.

"We're home!" Colin called from the entrance.

"Right on time!" Calder called back, giving Mia a devastating smile. She couldn't help but return it as Damek, McKenna, and Colin joined them in the kitchen.

"How cozy," McKenna grinned, coming over to smell Calder's cooking. "Is it time to eat?" she picked at the food and had her hand slapped by Calder.

"Five minutes- Grab Brisa, we can talk AFTER we eat." McKenna laughed, dropping her shopping bags next to the couch. Damek gave a half smile and headed out to get Brisa.

"Successful?" Mia asked Colin.

"Yes. We found maps of most of the North Atlanta area. We visited some hotels to get the tourist brochures in the lobby."

"Food," Calder interrupted, handing them some plates.

"Yes, sir," Colin saluted. Colin and Mia set the table. It wasn't long before the group was enjoying their first relaxed meal in days. The banter stayed light, purposefully avoiding all topics that would darken the overall mood.

Later that evening, the entire group camped out in the upstairs living room, going through the information they had gathered that day. McKenna and Calder poured over the maps, marking potential areas where the house from Mia's visions could be located. Colin and Damek searched travel websites for places to go in Atlanta. Mia and Brisa went through the guides. Brisa pulled the ones that would attract Sylph. Mia just kept reading through them and making a pile of the ones she wanted to see. Mia was so engrossed in one flyer, she didn't notice Calder until he climbed over the back of the couch, settling in next to her and grabbing the brochure she was reading.

"The Fox Theater tour? Really?"

"It was in Brisa's pile too," Mia retorted, as he laughed. "We might as well enjoy our recon."

"Sorry Mia, you aren't going to the tourist sites." McKenna didn't stop examining the maps.

"What?" Mia sputtered.

"You're the only one who has seen the house we're looking for." Mia tried to think of a counterargument for McKenna's reasoning.

"But…" She deflated slightly. Calder frowned.

"She couldn't draw a picture or something? We can text her pictures with our phones? I mean, who else will look like they're enjoying this stuff? And who makes sense for Brisa to be with? An Aether is believable."

"Colin," McKenna asserted.

"Wait, I get to go to the art museums?" Colin peered at the brochure over Calder's shoulder. "Cool." Calder shoved him. "What?"

"There isn't any way Mia can go to some of these things," Calder pushed.

"Unless she can start sharing images as well as words when she touches us, then no. Look on the bright side. When we get done here, we can take a day and tour around."

"It's okay," Mia sighed, putting down the other brochures.

"You passed thoughts or emotions on to Tana's parents. Why not images?" Damek mused.

"Give me your hand," Calder stated, turning to face her on the couch.

"What?"

"Damek's got a cool idea. You can talk to us. You can see through our eyes, maybe we can see through yours." Mia's stomach dropped out. This must be what it is like for everyone else when they take her hands. *What if he sees something he shouldn't? Like my view of Calder and Damek with their shirts off earlier that day or …* "You shared more than words with the family of Tana." McKenna stood up and walked over.

"I shared a feeling. It was like words, basically. You're talking about a distinct picture." She wasn't even sure how she did it!

"You think it's possible?" McKenna contemplated.

"Why not?" Calder shrugged. "It's worth a try." He held out his hand as Mia took a deep breath. This was the same thing they did for her. They trusted her. She needed to do the same. She reached out and grasped his hand. "Are you thinking about the vision?" Her mind immediately jumped to the guys fighting. Her eyes went wide as Calder chuckled.

"Right." Fighting an inflamed face, she focused on the vision of the resting spot. She tried to focus on the main points of the vision. *The breeze, and laughter, then looking up at the white house. The happy couple next to her, then the quilt. Down the lawn at the trees. Then she switched her thoughts over to the escape night. Moving down the yard, the panic gripping her and her heart racing.* She took a deep breath, releasing herself from the vision. Before she could let go, a searing pain, the same pain she felt when she first took Tana's hand, ripped through her. Then, it was done. When she focused back on Calder, his hand was gripping hers tightly. Then his eyes flew open.

"Holy… you… you feel what they feel." He took a huge breath. "Damn… I… I mean, you said you did, but I mean you really…"

"Wait you saw that? You… felt that?" Her voice trembled. He met her eyes and nodded slowly.

"Are all of your visions… that… painful?" He noticed her recoiling, and quickly continued. "I'm not… I… I am amazed… and impressed… how much… what you can see… what you went through to get that information… I'm sure you didn't show me all of it?"

"They aren't all like that. I… This was the first time I felt pain… real pain… I was thrown against a wall once…" Mia rambled. He just kept staring at her while she blushed.

"It worked?" McKenna finally interrupted. "You saw her visions." By this point, Damek and Colin had gathered as well. "I want to see."

"I'm not sure that you do," Calder warned. "That was intense. Thank you though… thank you for sharing."

"Let's try to simplify. When you were showing Calder, did you think of the vision or of an image?" McKenna paced.

"The vision."

"Okay, this time, think of just the image. The picture of the house, what you could see." Calder put his hand out to Mia. "No," McKenna stopped him. "It has to be someone who hasn't seen the vision. I'll try." McKenna sat down taking a deep breath. "Guess it's my turn," she met Mia's eye and held out her hand. "Okay, go for it." Mia braced herself, then grasped McKenna's hand. No images flooded her. With a sigh of relief, Mia thought about the vision. This time, she only thought about the image of the house. *She let her mind slowly go over the details; the balcony that spanned the length of the structure, the pillars that ran both levels, the white trim and woodwork, the stairs that led to a series of double doors leading into the building, the shape of the windows.* She opened her eyes and McKenna was staring at her. "It worked. Blessed be, do you realize what this means?"

"She can go sight-seeing?" Colin asked.

"No… the tactical… if we can share images. Okay, this time, let me see if I can show you an image." McKenna's mind wandered the room as she thought of what to share. "Let's try this one." Mia closed her eyes and tried to focus on the image McKenna was sending. *A picture of a crimson desert filled Mia's mind. Large stone fingers reached towards the impossibly blue sky. Short scrubby bushes were sparsely growing in the image's forefront. The greyish brown shrubs gave way to brownish green tops. A few small red stones could be found haphazardly between the bushes.* Mia described everything as she took the picture in.

"That's home," McKenna said wistfully.

"It's beautiful. Stark, but stunning," Mia pronounced. "Where is it?"

"Arizona. I've never been away for this long before," she shrugged. "Salamanders don't travel much." The comment made the entire group introspective for a moment, thinking of their own homes. "This is going to be an incredible tool." McKenna refocused on Mia. "Instead of searching for the house, maybe we will have you follow Brisa to some of these locations. You can scan the crowds. We can look at the images later to see if any faces show up multiple times."

"I'm not a computer, or a camera," Mia looked around, "I'm human. I can remember an image if I focus. I remember my visions because they're so…"

"Visceral," Calder supplied.

"But even they fade, like a dream or any other memory. There is no way I'm going to remember groups of random people after touring around all day."

"Guys, she doesn't need to do that," Colin interjected.

"It would have been helpful," McKenna shook her head, "Oh well."

"McKenna, she's going to tourist locations. She can just take pictures," Colin pointed out. Calder laughed.

"Valid point." Calder plunked back down next to Mia. "So, we get to go sight-seeing?"

"Hmmm…" McKenna reasoned. "Aether and Sylph are friends. Maybe you can sight see together?"

"The vision you had didn't include any Aether, did it?" Calder asked. Mia shook her head. "I didn't think so. If we have an Aether and Sylph together, the Sylph will never get approached."

"Brisa cannot go alone," Damek interrupted.

"What if we have a few of us following her as fellow tourists? Not together, but following discreetly? We can have a different mix of followers for each location," Colin recommended.

"Valid," Damek agreed. "We can do a tourist spot a day. Or should we do one each morning and one each afternoon? And we have a different shift following in the morning and in the evening?" The group murmured their approval.

"I think it would be better if we enlisted one of the local Sylph to go with Brisa. I would prefer someone was with her," Calder added.

"But none of the local Sylph have gone missing," Damek objected. "When we were talking to the doctor, she said that no locals are missing."

"So the people taking Sylph either know who is local or locals don't go to the tourist spots and therefore aren't approached," McKenna pondered.

"It's a 50/50 shot," Damek confirmed.

"Do you know any Sylph from your own clan that we can trust?" Colin turned to Brisa.

"I haven't been… I mean… we…"

"We get it," Mia stopped her. Brisa sent her a grateful look.

"Could a local Sylph go undercover? Change the way they look so that an acquaintance may not recognize them?" Colin recommended.

"How would they change how they look? They all have blonde hair. They all have blue eyes. They can change their type of clothes… hair cut?" Damek asked.

"Sylph can change their appearance. It's a basic glamour. It will fool anyone who isn't a Sylph. But if a Sylph is behind this… they will see through the glamour and notice we are using one. That will let them know we are hiding something," Brisa offered.

"A glamour?" Colin asked. It was nice when someone else was as lost as Mia was.

"It modifies the way we appear. Sylph used it at one time to help hide their nature."

"Any other talents the Sylph have that we don't know about?" McKenna asked testily.

Brisa responded warily. "I don't know what you know about us. I haven't had contact with the other clans until now."

"I don't think any of us have," Calder remarked, trying to keep the peace. "I have a feeling there will be many surprises from all of us in the weeks to come."

"Sylph can manipulate the air. We can ride on the breeze, allowing us to… well, kind of, fly. We can glamour to change minor aspects of our appearance. We can hear things over far distances, and we can use the wind to hide ourselves. It seems like we disappear to non-Sylph. But all our 'talents' are pretty much useless in fooling other Sylph. They can see us hiding in the wind. They can see through the glamour."

"Wow," Colin muttered.

"Definite tactical possibilities," McKenna's gaze turned inward as she worked out scenarios in her head.

"Just like with any Elemental, the Element is stronger in some than in others," Brisa added.

"How strong are you?" McKenna focused in again.

"I can do all of those things," Brisa admitted.

"It all comes down to whether or not Sylph are involved," Damek steered the conversation.

"I think changing my appearance, without the glamour, is the better way to go," Brisa proposed. "Maybe a minor glamour, but the more I can change with make-up and clothing the better."

"I still think she needs a partner," Calder persisted.

"We can ask Vi," doubt met Mia's comment. "We can trust her. Plus, she wants to help. She may know someone who can help us."

"Okay," Damek agreed. "Let's call her. You said that Tana went missing with her brother and his girlfriend. That means they were in a group. They might be searching for groups, not a single Sylph. People probably worry and check in less when traveling in groups." He turned to Brisa, who hadn't offered an opinion on Vi. "Are you okay with this? I know you aren't to full strength yet but…"

"I'm ready," Brisa interrupted. "Or as ready as I'll ever be."

CHAPTER SIXTEEN

Vi agreed to help and said she knew the perfect Sylph. The next morning, Damek, Calder, Brisa, and Mia arrived at Vi's address in the Poncey Highlands area after a grueling morning session with McKenna. Brisa had been correct. McKenna started Mia off with basic self-defense moves, weak points on her attacker to target, mainly ways to get away as fast as she could in a bad situation.

They arrived at an old brick building. It was an old motel from the thirties that had been converted into apartments. As Vi buzzed them in, they arrived in an open-air courtyard. There was a small garden at the bottom and three levels which opened up in the middle so they could see the sky. Mia limped up the wrought iron stairs to the third floor. In Damek and Calder's defense, they tried to keep from smirking as she grunted in pain, but they weren't overly successful. Somewhere in the back of Mia's head, she hoped that McKenna was suffering too. McKenna had worked out with the boys and then Brisa and Mia. In Mia's mind, McKenna was shuffling stiffly around the lake house, cursing them as much as Mia was cursing her in her head. But at the same time, Mia knew it was wishful thinking.

Down a cement hallway they went until they reached 312. As soon as they knocked, a Sylph wearing a tank top and ripped jeans opened the door. Her black nails ruffled her cropped hair, following the streaks of purple and blue running through it. Dark eyeliner made her eyes pop and rich lip color stood out against her pale skin.

"So… What do you think?" Mia stared at the strange lady with her confused companions. The lady's lips twitched, which clued Mia into looking at her aura.

"Vianca?" Mia squealed. The doctor winked. "Oh my Lord, I would never have recognized you!" Vi looked down the hallway, as she ushered the group into a small living room. The walls were painted a bright peach, the floors a warm wood, and an overstuffed purple couch dominated the room.

"You think I would fool anyone who knows me? I mean, not someone who *knows* me, but anyone who knows of me? Does that make sense?"

"Absolutely." Mia turned to Brisa. "What do you think?"

"It is so different. When did you have this done?" Brisa reached out to touch the doctor's colorful hair but stopped just short.

"Last night, after you called. I'm fortunate to have a brilliant roommate," Vi smiled to the door where an Asian woman with long brown hair was standing.

"I'm a hair stylist," the woman offered.

"You're a Gnome," Damek stated astonished.

"Yes," she confirmed, straightening her spine. Then curtly added, "So are you."

"You did an incredible job," Mia interrupted.

"Yes, she did," Vi agreed. "I was thinking about what you said. About a local potentially being involved. Or someone who knows the locals. And then I realized that most of the local Sylph have now met you. Brisa may need a bit of a disguise as well."

Damek joined the conversation. "We discussed this very valid point. I take it you have a suggestion?"

"This is Jules." Vi guided the Earth girl forward. "She's a brilliant hairdresser. And I was wondering if you needed a makeover?" Vi winked at Brisa.

Mia watched Brisa's aura panic. Before Mia could intervene, Brisa had it under control.

"I think… I think I could use a new look," Brisa decided. "What do you have in mind?"

"Well, we don't think you need anything as drastic as Vi," Jules studied Brisa's hair. "Maybe cutting it a little shorter than shoulder length, adding a color stripe, maybe red? That way you go together but are different — You don't match too much." Jules rambled nervously until Vi placed her hand at the small of Jules' back in a show of support. The connection between the two made Mia smile. Then she realized the tension in the room had gone up. Calder was determinedly examining a picture on the wall. Damek was observing the two women with a half frown on his face. Brisa was gawking at Vi's hand. Noticing Brisa's stare, Vi dropped her hand quickly.

"How about we get started?" Jules quickly left down a small hallway. Brisa took a deep breath and followed.

"Do you guys want anything to drink?" Vi didn't wait for a response. "I'll bring a pitcher of sweet tea." She disappeared as quickly as Jules did. The boys were exchanging a look.

"What's going on?" Mia whispered. "Are you homophobic?"

"What??" "No!" the boys exclaimed in surprise.

"Then what is your damage? Do they seem untrustworthy to you? Do you not trust Jules? I read nothing negative off of her and I trust Vi. If she trusts her girlfriend, that's enough for me." Calder's neck tensed at the word girlfriend.

"I don't get it. What is the problem with their dating?" Mia looked back and forth between the two. Despite the lack of Aether powers, they were silently communicating perfectly. Finally, Calder turned to her.

"They're two different Elements," Calder whispered. "They're also from two different tribes."

"So?" Mia whispered back. "You guys told me those other Elementals were hitting on me and we were different Elements..." Her voice raised, but Damek took her arm and shh'd her.

"Aether can marry other clans. Like I told you before, it's how each clan has priests. However, the other Elements... They are not allowed to intermarry. If the council found out about those two..." Damek grimaced.

"Well, that's a stupid rule. Do their kids become weird monsters or something? What's the point?"

"It's the law. It's upheld by the council. It has been for four hundred years." Mia's mind went wild with the injustice.

"Well, that is a stupid racist rule that has no place in the world today. So what? We don't accept their help? We tell the old council about them?" The boys exchanged a glance again. "No! Any law stating who you can love is wrong. Besides, they welcomed us into their home and are willing to help us. I won't hurt them." Right then, Vi returned. She stopped, taking in the atmosphere.

"Are you going to report us?" Vi asked silently, placing the tray of iced tea and glasses on a coffee table.

"No," Calder announced. Mia let her tension go.

"On this issue, we have chosen for the moment... to keep an open mind." Damek sat down and reached for a glass.

After a few moments, Vi sat down in shock, "Thank you."

"If the old council finds out, they'll banish you," Calder warned. "We have no control over that."

"Well, I've been with Jules for eight years. They haven't found out yet. There is a community of those who... well... don't agree with the rules. We support each other. If the council rejects us, others won't."

"The tribes mix here?" Damek inquired.

"This is Atlanta. The city is wildly diverse, as is the Elemental population. The majority stay with their tribes, but here in the city... that isn't something that keeps us apart. Other tribes do not have the same taboos that the Europeans do."

"You're still willing to help us on this mission?" Calder asked.

"I'm a doctor. I have pledged my life to helping others. If you find out where the girl was being held, you'll need someone who can care for any other victims. In the end, if it saves lives, it's more than worth a few days and a haircut."

"Then maybe we need to focus on our plan." Damek took a sip of the tea. His face twisted as if he had sucked on a lemon. "Blessed be, that is sweet!" Vi laughed.

"Welcome to the South." Calder and Mia tentatively took a sip. It *was* sweet. Calder put his down, but Mia enjoyed it.

They settled in on the couch as Damek went over the itinerary for the next five days. "We figure if they do not approach us within the first ten days, it will be too late. Tourists don't stay longer than that, usually, and they would have already hit the major sites. The question that comes up next is hotels."

"Hotels?" Vi repeated.

"You're travelers. You can't stay in an apartment or the house in Berkeley Lake," Calder chimed in.

"Most of the Sylph who come through try to stay with other Sylph, if they have family nearby."

"However, we doubt that someone staying with family is a likely target. There's someone to miss them," Damek explained.

"Okay, well… Sylph stay in hostels. There aren't many in Atlanta."

"We have a couple of theories," Damek sought Mia and Calder's approval, and with it, he continued. "Based on what we could see in Mia's vision, it's probably one of three possibilities. One: they lure Sylph to this location, thinking they are just sight-seeing. Two: Sylph go there because it's a Sylph 'gathering place'. Three: they lure Sylph there with the promise of nicer accommodations than the ones they are staying in. If they're in a seedy hotel or a hostel, they would jump at the chance to stay at what seems like a wonderful deal in a great location; especially if other Sylph are already there. However the Sylph end up there, they stay because they or someone in their group is ill."

"And we are covering as many bases as possible," Vi processed.

"You're sightseeing during the day, and at night…" Calder hesitated.

"We're staying in the hostel," Vi stated wryly.

"Sorry, but…" Mia started.

"No, I get it," Vi moaned. "I'll pack a bag."

"Remember, you're a traveling Sylph. They aren't big on lots of luggage," Damek prodded.

"I *am* a Sylph…. Remember?" Damek blushed. "How soon do we start?"

"How soon can you?" Mia replied.

"I can go today. I cleared my schedule for the next two weeks." Vi stood up. "It'll just be me and Brisa at the hostel?"

"No," Damek stated.

"We are rotating who is following you during the day," Calder explained. "However, Colin and McKenna are staying in the hostel too. McKenna is our best warrior and Colin is an Aether, so he can get a feel for the people who come in and out. McKenna and Colin are scouting the houses and local areas during the day, while the rest of us follow you," Calder explained.

"Isn't Mia a stronger Aether?" Vi asked. "Why aren't you staying at the hostel?"

"I…," Mia floundered.

"We need her to read the crowds during the day. We don't want anyone to recognize her at your hotel," Damek supplied. Mia looked at him gratefully. The group had wanted her at the hostel, but she had to admit the truth. She could only be surrounded by groups of people for so long. If she was going to crowded tourist sites during the day, she couldn't stay in a hostel full of people at night. She wasn't able to protect her mind from that kind of onslaught. Periodically, she needed solitude.

"Okay," Vi was unconvinced, but didn't push. "Will you be nearby?"

"We'll be at the house in Berkeley Lake. It's closer to the site we're trying to find. If you should be 'convinced' to go to the mansion, we'll be able to get to you faster from there," Damek reassured her.

"We have a GPS locator in Brisa's phone," Mia added. "You know, the kind parents put on their kids' cells."

"Okay." Vi moved towards a doorway to the left of the hallway. "I'll pack my things. I bought some clothes that would fit the part. I bought a few for Brisa, but I'm not sure about the sizing. I guessed. You guys will be recognizable now, too. The Sylph memorial had reps from all over the Atlanta area. If you're following us, and they know what you look like, we may be doing this for nothing," Vi left for the bedroom.

"She's right," Damek acknowledged. "We need to disguise ourselves."

"Not being in a group will help," Calder offered.

"If they have an Aether working for them, it won't matter at all," Mia scowled.

"Luckily, most Aether aren't as powerful as you," Calder poured another glass of tea and handed it to Mia. All three sank into their own thoughts as they waited.

About an hour later, they were still in their own worlds. Vi had rejoined them, putting a knapsack by the front door. Then Jules appeared in the doorway. "Attention, one and all... Presenting the new... the one... the only... Brisa!" Jules darted aside. Brisa entered hesitantly. Jules cut Brisa's long blonde locks into a sharp bob. A thick streak of red wound its' way from the undercarriage of her hair. Her plain autumn yellow t-shirt had been ripped up, now barely skimming the top of her jeans and scooping low in the front. A black duster sweater was covering the shirt sleeves. They had ripped the knees in her jeans, too. Black boots replaced her sneakers. In a crowd, Mia would never have recognized her. Calder gave a whistle.

"Wow," Damek stood up. "Brisa, you look amazing!" He grinned.

"It's really okay?" Brisa asked him.

"Definitely!"

"You'll be fighting guys off with a stick," Calder teased as Brisa blushed.

"I packed our bags, Brisa," Vi remarked.

"Already?" Jules interjected. Vi embraced her.

"Yes, the sooner we start, the sooner it finishes," Vi rationalized.

"I have a bag in the car but I think it will need some editing." Brisa considered her remodeled outfit.

"McKenna and Colin are already at the hotel," Damek grabbed his things. "We will drop you off at the bus station so you can make your way there. There's a stop close to your destination." Calder joined Damek exiting the apartment.

"Take a hat by the door," Jules said softly. "No one can see you leaving this apartment in those clothes. Just in case…." Brisa grabbed a hat while Mia gave up her hoodie to hide Brisa's outfit. Brisa left. Mia stood in the doorway.

"We'll wait downstairs," Mia offered. "Take your time." Mia closed the door behind her and found Calder waiting with his head cocked to one side. "We don't know how long this will take, or how it will end. They should get time to say their goodbyes. Just in case." Mia could feel the panic in Jules and the fear in Vi, even from a distance. Calder just placed his arm around her and escorted her out.

As Brisa and Vi walk away from the car at the Marta station, the rest of the gang were astounded to watch their walk and gait change automatically to fit their new personas. Brisa was more confident than Mia had ever seen her. A wide grin lit up her face. It took her a minute to realize both boys were staring at her.

"What?" she responded. "It is awesome to see Brisa gain confidence, even if it is just from a haircut!" She sank back in her seat.

"Now what are we going to do about us?" Damek asked Mia in the rear-view mirror as he pulled out onto the road again.

"I don't think dying our hair the same way is an option. I mean, if we all look the same, I think they'll notice," Calder commented.

"Well, maybe we just need to find other personas." Mia examined people out the window. "What things change the way people look the most?"

"Hairstyle," Damek brainstormed.

"Make-up?" Mia thought out loud.

"Well, unless we dye our hair, I don't know if hairstyle will make too huge a difference," Calder contradicted.

"We can add glasses to the look," Mia brainstormed, "or use a wig."

"Very few Elementals need glasses. Those who wear them usually do so as a fashion statement," Calder explained.

"So obvious glasses instead of trying to make them look real," Mia mused.

"How come I have a feeling we're going shopping?" Damek sighed.

"It won't be so bad," Mia needled. "I promise to hold your hand the entire time." Damek blushed.

"It might be a good idea to people watch for a while, see what strikes us," Calder suggested to Mia.

"How about a food court dinner?" Mia asked.

"A food court dinner?" Damek looked back quizzically.

"Like at the mall." Calder and Damek exchanged a glance. "You guys have been to a mall before, right? I mean I've only gone recently but I've been…" They remained silent. "Have you seen any of the thousands of movies that have scenes at a mall? Or a food court? Oh guys, this will be a treat."

"Really?" Damek queried.

"Really!" Mia reassured them. "Plus, there is no better place to people watch. I promise!" She settled back to search for local malls on her phone.

"Maybe your new look will give you confidence, too," Calder teased Damek, who returned the comment with a glare.

"Is there a look that might take away some confidence?" Damek scowled.

"I don't know if it is possible to hide this kind of natural sex appeal," Calder grinned.

"I think we will find a way," Mia said wryly. Damek struggled to contain his laughter.

"Thanks, guys. It is so nice to have such kind and supportive friends," Calder frowned as Damek's laughter erupted and filled the car. Mia chuckled. "Guys…" Calder whined, causing Mia's chuckle to turn into a full-fledged laugh. "I really don't see what's so funny." Which only made them laugh harder. Calder sunk into his seat as he struggled to keep a grin off his face. It only lasted a moment. Soon, the car filled with his laughter too.

The food court did not impress the guys, but the incredible amount of people did. The trio decided the most distinct thing about any of them was Mia's hair. Which, without dying, would be hard to hide. Thanks to a YouTube video and Damek, Mia could twist her hair into a French braid and cover it with a dark brown wig. After a trip to the thrift store, a pair of tight jeans, a beige tank top, and a long cardigan was added. With Jules' help, Calder shed most of his blond curls, leaving only a few at the top. He also layered up in neutral colors, fitted enough to make him cringe. Damek had the lucky addition of glasses and a skullcap. Since Damek's hair was already short, Jules couldn't do much with it. Damek was also uncomfortable in clothes so fitted.

Someone new waved at Mia from her mirror. She changed her posture to accommodate the new character. With Damek and Calder, she couldn't tell if the tight clothes, or the look itself, created the same effect.

CHAPTER SEVENTEEN

With a groan, she sits up. Shot... I've been shot... Blessed be, it hurts! She looks around fearfully... They are probably long gone... she looks to the left, the cars are still there, everything is where she remembers it. How much time has passed? She staggers to her feet looking towards the sedan. The man who shot her is on the ground, all the men that had been pouring out of the van, are slumped over and littering the area. What happened? Everyone seems to have passed out at the same time.

In the middle, she can spy a pair of dark blue scrubs... Mia! She moves forward ... it seems so far away... the throbbing in her left side is begging her to stop but she can't.. She has to get to... Mia... closer... her attacker is only a few feet from her and he is starting to move...she stumbles down onto the ground next to Mia's prone form.

"Mia!" Calder's voice pierced the dream this time. The image of looking at herself on the ground wouldn't go away, even after Mia opened her eyes. Mia was shaking. Was she dead? Was she seeing her own death? Calder enveloped her in a hug and didn't let go until the shaking subsided. Mia realized she had fallen asleep on the sofa. No wonder the dreams had returned. Her crystal grid was set up in her bedroom. "Nightmare?" Calder questioned. Mia couldn't reply. This one shouldn't be shared. Mia went to her room and dressed for a jog; the way McKenna had taught her to.

The team split up morning and night. Mia insisted on going to both, hoping the activity would erase the image of her wounded body lying on the ground. The first day, Mia and Damek went to the Fox theater tour during the morning. The tour guide didn't seem to know as much as Damek about Islamic and Egyptian architecture, but the history was fascinating. The opulent gold gilt was everywhere. It made her feel transported back to the age of the Great Gatsby. At one point of the tour, they sat and watched a fake sunset travel across an Arabian sky. It was beautiful.

The afternoon was spent with Calder at the Georgia aquarium. He pointed out the names of several major Water Elementals on the center's sponsorship wall. As much as most Water Elementals abhorred captured sea creatures, if there was going to be a major aquarium in Atlanta, they wanted it done right. They had done their best to influence the design and practices of the aquarium to make it more of a hospital and care center than a profit-driven zoo. Vi and Brisa were always in sight. By the end of the day, they had over two hundred random pictures of crowds from both locations.

Later, they arrived back at the house in Berkeley Lake to sift through the images. They didn't find anything suspicious in the day one pictures. Mia was grateful to have the first floor to herself. After dealing with hundreds of tourists with cell phones and having to use a cell phone, Mia needed the isolation. The check in with McKenna was brief. They had found nothing during day one either. McKenna and Colin had taken naps, allowing them to take shifts during the night. Mia double checked her crystal grid, then passed out.

On day two, Calder and Damek followed Brisa and Vi on a walk in Centennial Olympic park. They checked in by pretending to hit on them at a coffee stand. Mia used the time at a local thrift store, supplying their alter ego wardrobes. Buying for the guys proved difficult. How do you buy things you know they won't like even though it's the right thing to do?

The afternoon was spent at the Center for Puppetry Arts. Luckily, Jules partnered Mia that afternoon. Since Jules only had eyes for Vi, Mia didn't worry about spending too much time enjoying the exhibits. It was crazy being so close to her childhood Henson heroes like Kermit the Frog. That night, during the picture sift, nothing unusual was found. They didn't even see anyone that matched from day one to day two. McKenna was disappointed on the phone and getting pensive. Time was running out. After another day, they would be positive the hostel had nothing to do with the abduction.

Calder, Damek and Mia began day three with a hike up Stone Mountain. The banter between them grew more and more relaxed. With Calder and Damek, Mia had a weird comfort level. It wasn't as if she didn't think they were attractive. She wasn't dead. Though she usually regretted opening her mouth around guys, she didn't hesitate to offer an opinion to Damek or Calder, or just join in the conversation. Admittedly, Mia rethought everything she said. Still, it seemed like a step in the right direction. Afterwards, they went to their respective rooms to clean up. They spent late afternoon at the High Museum of Art.

Calder, Damek and Mia wandered slowly through the modern art exhibit at the High, taking an insane number of selfies to capture the people around the museum in their pictures. Brisa and Vi were laughing in front of a sculpture designed to appear as if it were coming out of the wall. Orbs, globes, circles, and signs burst with color, contrasting with the stark white wall behind it. While the guys argued over the merit of a piece that consisted of blocks of color, Mia watched a guy in his early twenties step over to hit on Vi and Brisa. She had seen it before. They were two gorgeous women, undoubtedly they would attract notice no matter what. However, after a couple of minutes of conversation, the stranger handed them a small piece of paper. Brisa signaled Mia before turning back to the lanky, dark-haired guy.

Mia quickly put up her camera and posed for a selfie but turned the camera to take a picture of the man with the Sylph. He didn't seem to be an Elemental at all.

"What is it?" Damek noticed the tension radiating from Mia. They posed for another fake selfie.

"Brisa indicated this may be the guy we are looking for," Mia told them. "I'll go see if I can hear anything."

"Be careful," Calder whispered as he took another fake selfie. She pushed her phone in her back pocket. She examined the piece of art near Brisa.

"No man, Edgewood is truly the place to see great art," Mia heard a masculine voice protest.

"Graffiti?" Vi questioned while Brisa giggled.

"It's an incredible art form, and the best part is, it's always changing. There's always something new. You have to see it. Come on, it'll be fun."

"Well, I guess we didn't really have plans for tonight," Brisa hedged.

"First round is on me," the guy jumped in. "The club is on Edgewood Avenue."

"That sounds like a deal," Vi replied.

"Awesome, I'll meet you out front." The man winked at Brisa and sauntered away. Brisa made a big deal of waving the paper at him and laughing with Vi.

"We need to see that paper." Just as Damek said it, Brisa texted a picture to Mia's phone. The florescent paper was a small hand flyer for a pop-up party that night at a bar on Edgewood avenue. A name, Dave, was scribbled at the bottom, along with 9:30. A text came through. *We are meeting him at the entrance to the club. He said to wear club clothes.* Brisa and Vi made their exit.

"Should we follow them?" Mia asked out loud.

"No. Text McKenna and tell her they are incoming. We should scope out the location and see what's going on. Then, we need to find some clothes." Damek placed his phone back in his pocket.

"Let's go get ready to party," Calder cheered, pulling Mia forward with his hand around her waist. Damek rolled his eyes and followed behind.

CHAPTER EIGHTEEN

Mia, Jules, and the boys followed at a distance as Brisa, Vi and the stranger from the High waited in line for a dance club. The guy had insisted they walk down the street inspecting Graffiti art. It had been hard not to be obvious about tailing them. The dance club should be considerably easier. Though, the chances of being inconspicuous was difficult when you had two men as attractive as Damek and Calder next to you. In club clothes, the two boys garnered even more attention than they had in the museum.

Mia pulled down on the short skirt Jules had insisted she wear. The two had fought over a midriff top, finally settling on a lace button up the front shirt, exposing her tank underneath. Jules deemed Mia's hoodie unacceptable and replaced it with a black leather cropped jacket that didn't fight against the cold sufficiently. Jules had helped Mia put black and green streaks in her hair and dimmed her natural red with a temporary brown spray. Mia hated to admit it, but she looked hot, and far older than she actually was. Mia couldn't tell if the butterflies in her stomach were because of the mission or because she was going to a club. She was almost seventeen. What would she and the others do if someone carded them? As they moved up the line, Calder stopped them.

"Let's go this way." Calder dashed into an alley, and the others followed. Down the backstreet, there was a wooden fence with a door. Unfortunately, it had a deadbolt lock. Damek sighed and pulled out a small kit of tools. He worked on the lock for about a minute before it gave.

"What in the world, man?" Mia looked at him with awe.

"Tools, metal… Gnome…" Damek shrugged as Calder pulled the gate open. They found themselves on the club's back patio. The man had hidden depths. There was a fountain with surrounding tables where couples were sitting and a few were smoking.

"Let's intercept inside," Calder recommended. As soon as they opened the backdoors of the club, a thumping rhythm assaulted them. Jules pushed inside. Calder grabbed Jules' arm and pulled her to his side. "Try to make it seem like your focus is actually on me." He threw her a devastating smile, which only caused Jules to roll her eyes. They grabbed a side table. The club was an abandoned factory that had been revamped. A high ceiling soared above them. Lights flashed in all directions. The center of the space contained a dance floor where massive amounts of people were gyrating to the pulsing beat.

Damek settled back behind the table with Mia. Calder stood in front of Jules. Since Jules faced the door, she could watch the entrance while seeming to talk with Calder. Soon Vi and Brisa entered. The man from earlier had one arm draped over each of their shoulders. Mia could read the revulsion coming from both of them. He quickly escorted them to the dance floor, where Vi jumped in and Brisa awkwardly tried to follow. Luckily, very little skill was involved with the dancing. Jules grabbed Calder's shirt and with a sly grin said, "Let's dance." Calder winked back at the table as they joined the masses.

Damek and Mia took in the atmosphere. "Have you ever seen anything like this before?" Mia yelled over the music.

"No!" Damek shouted back. "Gnomes don't do… clubs." Mia laughed.

"I'm very surprised," she teased, meeting his gaze. He held it for a minute, then looked away. "Do you want to dance?" Mia asked. Damek panicked.

"I… I…"

"Hey, no worries," Mia interrupted, reacting to his sickly green aura. It was probably better; all the electronics were creating a weird buzzing in her head.

"I just… I have… no rhythm," Damek disparaged himself.

"I think it's more moving with the crowd and trying not to get trampled," she joked.

"Right." The silence was deafening, despite the noise. "We could dance if you wanted to?" Damek asked, doubt in his expression. As much as she wanted to try, she couldn't do it to him.

"That's okay." The two sat and watched the others until Calder motioned them to the floor. Mia stood up. "I've been overruled," she giggled nervously. "Come on." She dragged him towards the dance floor where Calder was waiting. Calder drew Mia close. "I have no idea what I'm doing," she shouted over the crowd. He moved his hands to her hips, helping her find the rhythm. She threw her arms over his shoulders. The energy and sound coursed through her entire body.

Calder turned Mia around so he could see Brisa and Vi over her shoulder, but that left Mia looking at Damek. Jules danced with him, but he was so obviously uncomfortable Mia's heart went out to him. Calder noticed her preoccupation a moment later and said, "Switch," passing her off to Damek and taking Jules' arm. Jules and Calder started to groove together, dancing towards their target, leaving Damek and Mia behind. Mia chuckled at Damek's surprised expression, placing her arms around his neck, just like she had with Calder. Awkwardly, Damek positioning his hands on her waist. They moved to the beat a little slower than the rest of the crowd.

"This isn't so bad, is it?" she shouted.

"No…" he stuttered. "I'm sorry I'm not…" He shrugged instead of finishing.

"You're perfect," she refuted. Calder and Jules were right next to Brisa and Vi. When Mia turned back to Damek, he looked shocked.

"What?" she asked worriedly.

"Nothing," he shook his head and glanced over his shoulder. Since they couldn't tell what was going on with the rest of the gang, Damek and Mia spent their time watching the crowd. Soon the amount of energy around Mia felt like an attack. The pulse and the heat were making her nauseous. She tried to focus on a button on Damek's shirt, but her head wouldn't stop ringing. Noticing her discomfort, Damek steered Mia to the back door.

"I think it's time to go outside," Damek shouted in her ear. As soon as the door closed behind them, the music was muffled to a dull beat. Outside, there were tall metal heaters, metal chairs and benches around a variety of table types. Mia sank back into a chair with her eyes closed. It wasn't very crowded, so she could slowly put up her protective walls again.

"Are you okay?" Damek asked.

"Sitting is good… Air is good… Just give me a sec." A moment later, Vi led Brisa and the guy outside.

"Hey, grab a table by the fountain," the man said. Vi obliged. The three settled into their seats. A waitress appeared in front of Damek, bending over and smiling.

"Can I get you something darlin'?" she drawled, showing off her assets. Mia quickly leaned against him.

"Two sodas? Cokes?" Mia ordered. The waitress smiled, heading to the next table.

"Thank you," Damek colored.

"No worries." Just then, Calder and Jules sat down across from them.

"That was fun," Calder exclaimed. Jules turned her seat sideways so she could watch Vi. Calder leaned forward. "They didn't talk, just danced. Until the guy suggested they come out here."

Each took a turn watching as Jules described the club scene in Atlanta. She mentioned her favorite bars and restaurants. They discussed the sites they had seen that week and their impressions. The night air was getting nippy and the club clothes weren't keeping them warm. No matter how many times Mia rubbed her legs, she couldn't get the goose bumps to go away.

The waitress delivered their drinks and the ones for Brisa's table as well. Damek frowned as he watched the man take the drinks from the waitress to hand them to Vi and Brisa. Dave waved the drinks around dramatically before delivering them to the ladies. They then continued their conversation. A few minutes later, the man swung his arm, knocking Brisa and Vi's clutches into the nearby fountain. Brisa immediately leaped towards the fountain as Vi stood. Then Mia's vision went red. Suddenly, Mia reeled.

> She's standing, staring at the rippling water of the fountain. The ripples seemed to cross space and travel through her body. Her hand waves in front of her face. It is covered in rings, including her wedding band, her wedding band with Jules. The world went out of focus. The lights glare bright and then fuzz out. Her head is spinning. What is going on? Her drink. Someone must have spiked her drink. She reaches for it, but falls to one knee, trying to regain her balance. Where is Jules? She's watching... What is going on? Her heart races. She panics. What are the symptoms? Racing heart, blurred vision... she's been... drugged? Her mind fights for control, but her vision is fading. She tries to talk, to scream for help, but only a small trickle of sound emanates from her mouth. She's falling. Arms reach for her, but then there is darkness.

For a moment, Mia came back to herself. Then another vision hit.

> Vi is falling... what's going on? She turns away from the fountain, her blonde hair slapping into her face. She dashes to Vi, who falls to one knee. She panics. What is she supposed to do? Dave drops to Vi's other side. She knows he can't be trusted. Where are her friends? Dave picks up Vi.
>
> "I've got her," Dave leers.

"No, she should..." Dave glares at her for a second, then laughs. She grabs Dave's arm to pull Vi away from him, but Vi is dead weight and can't help. Dave knocks her into a table. Right then, a blonde man stands in front of him. His features are Sylph, but she doesn't recognize him.

"Put the lady down," the Sylph insists.

"Find your own date," Dave snarls.

"Put her down now," insists the new man. He doesn't raise his voice, but the power behind it is obvious. Dave weighs his options. Before he can react, she slams her foot into the back of Dave's knee. He buckles, dropping Vi, who lands hard on the floor.

"Bitch!" He yells. She braces herself for his retaliation, but the new guy seizes the man by the arm, yanking him around.

"Get lost," the Sylph growls. He throws Dave towards the far side of the patio. She immediately shifts to Vi's side. Vi is unconscious on the floor. Her gaze scans the crowd and her eyes meet Calder's and Jules'. Jules' hand balls into a fist, so tight her fingers are turning white. But Calder's hand on her shoulder holds her back. This is what they had been waiting for.

"We need to get her to a doctor," the blonde man says, kneeling next to her. "There's a Sylph care center close to here," he adds in a whisper. "I can get you help there." A care center? She agrees. "Don't worry everybody! She's my sister. I'll take her home," he announces to the gathering crowd. What is going on? Where is Mia?

CHAPTER NINETEEN

here is Mia? Mia found herself back on the patio. For a second, all the emotions and thoughts of everyone on the patio assaulted her. She grabbed her head in pain, trying to force up the walls she needed in such a crowded space.

"Mia, Mia?? Are you okay?" Mia opened her eyes to find herself on the floor. Damek was holding her up. His voice was full of panic. She focused on him, working her way back, shutting out everyone except the warmth of Damek.

"What happened?" Mia replied, trying to find her bearings.

"You suddenly stood up and then dropped like a brick." He scanned her face, trying to see what was wrong.

"I was…" Mia stopped. The table Vi and Brisa had been at was empty. Calder and Jules were also gone. "I was in Vi… then Brisa… they…. Where are they?"

"I am not sure what happened. In the beginning, we were taking care of you when you passed out. But then Brisa fought that guy. Before we could jump in, some blonde guy came in to save the day. Vi and Brisa left with him. I had Calder and Jules follow. Are you okay?" his voice returned to the panicky edge.

"I'm okay. I… Vi was drugged," Mia swallowed. Two visions, right in a row. She was dizzy. As she tried to stand, her legs gave way. Damek was quick to catch her. Shaking her head, she moved away. "We need to follow."

"They left a few minutes ago. They took the gate out of the patio." He offered his hand and Mia gratefully took it. He pulled her out the patio gate and down the alley towards the streetlights at the other end. Mia was dialing Calder before she stopped. If they were following, a ringing phone might grab attention. She deleted the number and then entered McKenna's instead. They sat on the street, unsure of where to go.

"McKenna," came a short bark of a reply.

"We're leaving the club, trying to find Calder and Jules. Any word?" Mia asked.

"Let me check their tracking thing." Damek paced like a caged animal. Mia allowed herself a moment of jealousy that Brisa would inspire such devotion from him. But having seen the hell Brisa had been through, she decided that Brisa deserved it. "They're four blocks north. But it looks like they are turning back and headed your way. What happened?"

"Vi was drugged, then a Sylph offered to take them to a Sylph clinic for help."

"Sylph clinic?" McKenna repeated doubtfully. "What did his aura say?"

"I don't know," Mia hesitated. "I only saw him through Brisa, and she can't read auras."

"You only… right," McKenna paused. "How did you get separated?"

"I passed out. Damek stayed with me. Calder and Jules followed."

"They must have lost Vi and Brisa," McKenna swore under her breath. Mia looked down the street and noticed the man named Dave. He was hitting on a girl in line for the club.

"I'll call you back. We may have another lead." She hung up and stood in Damek's path so his relentless pacing would bring him to her. Her attention stayed riveted on the man down the street. Damek quickly noticed where she was staring and stalked off in his direction.

"Stop!" Mia jumped in front of him.

"Why?" Damek growled.

"Because confronting him will tip him off," Mia whispered. "He's obviously a part of this." The girl Dave was talking to wasn't too interested. Mia hiked her skirt up and unbuttoned one button on her blouse.

"What are you doing?" Damek asked as his jaw dropped. He attempted to stand in front of her to block anyone's view. "Button your shirt."

"I need to get his attention," she insisted, trying to psych herself up.

"You don't need to unbutton your top to get anyone's attention." Her heart warmed as she realized he was protective of her too.

"Thank you."

"I…"

"Just watch my back and see if you can get his cell."

"What if it has a lock?"

"He's using it now. Just grab it and go to settings immediately. Remember the button that said settings- where we changed the ring tone? Change the code to one you know. It'll be fine."

Mia sauntered over to Dave and allowed herself to trip and fall into him, purposefully knocking his cell phone with one of her arms. "Oh no, I am so sorry," she gushed as the man leered over her. Just as expected, he immediately ogled her shirt and had a hard time lifting his eyes to her face.

"No problem," he insisted. Mia fought not to flinch at the oiliness coming off him in waves. He helped her up, but his hand stayed glued to her side. She giggled nervously and watched as Damek strolled past the two of them, grabbing the cell off the street. She placed a hand on Dave's chest, trying to keep his attention on her. She realized she had no idea what else to do. How does one flirt? Especially with a subhuman like the man across from her. "I'm Dave," he continued to gawk at her.

"Susie," Mia replied with another giggle. Susie? Where did she get Susie from?

"I was just going to have a smoke," he smirked. "Care to join me?"

"I think not," Calder appeared over Mia's shoulder. He forcibly removed Dave's hand from Mia's side. There was a cracking sound as he squeezed Dave's hand as hard as he could. Dave let out a small squeak of pain before Calder released his hand. "How about you go scurry under a rock." Dave stood at his full height trying to intimidate Calder, but the cradling of his hand ruined the effect. Dave was nothing compared to the muscular strength of Calder. "Stand down," Calder demanded over Mia's head. Mia felt herself pulled back into him. Her body relaxed. "Come on." Calder took Mia by the arm and practically dragged her over to Jules. When the three of them walked around a corner, they found Damek examining the cell phone.

"Why did you let her do that?" Calder hissed.

"Let her?" Damek replied, becoming flushed.

"Excuse me, it was the right thing to do," Mia interjected.

"No, it wasn't," Calder argued.

"Actually, as much as I want to agree with you, she's right," Damek disputed. "The texts and emails on this phone are rather illuminating."

"Did you lose Brisa?" Mia asked Jules. Jules looked away. Jules' fear hit Mia hard. "Oh no," Mia murmured. Calder was angry, and right now his frustration centered on Damek.

"There were other ways to get the phone... you shouldn't have sent her in there."

"I didn't send her in there. She went in herself. Mia's an equal member of the team, and she made a call!" Damek ran his hand through his hair. "I didn't like it either, but..."

"But nothing," Calder ranted.

"Stop it," Mia demanded, raising her voice enough to capture the guys' attention. "Calder, I am not a child. Damek was following me the entire time.

It was the best lead we had. You're not here to just protect me. You are here to be my partner. Let it go." Calder scowled.

"Let's call McKenna and decide what we do next," Jules jumped in.

"We can call from the car," Mia stated. She headed that way. Behind her, she could hear Damek go up to Calder.

"I hope you broke that guy's hand," Damek remarked. "She told me to stand aside, but as soon as he touched her…"

"Yeah," Calder agreed. As happy as their truce made Mia, it didn't last. Jules' panic kept Mia tense. Mia started dialing McKenna as they rushed to the van.

"McKenna," the warrior's voice barked again.

"We lost them," Mia said briskly. "But we got a cell phone from the guy who lured them to this club." The phone hooked up to the car, allowing everyone to listen. "Damek?"

"There are quite a few people involved with this. He was texting a circle of people updates. This afternoon, he was notified by someone who had spotted two Sylph at the museum. Dave arrived and sent in a picture of them to confirm, then received approval. He sent in a notification that he had set the trap. He sent another message before he picked up the ladies, then one when they arrived at the club. A final one was sent before they had their drinks delivered. Final message was received from another number– it said the package has been secured. I am assuming they mean Brisa and Vi."

"The Sylph that led them off was in league with this scumbag," Mia stated. For a moment, she relived Brisa's relief at his arrival. "When attacked by someone else, the sight of a Sylph there to help is an overwhelming relief. It makes the victim immediately trust and they're willing to jump into a car to get away, even though it's with a stranger."

"You are sure it was a Sylph?" McKenna's voice was obviously puzzled.

"Yeah, I'm positive," Mia confirmed. "I watched his defense through Brisa. She was freaking. She wasn't sure if she should stick with Dave thinking that's the person we were looking for, but Vi was ill."

"She waved us off," Calder added. "We were there for help, but she went with the Sylph."

"Maybe she still trusts her kind over us," Colin's voice could be heard over the speaker.

"No," Mia placed herself back in her vision. "She looked for us, to make sure we were there. I think her automatic reaction was to trust the Sylph, but she didn't give us up or blow her cover. Then the Sylph said care center, which sounds like resting place. She thought the Sylph may be a bigger lead. So she accepted his help. But she made sure we were there. It was the first thing she searched for."

"I'm not getting a signal from her phone," McKenna jumped in.

"Dave dumped it in a fountain." Damek pointed out. "It's probably fried." They all sat for a second.

"Okay, head to the house." McKenna ordered. "We will meet you there in an hour. We can plan our next step there."

CHAPTER TWENTY

The ride back to the house was done in silence. Damek kept fiddling with the phone, going through emails and texts trying to find any clues that could help them. Jules was almost frozen with anxiety. She rocked softly in the back seat watching out the window. Calder was driving, his knuckles white on the steering wheel. Good Lord, what do we do now? Mia curled up in the back seat, trying to block their worry. She was producing enough of her own. A moment later, Mia's phone rang. "McKenna," Mia said out loud as the name flashed across the screen. Answering, her greeting was cut off.

"We have a situation here," Colin's voice came out over the speakers. "A Sylph female just walked in and introduced herself to the front desk with Vi's alias. She told them she had a key but the number was rubbed off and she couldn't remember which one was hers. I followed. They helped her with the locker and she's been in the dorm room for about fifteen minutes. We are waiting on the porch to see what happens next…"

"How did she get the key? Did you see anyone lift it?" McKenna's voice came through loudly as she took the phone from Colin.

"No," Mia responded. "But there was a lot of confusion, especially when Vi became ill. It wouldn't have been hard to steal the key in the crazy."

"She's right," Damek confirmed.

"Keep heading to the house. I'll call once we have more information. Wait for us there." The phone disconnected.

As soon as they arrived at the lake house, the entire group changed to get the smell of sweat and smoke off of them. After Dave's sleazy perusal of her person, Mia wore extra layers. She sat on the couch, within the comfort of her hoodie. She also wrapped a blanket around her, creating a cocoon to hide in as she recovered from the onslaught of the night. Everyone stayed within sight of each other but remained in their own world.

Finally, with a deep breath, Mia started, "Are there such things as Sylph care centers?" Mia focused her question at Jules, begging her to rejoin the group instead of staying in her head.

"Yes," Jules answered. "In cities near the National Parks. The Sylph keep a house specifically to allow Sylph somewhere to meet with doctors or the local tribe's Cailleach, if they prefer. It maintains the front of a residence. Usually, a doctor and his family live there. We have one in Atlanta, off Ponce. It's why we live where we do. It's an easy commute for Vi."

"Is there any chance they will be brought there?" Mia asked.

"I doubt it. If this guy was a part of a team, they wouldn't bring them to someplace they could be recognized or remembered," Calder commented as he paced the room. "We should probably check and make sure though." Jules pulled out her phone. She withdrew to the balcony.

"Jules, Calder and I all had a good look at the Sylph that came in to 'help' Brisa. He wasn't familiar to me, but I didn't mingle much at the Sylph funeral. What about you?" Damek asked.

"I don't think so. They all have very similar features. It was easy for the crowd to believe he was a relation because of the blonde hair, blue eyes, slight build," Calder growled. "There wasn't anything distinguishing about him."

"Which was probably the point," Damek conceded, "the Sylph were parading men in front of you, Mia. Did you find him familiar at all?"

"No," Mia swallowed, thinking of the awkward night. "Honestly, there were so many people, they all blended together. What have you found on the phone?" Mia asked.

"Not much. Lots of personal emails and such. The guy's name is Dave Ranieri. I doubt he knows much. He gets a message when he should go meet someone at the High. He goes, emails a photo to check and is given an okay or a no. In his photo storage, there are pictures of hundreds of girls. Most aren't Sylph, but there is a picture of the newly passed. She is with another girl. There is also a guy in the picture."

"Let me see," Mia sat by Damek. A quick glance at the photo revealed the couple from her vision, sitting on the lawn with Tana. "That's her brother and his girlfriend."

"Then, someone kidnapped them from here. As were the other Sylph. I counted forty-three on his phone. But not all of them were European. Every tribe is represented in there," Damek informed them.

"Well… we're in the right spot," Calder repeated.

"And at least two Sylph are involved," Mia added. Silence fell on the group as they considered that. A moment later, Jules reentered.

"The Ponce center has had no activity tonight. It's been quiet." Jules paced behind the couch.

"They're taking them to a fake Sylph center. That would take a huge amount of money," Damek pointed out.

"That's true. Whoever is bankrolling this operation is loaded. A fake center which from Mia's vision, is a mansion. A crew of people to kidnap each person. We have the pick-up, the guy that saves them, someone who goes to the hotel, any doctors or nurses they have at the fake center. More and more people keep showing up in this and they must pay them," Calder reasoned. "What makes a Sylph worth so much money? What are they doing with these people?" No one had a response.

Horrible images flashed through Mia's mind. Were they being sold into slavery? Imprisoned? Abused? Were they being experimented upon? She shivered. Her cellphone ringing made Mia jump. "Hello?"

"The Vi imposter packed up all of their stuff and then checked them out of the hostel. We're following her. So far, we have taken 400 north way out of the city. I think we were searching too close to Atlanta, or the lady isn't headed to where they're keeping Brisa and Vi. I have you on speaker so Colin can hear you. What have you learned?"

Mia turned her own phone on speaker. She allowed Damek and Calder to take over the call and repeat their earlier discussion. Her head had started pounding again. Finally, she heard McKenna's response.

"This is even bigger than we thought. Okay, we're getting off the highway. We'll follow until their destination, then scope it out. We'll call with details. There's no point in going back to the hostel. Stay where you are." Abruptly the phone hung up, leaving the group flabbergasted. The stillness broke finally with Jules' voice.

"We can't leave them there. What if they're blocked from the wind too?" Her voice was trembling.

"We will not leave them," Calder stood and embraced her. "Tana had tons of needle marks on her arm. Whatever they did, it wasn't a fast process. She'll be okay."

"It will be a long time until they call again," Damek stated. "McKenna won't leave until she has every bit of information on where they are at. She won't call us until then. Try to get some sleep if you can." Damek's voice didn't hold conviction. The chances of sleep arriving were almost nil. The group separated to find their own peace for a while. Mia retreated to the upstairs couch. Her muscles were cramping from the stress of the evening. Slowly, she went through everything that had happened that day. She tried to reach back and see the auras on people, going back over her visions to make sure there wasn't anything she missed.

She looks down at the bodies lined up on the floor. They are deathly still. She crosses to the first one and checks their pulse again, just to make sure. She's still alive. They're all alive. Thank the Goddess... One of the boys starts to stir in his sleep. She rushes over, trying to wake him up. She needs help. She's all alone. What made her think she could ever be a hero? These people will probably die, and it will be her fault. Suddenly, there is beating on the door. "Mia sent me," the voice claims. Her heart is pounding in her chest. What should she do??

"Brinnnnngggggggg!" Mia woke with a start. She was still on the couch. It was eight the following morning. The cell phone rang again.

"Hello?"

"I am texting you the address. We will take shifts watching the mansion. I've seen no signs of Vi or Brisa. Pack a bag. We'll rent a hotel room near here so we won't have to travel too far if a need arises." Before Mia could respond, McKenna hung up, and an address popped up on the screen. 2400 Mackenzie Dr., Dahlonega.

"Guys!" Mia yelled. "We're headed out!"

CHAPTER
TWENTY-ONE

They didn't take long to pack, maybe twenty minutes. Calder brought some granola bars from the kitchen to tide them over in the car. The trip north was over in approximately an hour and a half. The trip would have been faster, but there was a lot of traffic. It gave Mia time to think about her dream. There were lots of people prone on the floor and they weren't dead. *Maybe she hadn't been dead in the other dream? She couldn't be dead- no one can see their own death... can they??* The thoughts pestered her.

As they reached the address, the group did a straight drive by. A series of wrought iron fences contained a brick mansion with large white columns in the front. They found a huge gate off to the left side of the house with a call box. They slowed down long enough to take it in, but hopefully not long enough to arouse suspicion. They finished going down the road. The house was relatively remote. It was far from the city, with lots of untamed wilderness surrounding the perfectly manicured lawn. The next house down was almost a half mile away. There was a driveway going off into the trees, but no sign of the actual house. Past that, there were smaller houses at least a hundred years old. On the far side of the road was the rental car that McKenna and Colin had been driving.

A sign in the window proclaimed – "Sorry, engine trouble. Will return with a tow truck." As they pulled in behind the car and parked, Mia's phone beeped.

We will be there in ten. McKenna texted.

"Ten," Mia announced to the car, but no one responded. Damek was driving. He watched out his rear-view mirror until Colin and McKenna came into view.

"Here they come," Damek stepped out of the van and opened the back door for McKenna and Colin. Colin sank into the cushioned seat with an exhausted sigh. McKenna just looked focused. Rings under her eyes proclaimed the strain she was under, but she started talking almost immediately.

"We followed the faux Vi back to that mansion around three last night. Most of the lights were out, and only a few came up at their entrance. It has been quiet since we arrived. We scoped the compound. There are cameras on the back porch, surveying the yard. Several cameras around the front focusing on the gate and the fence. There is a fence in the back, but it isn't very tall. I supposed any Sylph could easily go over it. It's lined with manicured trees or bush things. And there is a huge yard. It's definitely the one from your vision, Mia," McKenna verified. "I haven't seen any sign of Vi or Brisa though."

"The best plan is to keep vigil over the place until we can see them," Calder proposed. "Teams of two? Or three?"

McKenna barked orders. "Teams of two. Split our powers. Colin and Mia on different teams, Jules and Damek on different teams. Jules, why don't you come with me? Colin can go with Calder, Damek with Mia. Damek and Mia- you have first shift. Colin and I need some sleep so the four of us will find some new accommodations."

"I want the first shift," Jules insisted. "I need to see if she's okay."

"Jules, you're… too close to this. Let someone else see them first, so you don't go running in their direction," Damek reasoned.

"I would never take a chance of hurting Vi."

"I know but trust me when I say one bad reaction without thinking could give up our position and alert them to our presence. Let us take first watch. I promise we'll do anything we can to help her. If there is any sign of her, we will try to get video on our phones for you to see." Raw emotion passed across Jules' face. She controlled it and agreed.

"Stay in the woods, be careful," McKenna admonished, "we don't want to tip them off. First priority is confirming Brisa and Vi are there. There are more windows in the back than the front so I would watch the rear."

"Wouldn't it be better if two teams are here? One to watch the front and one for the back?" Jules quickly proposed.

"Yes, but Colin and I need rest…"

"Then rest. Calder and I can watch the front from across the street. Then, when one of you returns, they can send the correct person back. I can work a double shift so we always have two teams ready to go." McKenna turned red at being questioned. She was about to argue when Calder placed a hand on her arm.

"It won't take four of us to get the hotel. You guys need rest. We would just be pacing at the hotel. At least here, we can be of some use. We'll take the front and split into our final teams after the first shift." Calder tried to reason. The muscles in McKenna's neck bulged as she struggled to contain her ire. She looked to Mia. Jules needed to do something and to have her at a hotel would be torture. Mia nodded to McKenna, signaling her to agree.

"Fine," McKenna snarled, "Report back anything you see." McKenna stood up but hit her head on the top of the van. Muttering a curse, she quickly headed back to the rental car. Colin followed in her wake. They were soon on their way. Calder and Jules trekked into the woods across the street. They planned to make a loop and come straight at the mansion from the front under cover.

Damek and Mia walked through the woods between the estates to reach the back of the mansion. No matter how hard Mia looked, there was no sign of the second house. The foliage was still dense despite it being November. The trees were thick enough to provide ample coverage. The sound of the leaves cracking beneath her feet was like an alarm in Mia's ears. It reminded Mia of the first walk toward the camp at Samhain.

About five minutes in, Mia noticed that Damek wasn't making any sound. She listened as hard as she could, moving a little closer, but nothing. Finally, Mia stopped to listen, but he almost immediately matched her. At his questioning stare, she quickly moved forward, leaving him to follow. She would have to put it on the unending list of questions for later. Finally, they found a large tree behind the far end of the backyard and settled in. They found a place to sit, but soon ants and bugs attacked. This wouldn't be as easy as she first thought. Mia stood up next to the three, watching the ground for crawling things that came too close to her feet.

They stood, leaning against the trees periodically, without talking for the first hour, the gravity of the situation holding their tongues. By eleven, some Sylph ambled onto the field of green, bringing blankets to sit on and lunches to eat. They appeared relatively happy, enjoying the sun and weather. Brisa and Vi were not among them. They captivated Mia. Black teens lounging with light brown hair, golden in the sun. Asian teens with straight white snowy hair talking. Teens with pale blonde hair, identical to Brisa's, eating snacks. All of them with the startling Sylph blue eyes. The teens were interacting, enjoying the opportunity to explore so many distinctly different cultures. The attraction of staying here was becoming more obvious.

"Psst," Damek hissed. He gestured up towards the balcony. There was Vi, sitting in a wheelchair, an IV attached to her arm. Next to her, Brisa was sitting in a patio chair. They talked freely. Vi was a little pale, but otherwise okay. Mia moved forward a few feet, but Damek stopped her. Shaking his head no, he pulled out his phone and started taking pictures of the scene in front of him. Mia's eyes stayed on Brisa.

The manicured trees at the south end of the yard obscured Mia and Damek's position. Mia stepped between them, willing Brisa to look her way. At some point, Brisa walked to the railing. She was facing their direction. Could she see them from so far away? Mia quietly whispered, "Brisa," willing her to hear. Brisa had said Sylph could hear over great distances. At that moment, Brisa waved as if she was gesturing to the picnickers on the lawn below, but her face lifted higher in their direction.

"She doesn't seem too distressed," Mia commented. Mia and Damek stayed still as Brisa talked to Vi, then disappeared. Riveted to the spot, Mia and Damek continued to watch the playful banter of the picnickers as they hoped to get another Brisa sighting. In each group, there appeared to be one person who was sicker than the rest. Often, there was a taped off IV on their arm, waiting to be used again. No one seemed bothered by it.

Before long, Brisa entered the yard and walked around the perimeter, stretching her arms above her head. Her pace was relatively nonchalant. As she neared their position, Brisa slipped between the trees and quickly went to the gate.

"Mia?" Brisa whispered.

"I'm here. Are you okay?" Mia stayed next to a tree outside the gate.

"Yeah, I only have a moment. This is a hospital of sorts. They admitted Vi and started giving her fluids last night. But they had me donate blood. They've been drawing her blood this morning. Vi says it is considerably more than they should be taking. There are a lot of Sylph here, patients and their friends. Most have been here for at least a couple of months. The weird part is this seems normal to them. It's not. Sylph don't stay anywhere for more than a week or two, especially on a rata. But they are releasing one of the Sylph today. A friend of hers is leaving with her. We don't seem to be prisoners."

"How many people are working in the hospital? Are they all Sylph?" Damek asked.

"We've met with a receptionist, two different nurses and a doctor. I have seen one or two orderlies in the hallways. I can try to take a better count. But they're mostly humans working here. All the patients are Sylph, though."

"Do you have any idea why they have you here?" Mia wondered. "Is there any threat to you?"

"Not that I can tell. There are no phones and the water destroyed ours last night. A few people made it through with cell phones, but there's no service anywhere in the building."

"Has no one noticed their inability to contact the outside world? I mean, red flag."

"Sylph don't contact home often anyway, so it isn't a major panic point. And they have collections of postcards that people send to family just to keep them updated," Brisa shrugged. "They're strangely complacent though," she looked back over her shoulder.

"Could they be drugging them?" Mia enquired.

"Be careful what you eat and drink," Damek advised. "Companies coming," Damek whispered before Brisa could respond. Mia noticed an orderly heading their way. The man was huge, muscles bulging within the too small sleeves of his scrubs.

"I think we're okay for now. I will try to take a walk again, around nine tomorrow morning. Now Hide!" Damek and Mia hid behind two of the larger trees and waited as the beefy orderly barreled down upon them.

CHAPTER TWENTY-TWO

"Hey, Miss," the orderly walked up, a menacing smile twisted his lips. "We don't recommend people going back here, there are snakes and…"

"Deer!" Brisa hit him with a 100-watt smile. "They are so beautiful, but they ran away." She pouted. "I need to borrow a camera next time!" As she started walking the perimeter of the lawn, the man came up to the gate and looked around. Apparently, he saw nothing amiss. Damek and Mia stayed frozen in place for some time. Eventually, Damek walked away from the yard towards a bigger tree and crouched behind it. A second later, Mia followed his lead, meeting him behind the tree. He had his phone out.

"No service. We should move farther away and then call the others," Damek advised. He was obviously torn between calling and leaving Brisa behind.

"She said she was safe," Mia reminded him.

"For now," Damek finished the sentence ominously. Brisa was back on the balcony with Vi. Damek and Mia hiked through the woods, checking their phones periodically to find service. As soon as they were free of the trees, their phones had two bars. They immediately called to report in.

"She said she was safe?" McKenna repeated.

"She thought they would be okay," Mia confirmed.

"Okay, we'll have to trust her on that one. She said they would release someone today?"

"Yeah," Mia watched as Damek's hand opened and closed into a fist repeatedly.

"Let me call Calder," McKenna's speech was slow and deliberate, thinking things through as she talked. "You two head back to the car. Be prepared to go as soon as Calder calls you. Follow the people released and see where they're taken. If possible, try to talk to them and get any additional information you can about the care center. Also warn them to call their parents as soon as possible. Their parents may think they're missing."

"Okay, but-" Mia's words halted as she realized McKenna had already hung up. "I really need to talk to her about that," she scowled. "McKenna... thinks we should follow the other patient when they are released and see what they can tell us."

"Let me guess, she ordered us to do so?" He rolled his eyes and started striding down the road to the stashed car. As they moved without any conversation, Mia frantically tried to come up with anything to say.

When they arrived at the car, she put her hand on his arm and gave a sympathetic smile. "She'll be okay." His brow creased as he looked down at her hand.

"I know."

"I..." Mia's brain stalled for a moment as she quickly removed her hand. "I'm sorry. I just... you seem upset and... I know you care about her... or you seem to have this... bond... and..."

"Mia," Damek interrupted. "We all vowed to protect her, from her father, from anything. So yes, being unable to be there is frustrating. I... don't understand what you're getting at."

"Nothing," Mia blurted out, blushing furiously. How could she make such a mess of things? "I... I'm sorry. I haven't been around other kids my age much... I guess I just read the situation wrong." She darted around the car quickly and tried to open the passenger door. It was locked. Damek stared at her, his face blank. "Ummm… the door?" After he unlocked the car, they both slid inside. It wasn't cold enough to warrant turning on the car, so they just sat there.

"You haven't been around kids your own age?" Damek finally asked.

"I…" she hesitated, "I wasn't allowed to go to school because of my gift. My mom was afraid I would say or do something that would expose us." He absorbed that. "I figured it was kinda obvious, with how awkward I've been around… well… everybody."

"No," he replied. "I had no idea. You always seem very comfortable."

"Oh good, I was trying to seem that way!" She gave him a self-deprecating grin.

"You always seem pretty confident, actually," he puzzled. "In charge… I mean… not like McKenna take charge… trying to be the boss… just in control… knowledgeable?? I'm not sure of the word."

"Oh…" she blushed again, "I… thank you. I think that's good?"

"No, it's good, definitely good," he sighed with frustration. "Obviously, I'm not very good with people either. Calder's right. I should just keep my mouth shut." He was lost in his thoughts for a moment. Mia stayed as quiet as she could not to wake him from his reverie. They sat silently for quite some time. The only sound was the birds. "It doesn't matter what you say, you know," he finally remarked.

"Say about what?" she pondered his context.

"About anything," he paused, trying to find the right words. "Even if you did say something pathetic or weird, it doesn't mean *you* are pathetic and weird. Everyone says stuff sometimes they wish they didn't. A true friend doesn't care."

"We're friends?" she asked, startled.

"Well… yeah… I mean… I thought we were…" At that point, he moved back as if he had overstepped, "Aren't we?"

"YES!" Mia responded, perhaps a little too loudly, and then blushed profusely. "I mean, I would like that... a lot... I... I've never had friends... well... in person... friends."

Damek faced the front of the car. Mia watched as he blushed slightly himself. They both remained silent, waiting for the other to talk. *Well, this is awkward.* But he wanted to be her friend, she reminded herself. She watched a squirrel through the side window, a slight smile on her face. Eventually, Damek looked over, snorted, and matched her grin. Mia rested her head against the headrest.

"Damek?" she started tentatively, "Why were you and McKenna fighting at Samhain? You don't act like the kind of guy that would throw someone into a fire." He scowled.

"I was defending Solange," he sighed. "I don't know what from, I just... wanted to prove... I was trying to show..."

"That she could depend on you?" Mia offered, thinking of their earlier conversation. He sighed, again.

"I don't even know what their fight was about, but then McKenna was in my face, and I was frustrated and angry..." His face was slightly red with embarrassment. "I have a bad feeling about the whole thing... I don't usually... I never get into fights or anything like that... I just..." he stopped, full of frustration.

"It's okay..." Mia started, trying to find a good response. *Solange... she didn't seem very ... kind? Nice? Trustworthy?* Mia kept her thoughts to herself, afraid to raise his ire at her. Damek was obviously conflicted about Solange and that was not something she wanted to put herself in the middle of. The phone disrupted her thoughts.

"You guys ready?" asked Calder, cutting straight to the point.

"Yup," Mia replied.

"Okay, they are pulling out of the drive." Mia nodded to Damek who started the car. After a moment, Calder said, "Black town car, GA Plate, 957 CDC. Go now." The line went silent. Mia put down the phone, repeating the information about the car to Damek. They slowly went down the road. Since there was only a single road leading out of the area, they knew they could catch up pretty easily. Soon they could see the car far ahead of them turning onto a larger two-lane road. Without picking up speed, they continued to follow. Adrenaline rushed through Mia's veins. As they reached the highway, her mind went into overdrive. Were they heading back to Atlanta? The airport? Bus station?

"How do Sylph usually travel?" she asked.

"I don't know… Bus, I think?" Damek answered, pondering the question. They drove down the highway for about twenty to thirty minutes. Soon, the car pulled off the highway and onto back roads. It was doubling back. Mia took out the phone to call McKenna.

"They are heading north again. If we do the same, they will notice us."

"We'll pull our car to the highway. If they get off at the exit, we will follow them. You just keep going so they won't realize they're being followed. I'll call you." Mia relayed the message to Damek. They followed the car until it took the exit for the mansion. Mia and Damek stayed on the highway until the next exit and then turned around.

"Why would they go back to the mansion? Did they forget something?" Mia mused aloud.

"Or maybe they never intended to release the Sylph," Damek commented darkly.

"They just wanted it to seem like they were being released?" Mia asked.

"No one has ever heard of this 'care center'. There are a ton of Sylph there who they release regularly. Someone should know of this place. Unless all the Sylph who stay there never return." The implication was big. All those picnickers were doomed, and they didn't even know it yet. Which meant that they never intended to release Vi or Brisa either. Panic gripped Mia as an echo of the torture Tana suffered lanced back through her mind. Suddenly, a warm hand engulfed Mia's, pulling her out of the hell she had placed herself in.

"We will get them out," Damek said, glancing at her with a worried expression. She nodded, but her chest still felt constricted. They would save Brisa and Vi. It wasn't even a question. *They would save them,* Mia repeated. They continued on their way to the mansion, parking in front of the next mansion down. The other car was nowhere in sight. Another half hour passed before the phone chirped.

The instant message read: *We are coming to you. Stay in the van.* Mia showed Damek, and they waited. Soon, the other car pulled behind them. McKenna, Jules, Calder, and Colin jumped out and quickly entered the van.

"We followed them," McKenna said without preamble. "I called Calder and Jules when it was clear we were heading to a back entrance. They stationed themselves at the back of the house and found an underground garage. Colin and I weren't able to follow them into the back drive, but Calder and Jules could get close enough to see them park. They carried two unconscious Sylph back into the building. Colin and I waited on the back road and gave the two of them a ride back around instead of waiting for them to hike it."

"Again, great thanks for that one," Jules replied. "My hands still feel a little numb from the cold."

"They're keeping all the Sylph that enter," Calder voiced the opinion Damek and Mia already shared.

"We need to get them out of there," Jules' voice did nothing to hide the fear that was welling inside of her.

"Even if we get in, we don't know what kind of security they have. If we can find them, we still may not get out again," McKenna commented.

"We could try to get them a message," Colin offered.

"It could be seen or heard, and then they will know we are here," Calder replied.

"If I could get in and just touch her, we can communicate with no one knowing," Mia offered.

"We have a set meeting for tomorrow," McKenna reasoned. "Most of the Sylph there have been in residence for weeks. And they seem fine. I think twenty-four hours will be okay to get her the message."

"What is the message?" Damek asked. "Run for it? Get out? What will happen to the imprisoned Sylph if they leave?"

"What do you mean?" Mia asked.

"If they have a security breach that bad, will they shut down operations? What will they do with the Sylph inside? Move them? Execute them? We don't really know what we're dealing with here."

"Vi seems to think they are draining their blood," Mia added.

"Could that be what severed Tana's connection with her Element? Losing blood?" Jules pondered.

"We consider our blood sacred. Our Element could be in our blood," Colin theorized.

"How much blood do you have to lose to hurt your connection with your Element?" Mia asked.

"I have no idea," McKenna looked around the circle and everyone shook their heads. "I've never heard of anything like it. Besides torture, I don't see any point in it. But if they were here to be tortured, why keep up the ruse of a pleasant care center for those coming in?"

"It doesn't make any sense," Colin commented. They sat quietly trying to find a reason behind the madness, but nothing came to them.

"We need to get into the underground garage and see where they took the unconscious Sylph," McKenna asserted.

"Perhaps we need to try to find a way into the base," Mia suggested. "Perhaps some motorists are stranded and walk up the back way, searching for help?"

"We could try. If nothing else, it will get us a look at their security," Calder agreed.

"We still need to get a message to Brisa and pull her and Vi out," Jules insisted.

"I am not sure that's wise," Damek shook his head. "We need them on the inside finding out as much as they can."

"It isn't safe," Jules hissed.

"No, it's not," McKenna agreed blatantly. "But they knew that going in." She looked around the circle. "When we took on this mission, we knew we were placing ourselves in potential danger. Now the danger is here. Do we run away or do we follow through?"

"I didn't sign up for this mission," Jules argued, raising her voice.

"No, but Vi did," McKenna countered. "She was bravely thinking of the greater good. There are forty plus people in there who may be disconnected from their Element. We have to help them."

"That's easy to say when you aren't the one in danger," Jules snapped.

"I would be willing to-"

"But you're not... she is." Jules' voice quavered as she cut McKenna off. Mia automatically grabbed McKenna's arm. McKenna swallowed, biting back a retort. McKenna felt the need to defend herself, but it wasn't the right time. Jules pulled out her cell phone and retrieved a photo. She handed the phone to Mia. It was a picture of the mansion. "While we were watching the place today, I took this photo." Mia saw nothing unusual about it. After a pause Jules pointed out, "the crows." The other Elemental's eyes went wide in shock.

"It can't be," Damek murmured. On second glance, Mia noticed there were seven crows in front of the house. Calder took a deep breath.

"When I was little... "

"When all Elementals are little..." interrupted Colin.

"My mother used to sing a nursery rhyme about crows to me and my sisters," Calder continued. "It went 'One is for Sorrow, Two is for Mirth, Three for a Funeral, Four for a Birth..."

McKenna continued, "Five is for Magic, Six is for Plague…"

All four of them finished at slightly different paces: "Seven is for a Curse that has been laid."

"It's a nursery rhyme… we can't…" Damek dismissed the idea.

"I don't think it is!" Jules exclaimed. "In my culture, we were told stories of the crow. Crows on your threshold are an omen of death. Every generation passes on important information through stories to their young, so we will always know what to look for. And if they are right, that 'care center' or whatever it is, has death waiting at its doorstep," Jules declared. "We need to tell the council, tell the local Sylph so they can shut them down. We don't have to have anything to do with this," Jules insisted. It seemed like the easiest solution. But something was wrong with it.

"We *are* the council," Mia replied. "If we leave, especially if we take Brisa and Vi, they will shut down before we return. They will disappear."

"Then we leave Brisa and Vi inside, but we go for help now," Jules demanded.

"Sylph are running the center. They are mostly human, but it involves Sylph. We have no idea if they're connected with the local community or not. We don't know who we can trust. What if our going for help tips them off while Brisa and Vi are still in there?" Damek questioned grimly. Jules was silent.

"Okay," Jules whispered, committing herself to the cause. "Tell me what we need to do." Mia's respect for Jules and Vi increased exponentially. It must have been clear in Mia's face because Calder nodded his agreement. Maybe multiple battles would be won today.

CHAPTER TWENTY-THREE

After hashing it out, they decided Jules and McKenna would fake a car breakdown and walk up the back road to the house. Mia and Colin would return to the woods to meet with Brisa, while Calder and Damek would provide backup. Calder and Damek stayed through the night, taking turns sleeping in the van in case of an emergency. The rest of the crew headed back to the hotel and tried to get a good night's sleep.

Mia stared at the ceiling, thinking of everything that could go wrong. Sleep was long in coming. Only a few hours later, she was up again, dressing in dark clothing so she would blend in as much as possible. Knowing she would spend a good portion of the day outside, she layered up. She pulled her hair back into a ponytail and put on her hoodie, hiding as much of her bright hair as possible.

The sun was barely up before they found themselves on the highway, headed north. The road was busy, but nothing like the slow-moving traffic headed south towards the city. Jules and McKenna were wearing make-up, jeans, and neon colored t-shirts that could easily be hidden with dark-colored hoodies. They also kept a stash of darker clothes in the car, just in case there was an opportunity to change. After picking up a small breakfast from a drive through, they met Damek and Calder at the van. The boys were in rough shape, functioning on little sleep.

"Thank you for this," Calder chugged the coffee.

"I'm not sure I can eat anything," Damek's concern for Brisa was etched on his face. His hair was sticking up at weird angles from sleeping on the back seat of the van. Calder didn't look any better, but somehow the dishevelment suited him.

"Notice anything unusual?" Colin asked. He popped another hash brown into his mouth.

"Not much. No one seems to stir until around eight," Calder supplied.

"Another car arrived this morning. Some guys in suits went in. They had authority," Damek continued.

"If it's a big wig, they may be more preoccupied and might not pay as much attention to our motorists," Jules said hopefully.

"More likely, they won't give us the time of day," McKenna groaned.

"Well, let's get to it. You guys want to head back to the hotel?" Mia asked.

"Maybe after we've made contact," Damek answered after exchanging a look with Calder.

McKenna and Jules headed out to come in from the opposite direction. The two had pushed away their animosity and were working on their backstory by the time they got into the rental car. Calder hiked his way towards the rear entrance so he could watch from a distance when they arrived. Colin and Mia started toward the meet point with Brisa about an hour before the appointed time. They went slowly to keep from being spied from the house.

The morning was nippy. Mia pulled her hands into the arms of her hoodie. The leaves crackled beneath her feet, despite her best efforts to be silent. Colin frustration grew as a twig snapped under his foot. Somewhere far behind them was Damek. The thought made Mia feel better. Nerves made goosebumps raise on her skin, despite the layers. A chill went up her spine as she caught sight of the house. Something was wrong. Too many dreams and scenarios had gone through her head the night before and now, one by one, they danced in front of her eyes. They were just dreams. She stopped behind the tree they had used previously.

Shrugging off the ill feeling, she focused on trying to send the most concise message possible to Brisa. Probably best to throw a wrench in the works, especially if anyone was listening. The argument about telling Brisa and Vi to get out if possible had raged long into the night. In the end, they decided the best thing to do was to give Vi and Brisa the information the group had collected but let them choose what they wanted to do from there. Mia already knew the answer. Brisa and Vi would stay, but the choice needed to be theirs. Mia and Colin waited until the allotted time and then peeked around to see Brisa leaving the mansion again. This time, she was carrying a small camera and clicking pictures of the world around her. As soon as Brisa approached their meeting place, she ducked between the trees quickly. Mia rushed up, grabbing her hand as she greeted her with a furtive "hello!"

In case they can hear us, Mia explained. *This is the site, but after they saw you here yesterday, we thought we shouldn't take any chances.* "How are you two doing?"

"Fine," Brisa acknowledged Colin with a small wave. He stood by the tree watching the mansion for the guard to come running their way. "I... don't think this is the place we are searching for." *Is that what you want me to say?*

"Then we should probably check you guys out and see if we can find the missing Sylph elsewhere. McKenna thinks the guy that drugged Skye is the lead we need to follow," Mia proclaimed clearly. *They didn't release the two Sylphs. They brought them back to the mansion unconscious. We think there may be another compound beneath the mansion.*

"Skye is still not feeling well though," Brisa countered. "Perhaps we should stay a few more days until she's back on her feet." *Vi and I will nose around as much as possible in the next...24 hours... and then we will try to get out.*

"If you think it would help her, then that sounds like a good idea." *Be careful. McKenna and Jules are trying to get in the rear entrance. The rest of us will keep monitoring. We agree with Vi- it must be blood they're after.* "I don't think we can give her more than a day though." *Find an exit strategy. If the center is monitoring this, they may willingly let you leave. If they don't…*

We'll come up with something. If a Sylph out of her mind with the lack of Element could escape, I am sure two lucid Elementals can too. "I'll tell her the vacation is over tomorrow." Brisa stepped backwards, back onto the lawn. Brisa acted as if she was going over pictures on her camera.

Mia hoped she didn't forget to tell Brisa anything important. Then she felt the others. No wonder they didn't send a guard. The guards were already surrounding them. She joined Colin and took his hand. *We need to leave.* He nodded. Colin would panic and let the watchers know they were aware of them. Her eyes swept through the woods, finally catching the figures camouflaged in the trees. Only their auras gave them away. Mia's heartbeat was in her throat as she forced herself to match Colin's pace out of the area.

More and more light poured into the woods as Mia and Colin came closer to the road. Just a few more minutes. From across the road, Mia could see Damek about to head her way. She shook her head, trying to make eye contact from the great distance. A frown crossed Damek's face. He entered the van. The men probably saw him, but the less they knew the better. Also, the sooner the van was ready to get them out of there, the safer Mia would feel. As Mia got to the end, she picked up the pace. Colin was a little confused but matched her. They jumped into the van. As soon as the door closed, Mia blurted:

"They know we're here."

CHAPTER TWENTY-FOUR

"What?" Colin yelped.

"We were surrounded," Mia confirmed. "At least five men. They were camouflaged. Close enough to overhear our conversation."

"Did they hear anything pertinent?" Damek asked.

"No. Brisa told me this is the wrong location, and we needed to try elsewhere. That Vi was still sick, and they planned on leaving tomorrow."

"Do you think they believed you?" Damek probed.

"I couldn't get a good read on them or their auras."

"Let's go around the back, so we can help McKenna." Damek shifted the car into drive. Would they let Brisa and Vi leave tomorrow? If so, the council could regroup and hit the compound together later. If the kidnappers let them leave, they may let down their guard, assuming the council would go elsewhere. But if the council left, they could tell others about the care center, and then the entire operation would be exposed. Then again, that wouldn't matter if the captors were planning on closing down the operation now that someone knew about it. Or, they could decide to keep Brisa and Vi and move the operation completely. Either way, this location was doomed. The kidnappers couldn't take the chance of continuing if there was any way someone knew what was going on here. So how soon would they move out? Was there enough time to rescue the captured Sylph? The council had to do something before the abductors disappeared again.

The tension in the car was thick as each contemplated the possibilities. The van pulled up on the side of the road across from the back entrance. Colin, Mia and Damek scoured the landscape for signs of McKenna and Jules. Nothing. *I hate waiting,* Mia thought. The tension from her meeting in the woods hadn't dissipated, and she started rubbing her arms trying to warm herself from the outside in. Colin gave her a reassuring smile, but it didn't reach his eyes. Damek just watched for the first signs of movement. At least twenty minutes had passed before they noticed Calder moving out of the woods. Calder noticed the minivan. He stopped by the van, and Damek rolled down his window.

"They know," Damek said calmly. Calder's face took on an uncharacteristically grim expression. He headed to the car, lifting the hood to replace a spark plug. Then he hopped in and started the car, ready to go. Soon, the sound of McKenna and Jules joking as they walked down the driveway could be heard. They were still portraying the fun-loving teens with car trouble in the woods. The moment McKenna and Jules noticed the van, they went silent and jogged to the car. Damek pulled out, and Calder fell in behind. No one commented as they headed to a nearby diner. Once they had huddled together in the booth, McKenna interrogated Damek.

"What do they know?"

"They were waiting for us. The guards didn't approach, but they observed our meeting with Brisa. No important information was given, and Brisa and Mia did the best they could to throw them off the scent, but…"

"But if anyone even knows about the care center, it will shut down and relocate as soon as possible," McKenna finished.

"Plus, even though we said this wasn't the place with the missing Sylph, they would have to believe we're idiots to find that believable," Mia muttered

"The center may have already done most of the prelim work for a quick removal," Colin speculated. "If we assume they suspected from the point when we met with Brisa yesterday, then they have been contemplating and planning since then."

"How long could it take to move an operation like this?" Calder asked.

"Depends on several things," McKenna mused. "If there are forty plus Sylph contained on site, it comes down to whether they will remove the Sylph or set them free. Also, whether or not they already have another location. We didn't see much going in the back way. There was a guard at the rear entrance. He didn't even let us near the parking garage. But I only saw the one."

"There were at least five guys watching us with Brisa," Mia commented. McKenna's brow furrowed.

"I do not think they would release the Sylph. At least, not the ones in the underground compound," Colin stated. McKenna who gave him her full attention. "They know too much."

"We are going to lose them quickly," Jules swallowed. Her terror had returned in full force.

"No," Mia looked at each one of them. "We will not lose Brisa and Vi. We know where they are now. There is a limited amount of time. What do we do? All ideas on the table."

"I don't think there is a huge amount of security," McKenna started, "but we don't have any warriors, and we've lost the element of surprise."

"I don't know any fighters," Jules added. "Lots of medical personnel though."

"We need to go in almost immediately," Calder stated. "The whole operation could be gone tomorrow. And if they think they get to keep Brisa and Vi that way, the kidnappers may take the opportunity."

"Could they move out that fast?" Colin asked McKenna.

"They could. With enough people, definitely. If they didn't take the Sylph, it would be easy."

"If we are right and they want blood, they could try to drain them and run," Damek warned.

"Then time is of the essence," Mia's comment silenced the table again. "We need to go in. And we need to go in tonight." As she looked around, all eyes were wide except for McKenna's, whose had narrowed to slits.

"Then it is time to call in reinforcements." McKenna took out her phone. "It's all or nothing."

CHAPTER TWENTY-FIVE

The group planned for about a half hour and broke up around eleven. Jules left to gather the people that the plan required, people she was trusting with their lives. McKenna and Mia left to find the nearest Fire clan. The boys went to a thrift store to buy scrubs similar to those worn by the workers at the mansion and to find supplies. Then the boys went to the hotel to take a nap. Colin volunteered to stay across the street from the mansion and watch for unusual activity.

"Brand said that there is a small Fire clan just north of Milledgeville, Georgia. It's about three hours southeast of here. He is calling in an introduction," McKenna explained as they drove down the highway.

"Three hours? That will get us back here right before dusk. IF we spend almost no time there."

"They are the only warriors I have access to. We can't contact the Sylph. There is no water nearby so no Undines, there may be some Earth clan in the mountains, but frankly they aren't known warriors."

"But there are warriors in Milledgeville?"

"All Fire clans have a warrior contingent wherever they settle. It's tradition."

"And you think they'll help us?" Mia asked.

"No, not unless we prove ourselves."

"And how do we prove ourselves?" Mia wasn't sure she wanted an answer.

"You'll see," McKenna replied forbiddingly and focused on the road. Evidently, McKenna was thinking through the next few hours in her mind. This was McKenna's show; Mia was only along for the ride. Mia sat back and gave McKenna the mental space to focus. The van exited the city going a little faster than it should but staying within 15 miles of the speed limit hoping that would keep them safe from tickets. Every time a car sped past, they would speed up and go a bit faster until the other car outdistanced them. There were a lot of fast drivers in Georgia, which helped their travel time considerably.

The land was flat as they left Atlanta, heading east. After they passed the eastern burbs, the road became very monotonous. Soon they turned off the highway onto back roads. Lots of forest dominated the landscape, along with some small houses. Nice well taken care of ranch houses stood next to antiquated homes that had fallen into disrepair. Working barns were built next to abandoned ones. The variety was fascinating, but without McKenna's companionship Mia soon fell asleep, making up for the last two sleepless nights.

"Wake up Mia," McKenna barked. Mia jerked herself awake, reacting to the tension in McKenna's voice. They were on a country road, with trees surrounding them. They ended up at a large cabin. It appeared deserted except for a lit porch light. It was spooky, definitely spooky, and they were about to go inside. Cue the banjos.

"What do you want me to do?" Mia asked as she tried to calm herself.

"Watch, support, listen," McKenna took a deep breath, "And if this goes badly, get me out of here." McKenna sucked up her courage and opened the door. Mia exited on the other side.

Unlike their meeting with the Sylph, they hadn't dressed up, instead opting for cargo pants and t-shirts. McKenna had even dressed Mia as her more pathetic twin, but Mia's black t-shirt had the Beatles on the back covered by her hoodie. Mia tried to imitate McKenna's bravado, but frankly, it was lacking.

What Mia had learned lately was when she was threatened she acted with more courage than she had. It was like a twisted game of chicken. This time Mia had yet to meet the Fire clan, but knew that she would be the tiniest, weakest person here. McKenna really should have taken Calder or Damek, but instead here Mia was. Why was Mia of so much interest to the other clans? Another thing to ask about. Well, there would be the three-hour drive home… she hoped.

Instead of heading into the cabin, McKenna walked around it, dragging Mia in her wake. As they reached the backyard area, they found a small clearing. There was a fence enclosing a clear space where two men sparred. Several others were gathered, watching the match intensely. There was no yelling or jeering, just insane focus. McKenna stayed at the edge of the building, taking everything in. She watched the fight avidly. Better not to draw attention to us, Mia thought, frozen in place. The fight wasn't brutal, but it was quick. Both of the men in the mini arena exhibited a basic boxer stance. Each landed blows on the other, but neither reacted to the hits as the battle waged on.

There was an older man standing on the fence, periodically calling out points. "One to Flint!" came a cry. The spectators nodded, agreeing with the call. The fighting continued until a single voice sounded, "Visitors." As one, they turned and faced McKenna and Mia. Mia forced herself not to take a step back. McKenna's spine straightened. She allowed the group of Salamanders to approach her.

"You're McKenna." The older man approached, leading the younger crew.

"Ignatius," McKenna acknowledged him. "The new council needs warriors for a day. It would-be real-world training against an actual foe who is hurting Elementals."

"You're asking us to take over a task for you?"

"No, I am asking for a contingent of warriors willing to follow our lead."

"Why would any of my soldiers follow you? You're a kid and obviously not one of us." He gave a sneer, then turned away. Mia blinked at the racist slight. She opened her mouth but McKenna's hand was on her arm. *He is trying to provoke me. He will not succeed.* McKenna took a step forward.

"I intend to earn the right in the traditional way," McKenna announced. Ignatius stopped. All the warriors gave McKenna a slack-jawed look, then focused on Ignatius as he turned back.

"You want an Agon," he snorted, "You intend to fight my best," he looked back at his assembled crew. "I wouldn't put you up against my weakest."

"Ahh, afraid to give up your command." Her voice outdid his for condescension. Mia couldn't help but smirk, which probably wasn't a good idea. A couple of the behemoths turned their attention Mia's way.

"Ahh, goading me into it," Ignatius chuckled. "Why would I even consider putting my team in your hands?"

"Tradition. I formally submit my challenge. I will fight your best, or I will fight you. However, there are Elementals being tortured and dying. If you think I will walk away without a fight, you're greatly mistaken."

Ignatius paused, holding long enough for awkwardness to descend. "Challenge accepted." He strode to the small arena. "I'll give you a fighting chance. I'll let you fight my best. If you can defeat him, you can lead my team into battle. Otherwise, I wouldn't trust you with them." Mia was shocked. McKenna never mentioned a fight. Mia wanted to ask McKenna, but McKenna was steeling herself for what lay ahead. The team of warriors circled around the small arena. A large dark-haired fighter, around twenty-five years old, separated from the rest of the crew. He had stripped off his outer shirt and stood in the center of the small circle, muscles straining the fabric of his undershirt.

"McKenna?" Mia whispered. "Are you serious?"

"Pretty much." She removed her jacket. "I have the skills. I just have to keep my head. I can't lose my temper. As soon as I get angry, I lose." Mia could tell that McKenna was talking to herself, almost repeating a mantra. McKenna's face was grave.

"This isn't a fight to the death or anything?" Mia joked. McKenna handed Mia her overshirt. "McKenna, we are outnumbered by a group led by a racist old man. This isn't safe. We need to get out of here."

"Brand said I could trust him but expect a challenge. Apparently they were friends a long time ago. Besides, what he said isn't half as bad as what's Damek's girlfriend said. And you trust him right?" McKenna strolled into the arena. Oh, my Lord. Mia scurried after her, stopping at the gate. She was going to have some heated words for Damek about 'Solange'. All the warriors watching appeared certain of the fight's outcome. Mia straightened up and tried to come across unaffected, but she continued to send McKenna panicked looks.

The two warriors circled each other, doing a final assessment before shifting their arms into a defensive posture. McKenna's opponent shuffled in and swung in her direction, but she was too quick, ducking and pivoting behind him, landing a blow to his kidneys in the process. He turned immediately, assuming a defensive posture. They continued to circle. He feigned once, but McKenna didn't fall for it, nor did she make a move.

Use his strength against him. Mia heard the thought filter into her mind as Mia's hand instinctively clutched her necklace. Mia's brow furrowed as she tried to figure out who had spoken. Soon the man made another offensive strike. *Duck and cover. Make multiple blows.* Sure enough, McKenna moved into him, missing the strike and landing several hits to his body before dancing out again.

"Yeah!" Mia cheered, breaking the silence. Several spectators reacted, but the two fighters were too engrossed in each other. Mia swallowed and concentrated on the fight. McKenna was staying right out of his reach, waiting. He moved in with a volley of hits that combined boxing and a weird form of martial arts. McKenna weaved and avoided most of his blows, letting his own momentum aide her in the deflection of them. Mia's breath caught as he landed a hit to McKenna's side. Pain flickered across McKenna's face, but she smoothed it quickly. The sparring Mia had watched at the lake house was nothing like this.

As serious as the group had been in their training, no one was aiming to kill the other. This man wanted to destroy McKenna. It was clear on his face.

Soon, he attacked again. McKenna ducked, but he anticipated her, managing to get a strong hit to her face. It sent McKenna spinning. She was up again in seconds, moving out of his range. Rage pulsed through her aura. He smirked once, sending a knowing grin to Ignatius. *That was a mistake.* McKenna took advantage of his distraction and landed a kick to his solar plexus. He took the hit, but grabbed her leg, twisting it sharply as he flew backwards. She flipped sideways, then hit the ground. *Aghahh… knee…* McKenna was up again, trying to keep her weight off one knee. Anger was overcoming her again.

"McKenna!" Mia shouted, grabbing her attention. Their eyes met. McKenna took a deep breath, letting her anger go on the exhale. McKenna concentrated on her foe again. *Over show…* The man was rubbing his chest and confident in his victory over the wounded woman before him. They circled each other. As the small crowd watched and evaluated the fight, Mia was at a loss. Was McKenna winning? Or was her opponent? McKenna definitely appeared to be in worse shape.

At that moment, Mia was hyperaware of how truly helpless she was in this world of Elementals. The small amount of self-defense McKenna had taught her would never stand up in this arena. She would be dead meat.

The Fire Elemental dove in, aiming to sweep the leg, but McKenna saw it coming. Using her bad leg, she jumped, stepping off his shoulder and landing behind him. She then slammed her foot into his back. He careened into a fence post, hitting his head against the top rail.

McKenna stood still as he gripped the fence to help himself up… *Stay down… just stay down…* the voice in Mia's head chanted along with Mia. It had only been a few minutes, but the pain and tension in McKenna's body pulsed. Now, the other fighter was in much worse shape. A trickle of blood traveled down the side of his face.

Rage poured off of him as he faced the upstart female, putting him to shame. McKenna met his gaze and sunk back into her defensive posture, raising her arms to protect her body and face. The young man snarled and immediately tried to rush her. *Mistake,* the voice said grimly. Mia could see how his anger made him sloppy. McKenna easily maneuvered out of his grasp, sweeping his legs this time and listening as he slammed into the ground. The sound of his head hitting making the viewers wince. Mia could feel it more than hear it. Something was wrong.

McKenna prepared for his next attack, but the man stayed down. Mia jumped the fence without thinking, running to the wounded man. His hand went up to his head, applying pressure to his forehead. *Oh good, he's not dead.*

Mia approached the man struggling to move up. "Mia, get out of here," McKenna shouted. Mia reached out and grabbed his hand. He immediately tried to swat her away, but not before a loud ringing pierced her ears and a pounding began in her skull. Other pain manifested in her leg, back, and chest. For the moment, she was one huge bruise.

"Ear ringing, pounding skull. McKenna, he's got a concussion."

"Concussion?" McKenna repeated, taking it in. *The face of a young girl with long black hair flashed in Mia's mind.* McKenna faltered. Her defenses dropped slowly as she processed the information. "Concussion!" McKenna said loudly to Ignatius. Despite her measured speech, the exertion of the fight could be heard in her raspy breath.

"He'll get up and fight," the man spat in her direction.

"I won't fight him," McKenna retorted.

"Then you've lost your assault team." McKenna steeled herself.

"I'll fight the next person in line." There were murmurs among the assembled mass. "Additional hits on a concussion can do long term and serious damage. In a battlefield, it's worth the risk. In a sparring match, to continue is foolishness and I will not potentially harm a... brother of mine." Silence fell as they waited for Ignatius to respond.

"You are a fool to take on another after the hits you've taken. I will not send my fighters to follow a fool." He turned to leave.

"No," she yelled, forcing his attention. "There are Elementals in danger. My life is meaningless if I fail to protect those in my care." The young girls' face flashed through McKenna's head again and again. Maybe the girl had hit her head too.

"These are Salamanders in trouble?"

"No, Sylph."

"Why would you care about the Sylph?" His voice dripped with derision, showing he couldn't care less about them.

"We are the new council. All Elementals fall under our care. We took an oath to protect any and all. I will not give up. I will continue to fight until I cannot continue. I have issued the challenge… I have not lost. Therefore, the challenge continues." The murmurs started again. Mia stood up and stood next to McKenna to show support.

"And you are the leader of the council?" Ignatius asked.

"No," McKenna responded. She gestured to Mia, "She is." McKenna gave Mia a nod of approval. Mia took a huge breath and then turned to face Ignatius, meeting his stare. *My God, I hope McKenna knows what she is doing.* Hopefully, this bluff wouldn't go so far.

"What's so special about her?" Mia didn't blink and didn't respond. How do you respond to that? Nothing special, just a member of the team.

"She could read Malta," McKenna said simply. Mia tried to raise an eyebrow the same way McKenna had earlier. All Mia managed was to make her face twitch.

Everyone waited. After a minute or two, Mia asked the other warriors. "Do you have a medic? Your man needs to be seen."

"I will not fight him. Whoever I need to fight next, take the ring. Time is of the essence!" McKenna indicated the side of the arena with her head, signaling for Mia to leave. Mia was about to refuse when the deep voice of Ignatius reverberated through the clearing.

"Stop. I dare say my warriors have seen enough to make an informed decision." He surveyed his students. "The Salamander of the new council is asking for warriors to assist her on a mission. This mission will take place…"

"Tonight," McKenna finished.

"You would be under her leadership. I allow you to decide if you will join her." He then answered their unasked question, "I will not hold it against you." He scowled. "If you will follow… McKenna," he said grudgingly, "enter the arena." There was a pause. McKenna lifted her head proudly, meeting the gaze of the assembled. Then one of the smallest, a woman with short black hair, jumped the stile, taking a step in McKenna's direction.

"I will follow," she stated, lifting her hand to her heart and bowing slightly. As she bowed, a man taller than most jumped the stile, shadowing the first woman.

"I will follow," he announced. One by one the others jumped the stile. Eventually, all but the fallen warrior accepted McKenna's leadership.

"I thank you," McKenna said, looking to Mia.

"The council thanks you," Mia announced, hoping that was McKenna's secret message. Immediately, McKenna stepped over to the man who at this point had sat up. He had watched the proceedings, still holding his head. She offered a hand. He grasped it and allowed her to assist him to his feet. Then McKenna took a step back and bowed, holding her hand to her heart in the same fashion the other warriors had used with her. The man hesitated, then bowed slightly back. He reached out his arm, which McKenna grasped by the forearm.

"I would be proud to follow," the warrior said.

"I would be proud to have you with me," McKenna allowed. "But see the medic." She grinned. He responded with a matching smirk. McKenna announced to the others. "We leave in twenty minutes." They went running to grab gear. Ignatius walked up to McKenna.

"Good show," he nodded his approval. "Brand said you were a spitfire when he asked me to help you."

"You were going to help us?" Mia exclaimed. "Then why the fight?"

"I didn't ask for a fight. She did. My trainees aren't fools. They have to respect those I ask them to follow. Brand said she would hold up. He was right." Before Mia could respond to such an asinine way of proving yourself, McKenna ended the conversation.

"Thank you for the opportunity." Signaling to Mia, McKenna walked with as much strength and conviction as she could back to the van. The pain in McKenna's leg was obvious. As soon as they were out of sight, she leaned heavily on Mia.

"Who was the girl?" Mia asked. McKenna swung her head up, cringing.

"My… sister… had a head injury when she was young… she… never fully recovered." Mia nodded. That didn't explain the guilt, but at least the association. At last, they reached the van. "Can I sleep on the way back?"

"Are you sure *you* don't have a concussion?" Mia asked. She nervously approached the driver's side… Mia could drive… barely.

"He didn't get my head… my leg… yeah, gonna feel that one for a while." McKenna grimaced as she bent over awkwardly to get into the car. Mia watched as McKenna relaxed backwards into the passenger seat, pain still touching her face. Mia wouldn't force the confidence… It wasn't her business.

CHAPTER TWENTY-SIX

It was dusk before people arrived at the agreed upon meeting point, the hotel. A manager had agreed to allow them use of the breakfast room to organize, though he thought they were a group of students trying to assemble a lacrosse team.

The Salamanders had followed in their own van back to Atlanta. At some point, the Salamanders decided Mia was too slow and took the lead. She followed behind them in a panic as they sped through Atlanta. McKenna slept, oblivious to Mia's anxiety.

The warriors climbed out of their van and were pulling weapons and arming themselves. McKenna let out a stream of curse words Mia couldn't understand as she stepped out of the car.

"What's wrong?" Mia rushed to McKenna's side. McKenna wouldn't look her in the eye.

"I… my knee… it… tightened up… the pain… I have to walk in there Mia, without help… but…" McKenna glanced over to the Salamander van where the warriors were finishing their weapons check. McKenna finally looked Mia in the eye. McKenna was scared. That scared Mia. "Is there anything you can

229

do… like what the old lady did?" Cailleach Ilma's words popped up in her mind unbidden.

"It's all about intention," Mia whispered. She took a deep breath, trying to give herself confidence. She manipulated her t-shirt to come out from under her hoodie and over her head. With a silent word of apology to the Beatles, she ripped the shirt into strips. "I don't know if this will work." She looked at McKenna.

"Do it," McKenna whispered after trying to put weight on it again.

"Where is the pain?" Mia examined the knee. The swelling had started in earnest. McKenna indicated the base of her knee. "I have to believe I can do this." Mia thought over the things she had accomplished to that point: saving Lucy, speaking for Brisa, connecting with Tana. She may not have control over her gift, but her gift was helping people. Mia sent a quick prayer to the heavens- *God or Goddess or whatever force is out there, please help me help my friend.* Kneeling, Mia tied a strip of the fabric around the knee. "Bind the pain in the knot, not the knee. Please bind the pain in the knot, not the knee." She tried to visualize the rope working like a sponge, pulling the pain out and absorbing it. She repeated the mantra again and again. After three ties, Mia let out a breath and looked up at McKenna. McKenna tentatively put pressure down on her foot. She flinched but nodded.

"Pain is still there but… I can walk on this." She helped Mia up. "What did you do?"

"Good question." Mia sent a quiet prayer of thanks as she trailed McKenna into the hotel. Eight warriors followed them into the meeting room. Calder rushed over, trying to get a better look at the damage to McKenna's face.

"What happened?" he murmured as McKenna pulled her face away.

"Tradition," McKenna said succinctly. Calder's face demanded an explanation.

"Later," Mia mouthed. Reluctantly, Calder agreed. Damek didn't even comment. He just gave a greeting, allowing McKenna to appear tough in front of her assembled crew. She led them to the crude map Colin had created of the grounds around the mansion.

"How many of you are Heaters? Protectors?" McKenna asked. The warriors began to debate strategy while Mia welcomed the next group of people. Jules was the leader this time; behind her walked five plain clothed doctors. If people were being held against their will and possibly drained of blood, having a Cracker Jack medical team would be invaluable. Jules swore these were some of Vi's closest friends and colleagues. It said something that they were willing to show up in the middle of nowhere to help Vi out. All were Elementals, but not all Sylph. From their hair and eyes, Mia could easily determine that there were two Earth, a Water, an Aether, and finally one Sylph. They were to come in after the council and the borrowed Salamanders worked their way through the compound.

Colin had called to inform them that a van of several people in scrubs and one or two more security guards had shown up at the mansion around five. McKenna let a doctor fix her knee with a brace, a steroid shot, and painkillers. Mia went to a bathroom to change into her scrubs. The scrubs weren't enough. Damek and Calder also brought her wig to disguise the bright auburn hue of Mia's hair. When she looked at the final effect in the mirror, her stomach dropped out. This was how she had appeared in the dream… when she was… Her breathing quickened and her heart raced. Her dream was coming true. This was the moment. She had never avoided her visions… until Colin. Maybe she could avoid this one now! Should she desert the mission? Or should she help save Brisa and the other Sylph? Could she live with herself if she didn't help? What if not going makes her end up lifeless in the road? How do you want to die? Mia asked herself. With courage or with fear? She tried to slow down her breathing. There was pounding on the door. She opened it to find Calder on the other side. He was dressed as her security guard, having put on a dark grey suit. Jules had trimmed up his hair to make him a little more military.

"You okay?" Calder checked in. Mia nodded but couldn't get any words out. Her heart was racing a million miles a minute as they got ready to leave.

Watching the battle between the Salamanders was a blatant reminder of her complete and utter lack of training. She could go back and forth forever. Mia decided she could only do what she thought was right and that was helping the Sylph. They left the hotel in teams, then reconvened behind the mansion.

The large brick building was completely lit up. A gauzy curtain blocked each window of the mansion, allowing only shadows to pass through. Damek, Mia, and Calder headed in first. They shifted through the woods to the side of the house. Mia remained alert for any sign of auras. Damek scouted ahead since he could walk almost silently. He was able to do this, he finally explained, due to his Earthly connection. The only thing the others could see was darkness. Though Mia's eyes had adjusted, the twilight leeched the world of color. She stood in a gray, black and blue landscape. The familiar was now eerily menacing. Soon, Damek reappeared, reaching for Mia's hand. She grasped Calder's.

I didn't see anyone ahead. The back yard is deserted and no one is on the balconies. Damek informed Mia and she automatically relayed the message. *You ready?* Mia nodded but couldn't manage the reassuring smile she attempted. *We will watch as best we can from afar. McKenna's team will wait a half hour before they advance. Expect us inside within the hour, if all goes well.* Mia nodded again and let go of Calder and Damek's hands. The mansion was intimidating. What if alarms went off? What if anyone had a good look at her face? Damek picked up her hand again and met her gaze. *Be careful. No unnecessary risks. You find Brisa and Vi and then hide until McKenna's team has worked their way in. Okay?*

Okay. Again, Mia couldn't manage the smile. Suddenly she heard the flapping of bird wings and looked in the backyard. Three black birds were standing around on the lawn. *The bird song… what was three birds?* Surprised, Damek followed her gaze.

Death, he replied. *Are you positive?* Mia couldn't look away from the birds but nodded. The image of her own body on the ground paralyzed Mia for a moment. Damek squeezed her hand, pulling her out of it. Calder crept ahead, and Mia followed. Damek remained there until Mia and Calder were out of sight, working their way down the length of the fence towards the house.

Calder and Mia had agreed earlier to get about halfway to the house before scaling the fence. It wasn't electric, or even overly high. It was an old-fashioned black cast-iron fence with decorative swirls, making for an easy climb. They came down on the other side, still hidden by the manicured trees that lined the perimeter. Wedged between the trees and the fence, they came as close to the mansion as possible and waited. There was no movement through the glass doors, which opened into a large living room space. No one was watching the large TV. At any hospital, or even hotel, there should have been at least a few residents in the community room, but it was barren.

Viewing shadows through the upstairs windows, Mia and Calder crossed the small space of lawn as quickly as possible. The doors opened easily, with only a slight creak that sounded like thunder. When no one appeared, they moved inside, then deeper into the house. Through a very short hallway, they found a dining space. The empty room was full of large circular tables.

On the far side should be the kitchens. If there was no one dining, it was unlikely to be occupied. Their first priority was to locate Brisa. They headed away from the kitchens, searching for some stairs. Upon reaching the foyer, they could hear voices coming down the grand staircase. Calder pushed Mia through an open door. It was dark inside. Calder kept her pinned up against the wall as they listened to two female voices conversing. Calder's eyes met Mia's. She swallowed. He was close enough she could feel his breath on her face. He was breathing as rapidly as she was. She looked over his shoulder, breaking the connection and waiting for the women to pass. As the women reached the bottom of the stairs, Calder and Mia could hear the words.

"Most of them are out. If we help with loading the patients in the basement first, we should have little resistance from upstairs."

"I don't know. I'd rather wait with our patients. The ones from downstairs are…"

"I know," the first voice cut her off. "But they need our help." The voices moved away, echoing from the empty dining hall. Calder took Mia's hand intending to go through the door, but she stopped him. While they had been standing in the darkness, her eyes had adjusted.

Apparently the basement is through the dining hall, the upstairs has been drugged, but there will be little supervision for a while. Calder summarized. Mia squeezed in acceptance, then replied.

Look behind you. They were in an office, but it had been packed up. Boxes were stacked high against the wall. File cabinets were slightly open with nothing inside. Even the top of the desk was bare- no pencils or staplers. *They're clearing out*, Mia projected.

We need to hurry, responded Calder. They waited a moment, making sure no one was about to head their way. Mia and Calder dashed up the stairs since there was nothing to hide behind.

Upstairs, they came to a long hallway with several doors leading off. The bright cheery lighting took on a twilight zone feel. Stopping at the first door, they listened. No sound. They opened the door slowly and peeked inside. It resembled a basic hospital room. The walls were a pale blue with a TV in one corner and a hospital bed in the middle. A small blonde woman occupied the bed. Blood coursed through a tube hooked up to the woman's arm.

"How do we stop it?" Mia said out loud without thinking. The sound of her own voice startled her. Calder checked the door, but no one entered.

We can pull it out and apply pressure. Even if she bleeds, it has to be better than being drained, Calder suggested. With Mia's approval, Calder picked up the woman's arm, peeling off the tape. With medical gauze from a side table, Calder applied pressure while he slowly pulled out the needle. Calder held the woman's arm up. They couldn't stay long. They had to find Brisa. Mia picked up some medical tape and helped to tie the gauze on. Calder took the pillows from beneath the patient's head and put them under her arms, elevating it slightly. With unspoken agreement, they moved back to the door. No sound came from the hallway, so Mia and Calder moved to the next door down. Inside they found the same thing, only this time a male. In a chair beside the bed, a slumped individual was sitting. A tray with two bowls of mostly eaten soup and some crusts of bread sat on the table. Calder removed the needle again. Mia felt nauseous. It was one thing to talk about collecting blood, but it was another entirely to see people being tapped.

Mia left the room first, running right into another woman. The woman was older than Mia but not by much. Her aura was human. She wore a fitted suit, implying she was with security.

"I don't know you?" the woman scrutinized Mia, reaching toward a holster on her hip.

"Mary," Mia tried to smile innocently. "I was sent to help with the removal."

"I thought all the nursing staff were working in the basement now that the upstairs was out." Mia inched towards the stairs, drawing the security officer's attention away from the door hiding Calder.

"We were, but those patients… I wasn't handling their condition well, so they sent me up to double check on the patients here. I'm a little too new, I guess," Mia lied. The lady continued to stare at her suspiciously. The woman let go of the holster to grasp a shoulder radio. Before she could push the call button, a metal medical chart hit her upside the head. She fell sideways in surprise. Mia rushed to her side, grabbing the woman's gun. She leveled the gun at the woman but didn't have a clue what to do past that. Calder was immediately at Mia's side and took the firearm.

"Guns?" he tsked. "Sad. I think it's time you took a small break."

"They'll notice I'm gone."

"Eventually." He kept the gun trained on her then suddenly swiped down, clocking her on the back of the head. The woman collapsed. "Quick," he hurried into a room, returning with a sheet. He ripped the sheet on the grain, making a long thin piece of fabric. "Rip this up." Mia tore the sheet into pieces. The challenge was to start the rip, but once it started the fabric came apart easily, but loudly. Mia glanced over the balustrade. No one seemed to hear. Calder used the strips to tie and gag the guard. He then secured her in a hallway closet a few doors down.

Luckily, they found Vi and Brisa in the next room. Vi was in the bed with the familiar tube in her arm. Sitting in a chair next to the bed was Brisa. She was leaning against a table, her head resting on her arm. Calder and Mia dashed to the bed first, to get the needle out.

"Mia?" Came a fragile voice from behind her. Stifling a scream, Mia whirled around to find Brisa sitting up. They came together in a tight hug, immediately clinging to each other for a brief second as they gained their bearings. Mia slipped her hand down to Brisa's.

They didn't sedate you?

I was too nervous to eat at first. I had planned on breaking in downstairs tonight. Vi was able to get across the food was drugged before she passed out. I pretended to be asleep when the nurses stopped by. Brisa motioned to Calder. *Why are you here?*

They were watching when we met. Mia communicated. *It looks like they are closing shop and moving on. They are draining as much blood from everyone on the floor as they can. They said they are going downstairs to deal with the basement people now and will return upstairs later. I don't know if they are planning on taking people with them or...*

Getting rid of them. Brisa was visibly shaken. *Okay now is the time. What is the plan?*

Our plan was to get you and Vi.

Calder grasped her other hand. *We can't leave these people to be drained. We need to take out all the tubes down the hall.* Mia relayed the message and received a nod. Vi was unhooked but far gone.

We can't leave her. Brisa insisted to the other two. Calder pushed Vi's covers down and picked up the slight woman. Mia checked the door. She shook her hand, signaling the all clear. Mia and Brisa headed to the next room. Gradually, they worked their way down the hall, unhooking every patient they could find. Mia gave a time check gesture with her wrist as they came to the last room on the hall. The other teams would work their way in soon. The incapacitated patients were a problem. They couldn't leave them helpless. If the kidnappers were desperate, they could kill the witnesses to escape unhindered.

Calder placed Vi carefully in a chair and joined the other two. *I think our best bet is to carry them all in here and barricade the door.* They quickly agreed. Brisa and Mia pushed the hospital bed against the wall to make more space in the middle of the room. In the closet, they found extra blankets and pillows. They set up makeshift beds with the additional blankets, running from room to room to obtain their supplies. Calder steadily worked the rooms, bringing patients into the one room at the end of the hall. The sight of all the unconscious people lined up on the floor was ominous. They almost seemed like they had passed from this life and their bodies were left for identification. It was just like Mia's dream. Mia leaned against a wall for support. *Courage... I choose courage...* Mia chanted.

Fifteen people were in the room by the time Calder finished. Time was running out. As Calder shifted a small woman in between two others, Mia cried out in pain. Her head filled with a scream, reminiscent of Tana when she tried to communicate. One voice was soon joined by another in a lower pitch, screeching their torment. When Mia opened her eyes, she was seeing double. Calder was kneeling in front of her. Brisa was next to him, her hand on Mia's arm.

They are draining the others. Mia managed. *They have almost lost their connection with their Element. They are crying out. We have to help them.*

But these people?! Calder indicated the full room.

I will take care of them, Brisa decided. *Once you leave, I will lock and barricade the door. Hopefully, they will wake up soon and be able to help me. If you close the other doors on the hall, it will take them longer to find us. They may not even look this far if they keep finding rooms empty.* Mia and Calder looked at Brisa doubtfully. Brisa reassured them. *Help the others, you really have no choice. I can't leave Vi.* Mia searched Brisa. Fear was there, but more importantly there was a determination. She wouldn't let these people be victims. She would be their protector. Mia nodded to Calder.

We will direct the troops up here as soon as we run into them. They are coming from the backside. They should be in the house soon.

GO! Brisa urged.

Calder started moving a dresser towards the door. When it was as close as he could get it while still allowing for an exit, he caught Mia's hand. *Tell her to block the door with it when we go. If it is too heavy, remove the drawers, push, then return them. Then fill those drawers with everything she can find. Move whatever additional furniture she can.* Mia relayed the message as he crawled over the dresser and into the hallway.

As soon as Brisa acknowledged the message, Mia was over the dresser too. She fell off the other side as another wave of screams hit. Calder was swift to help her up. Mia shook off his concern and started down the hall. The door shut behind them. They heard the bolt lock, and the scrape of furniture sliding across the floor. Mia and Calder made it to the stairs before the next wave of pain hit. When Mia faltered, Calder placed his arm around her waist, helping her down the stairs. They stumbled through the dining space.

Mia, you need to wait here. You aren't strong enough for this. Mia knew he was right, but the Sylph were calling to her.

Let me help you find them. Then I'll stay back. Calder grimaced, but nodded. They found an open doorway on the side of the kitchen. Sound was originating from below. There were several voices. The loudest one was issuing orders. Mia and Calder listened. They could hear a tentative voice from a nurse.

"I think we should slow the dialysis on this one. She's starting to shake; the fevers are getting worse."

"Nurse... Lisa? I'll check on the patient. Why don't you check on the patients upstairs?" A commanding male voice replied. Silence reigned downstairs.

"Yes, sir," came the timid voice. Footsteps on the stairs echoed upwards, warning Calder and Mia to hide behind a counter. A young nurse in blue scrubs entered through the doorway, muttering under her breath. The noise from downstairs went back into a busy rhythm.

Mia pulled out her cellphone and texted to McKenna. *Brisa upstairs- last room on the right- 16 patients. Found entrance to basement- must move now.* Mia's skin was crawling. It pulsed away from the muscle below. So much emotion and pain emanated from the basement. Calder watched her, the worry clear on his face. The fences and blocks that Triana had taught Mia were breaking down. The screaming that had been a faint background noise with periodic eruptions was now a constant flood in her mind. Her phone vibrated. *Entering now.*

I will try to get more information. Wait here. Calder moved around the counter and towards the doorway. Right then, Mia heard yelling. It came from downstairs.

"Call Security. We have intruders from the rear," came the male voice from earlier. "Destroy the evidence. Kaden and Graham- upstairs! Find security and prep the other patients for transport." The noise from below became louder. Calder didn't have time to hide before two men came up the narrow hallway. As soon as the men were in range, Calder attacked. Mia's training hadn't passed defensive maneuvers, leaving her looking on helplessly from behind the counter. The men fought back, nearly gaining the upper hand. Mia couldn't stand feeling so useless. Not allowing herself to think it through, Mia threw herself on the back of one of Calder's opponents. She might not take the man down, but the distraction could help Calder. The man threw her off like she was a rag doll. She crashed into a counter, slamming her head against the wall. The man barely noticed, recognizing Calder as the bigger threat.

Turn your back on me?! Mia fumed, searching the kitchen for a weapon. Finally, she found a cast iron frying pan. Using every ounce of fury she possessed, Mia slammed the frying pan into the back of the attacker's head. Her entire arm vibrated with the force of the hit. He slumped to the floor, turning the tide enough for Calder to finish the other man off. Calder kicked the man Mia had hit to make sure he was out, then gave her a look of approval.

Calder started down the stairs first, with Mia only a foot or two behind. At that moment, the girl that had passed earlier returned and froze at the sight of them. "Are you here to help them?" she whispered. Mia nodded. The nurse paused a moment, turned and went back up the stairs. Mia exchanged a look with Calder, who shrugged. They had bigger problems. As they reached the bottom of the stairs, Calder motioned for Mia to go back up. He then marched into the room with as much confidence as possible.

"Security, what is the problem?"

"We are under attack you... wait... you're not... He's an intruder!" Mia jumped out behind Calder. In the room were several nurses who moved to protect their patients. The man bulging out of his scrubs from the lawn was there, moving menacingly forward. Another man in a security jacket started shouting orders, but the nurses stayed by the beds lined up against both walls. The guard called for backup on his shoulder radio.

The screaming was louder now. It echoed around inside of Mia's skull. She sank backwards to the ground. Calder was fighting the scrubs man, but a nurse was rushing to Mia. Mia tried to swing her frying pan, but she couldn't get her arm to move. She dropped the pan to hold her head.

"What's wrong?" The nurse was trying to get a good look in Mia's eyes. The screaming continued.

"Don't help her! She's the enemy!" A small sniveling man was throwing his arms in the air and moving towards them.

"There is something wrong with her." The 'Sniveler' pushed the nurse backwards. He grabbed Mia by the arm and pulled her up. Mia slammed her foot down on his insole, then kicked back, connecting with his knee. The man howled. Mia tried to punch his neck, but two security guards had made it down the stairs. One guard pulled her arms behind her. The screaming broke through her defenses. She couldn't move, the pain in her mind was excruciating. It was blocking out everything else, even her vision. She was vaguely aware that the scrubs man subdued Calder. The other new guard was barking orders, clearly in charge.

"The screams," she murmured. The world had a red filter over it. Black spots were dancing around in the redness. The leader came towards them. His hands clutched Mia's hair, pulling her face to the side.

"This is the Aether on the new council!" he sneered.

"The new council," the 'Sniveler' repeated. "This is horrible. Everything is ruined."

"Let them go," Mia gasped.

"Oh, I will," he chuckled, "but I think you will come with us." Calder yelled, but Mia couldn't make out what he was saying. "Tie her up and get rid of him." He pointed at Calder. Mia was nauseous. Her head lolled back but from the corner of her eye, she could see the scrubs guy silence Calder with his fist. The nurses were huddling together. "As for the rest of you. Your services are no longer needed." He turned back to the guards. "Take them to the back room." The nurses protested. One female and one male nurse tried to fight back. The guards restrained them, pushing them towards a large door at the end of the room. The guard pushed the five nurses inside and locked the door. "Doc, come with me."

CHAPTER TWENTY-SEVEN

The man holding Mia captive swung her across his shoulders, carrying her like a sack of potatoes. Mia could hear fighting from the outside.

"We have to leave through the front," the man in charge yelled.

"What about the patients?" Scrubs man replied.

"They can't talk," he glared. "Just leave them."

"The Master will not be pleased," another guard cautioned.

"Well, we will just have to hope our gift will appease him." *I'm a gift?* Mia managed to think before the screaming took over again. "Set the fires." Two men worked their way to the back of the room. The last thing Mia witnessed was gasoline being poured on the floor between the hospital beds. The goon holding Mia followed the leader up the stairs. They moved quickly through the downstairs towards the grand foyer. The lady from earlier was waiting on the stairs.

"Are the others ready to go?" The leader demanded. The nurse observed Mia, slumped over the goon's shoulder.

"Sir, they're missing. All the beds are empty." The nurse was petrified. A stream of curse words flooded the room.

"There must be more of them than I thought," the leader finished. He grasped Mia's head, pulling it up at an awkward angle. It would have been painful, but she was already in such agony, it went unnoticed. "How many of you are there?" he spat in her face. She let the screams wash over her, drowning out his demands. His arm flew through the air striking her, but she couldn't feel it. Her lack of response created a new litany of curses.

"Get the fires started on this floor while I have a car pulled around. Then bring her," the leader pushed one of his guards through the mansion's front door. He waited long enough to make sure it was safe, then followed the man out, pulling the 'Sniveler' with him. Mia was dumped on the floor as the men moved deeper into the house.

While she was alone, Mia struggled to silence the voices which would allow her to move. Using the wall for leverage, she managed to get to her feet. Her arms were tied tightly behind her back. When had they managed that? The lights from the chandelier danced in her vision. The smell of smoke arrested her. Brisa was trapped upstairs, Calder was down… how could she let them know? She tried to climb the stairs, but tripped on the first step, slamming her chin into the marble staircase. The red haze now featured stars. She focused on the cold marble to regain her balance. As soon as she could see straight, she rolled over to see the face of the young nurse from earlier. The nurse looked panicked.

"Let me get your hands," the nurse tried to untie them. Here was Mia's solution. The ropes were getting looser, but there was no way Mia would be free before the man and his sidekicks returned.

"Stop," Mia gasped, "You have to warn them. Fire… last room on the right."

"Last room?" The look the nurse gave Mia clearly indicated she thought Mia had hit her head too hard.

"They are in the last room." Mia's eyes closed from the effort the short sentence required.

"I'll do what I can," the nurse promised. The girl was obviously afraid but honest in her declaration.

"Her name is Brisa…Tell her Mia sent you," Mia groaned. The nurse sprinted up the stairs. Smoke was starting to filter into the foyer. She sat up in time for one of the guards to return.

"Time to go," the guard barked. He swung her up over his shoulder and exited the mansion. Outside the air was cool, helping Mia brace herself and regain some of her vision. The night was dark. Only the lamps that lined the drive were lit. A black limousine had pulled up front, followed by a van. The back door of the long dark car flew open.

"Put her in here," came a voice from the shadowed interior. The brute swung Mia down to the ground. A man from inside the limousine reached out and grabbed her by the shoulders, pulling her while the other foe picked up her legs and pushed. Her face was ground into the dark gray fibers of the car floor.

Mia took a second to observe her surroundings. The limousine had two sets of seats facing each other and she was in the middle. The only other person in the back of the car was the sniveling man the security guard had called 'Doc'. His shiny leather shoes were just within her peripheral vision. From outside the door, Mia could hear the security guard on a cell phone.

"They arrived too soon. I sent most of the paperwork out this afternoon. We have set fire to the residence. Hopefully, most of the older patients will disappear with it." There was silence. "Yes, sir." Silence. "It was the new council." A pause. "No, I am positive, and I have a gift for you to prove it." His voice oozed on the last comment. "Yes sir. We will be on a plane in an hour." The man leaned into the car. "Think you can handle the one prisoner Doc?" The 'Sniveler' nodded to the man in the suit who then closed the door.

"The new council," Doc muttered. Mia could feel the car humming, but it didn't move right away. Mia looked up to find the man staring at her with despair on his face. "How did you find us?" he asked. Mia just stared back. "The Sylph still think it's a drug problem." He contemplated her for a moment. "We will just set up again," he threatened. "But I must admit, I am curious." Mia pushed away as much as she could. "The Master will enjoy meeting you." His face glanced out the window. He nodded to someone, then tapped the glass.

The driver put the car into drive and headed down the driveway. Fear lanced through Mia. She shivered. What would McKenna do?

"Who is the Master?" Mia gasped. It was harder to get the words out than it should be. She realized her mouth was swollen. The punch from earlier must have done some damage.

"You will meet him soon enough," the man turned away to watch behind them.

"I thought the security guard was in charge," Mia managed.

"He *is* in charge… of security. This operation was mine, but we all work for the Master." He flicked a glance her way. Mia tried to focus. Doc had black hair and dark brown eyes. But he wasn't Fire clan… no, he was… just a normal mortal. Not an Elemental at all.

"Do you realize what you were doing to those people?" she asked aloud. Could he understand as someone who wasn't tied to an Element?

"Those people gave us a precious gift," he fretted. "And I made them a paradise to live in as they gave it to us. But the demand for Coro went through the roof, and the Master demanded more. It was too much… we couldn't get enough blood," he lamented. Mia tried to put together what she was hearing. The drug Coro… they needed Sylph blood to make it?

"We started losing patients. I couldn't keep up…" his voice trailed off as his eyes went wide. His arms flew up into the air to protect himself. Instinctively, Mia braced herself. Suddenly, something slammed into them. Mia's stomach heaved as the car swung around from the impact's force. The sound of glass breaking. Horns blaring, too. The car turned sideways, throwing Mia against the far door. She groaned and struggled to sit up, but at that moment the car fell back down again, flinging her to the floor.

The next thing she knew, there was yelling from outside the car. Doc was climbing through a door. Pushing herself against the seat to get to her knees, she crawled as best she could to the edge of the car. Then she got out, one foot at a time. Down the street, she saw the van. The front was crumpled in. Damek was stationed behind the wheel. He revved the engine for another go. The security man had joined them. He grabbed Mia by the arm, producing a gun and placing it to her head.

"Looking for this?" he yelled. The muzzle of the gun was cold as it touched her temple. Damek turned off the car and raised his hands in surrender. The door of the van flung open. Damek stepped out, keeping his hands in the air.

"Just let her go," Damek pleaded.

"I don't think so," the man laughed. Suddenly, the gun was no longer at Mia's head; it stretched out before him, aiming at Damek. "You're a member of the new council, and the man downstairs… So much for the new council," he chuckled and pulled the trigger.

Mia watched the bullet strike Damek. The left side of his body was thrown backwards. He twisted as he fell to the ground.

"No!" Mia screamed. Her sight went red, as fear and anger pulsed through her. Not Damek… The shrieks of the damned in the basement welled within her, mixing with her own pain as she screamed with every fiber of her being. Then there was blackness.

CHAPTER TWENTY-EIGHT

The blackness went from dull to glossy with sharp edges. The first wave had been easy. Luring the enemy out of the mansion with their guns was as simple as throwing a rock through a car window. The car alarm went off and a set of guards poured out of the building. From then it was a matter of infiltrating the building in sets. The Heaters pushed energy as they entered, causing the bullets to implode. A southern Fire Elemental, named Bobbi, was strong enough to stand in the open and thwart a barrage of bullets at once. Two others followed. They weren't as strong as Bobbi. They were able to push enough energy that they are safe drawing some fire. Then the rest of the team followed in their wake, until they were close enough to attack the guards.

She feels the adrenaline course through her body, lighting her veins on fire. All the training, all the practice, it comes back to her effortlessly. Her staff swings, and she can feel it cutting through the air. Stupid humans and their belief in guns. She wants to laugh, but then a bullet hits her from behind. What feels like a sucker punch pounds into her left shoulder. Her vision goes red.

The hit will not stop her. She turns. The enemy soldiers had circled, coming up from behind. She pushes as much energy as she can towards the guards. She has to protect her team. They continue to advance. The bullets are harder to push away. She uses the pain to fuel her rage and adrenaline. They are getting too close... She cannot hold them off much longer. She pushes again, vaguely realizing fewer bullets are being fired... they are running out of bullets. Push again. All the muscles in her stomach contract. Her lungs even feel the strain. The concrete of the garage is hard as she drops to her knees. She can't sense any bullets but continues to push towards her enemies.

"Akuji..." She hears sharply above her. The voice is raspy and impatient. "Akuji...." A pause. "Mick- enna". She looks up. Above her is a woman with skin as dark as the night that reflects the harsh lighting of the mansion's garage. Her eyes are dark and piercing, and her face looks disdainful. "Get up, girl. Your team needs you." The warrior starts to move away.

"Who are you?" she manages.

"Sempiira," The woman gives a twisted smile. "Call me Semmy," the woman adds, looking towards the battle with a fierce grin.

She takes a deep breath. Three guards are limp on the ground before her. A reminder to keep her head in the game. She ducks behind a brick pillar. Her eyes narrow; she will not be caught off guard again. Following the sounds of Semmy's foot falls across from her, she progresses from pillar to pillar going around the fire fight battle that rages in the center of the garage. She is at the pillar closest to the door. The guard is trying to reload but catches the movement and his head turns towards them. Instantly, she lunges, but the guard is already backing through a door, and slamming it shut. The sound of the lock echoes in the parking area. She turns on the other two guards that are still shooting at her compatriots. Semmy nods to the one on the left, and she nods to the one on the right. While their focus is towards the parking garage exit, she and Semmy hit them from behind.

"We need to get inside," she announces.

"Closer quarters," Semmy observes, watching the others join them.

A warrior named Rivin sizes up Semmy, "Our Heaters need to go in first."

"Pair up," she snarls at the sound of someone else giving orders to her crew.

"McKenna," the small female, Bobbi, grabs her attention. "I smell smoke."

"Stupid humans," she smiles. They laugh. "Let's break down a door."

Blue lines lanced through with gold flash before her. Then smoke is everywhere. One eye can't open completely, but she sees flames are licking the walls only a few feet from her. Her throat burns and her eyes water. She tries to push up but pain shoots through her body forcing her to collapse to the ground. She looks at her arm. Clad in the thick wool suit, no breaks are visible, but the agony is acute. At least the air is better down here. She tries to laugh.

There is no water left in the air, and her skin can sense the lack. The heat and lack of moisture cause her to feel on fire herself. She rolls slightly to look up.

She hears pounding not far from her. She tries to put down her other arm and can apply some pressure. Shuffling on her knees, she crawls out into the aisle between the beds searching for the noise. She struggles to move to the back of the room where the sound originates. Finally she reaches a solid door, shaking from the beating it is receiving from the inside. She focuses on the lock. The guard left the key inserted. She turns the key and the door flings open, slamming her in the face. With a groan, she tries to sit back up. A nurse is at her side, helping her stand.

Several nurses run ahead trying to get out of the burning building. One or two of the nurses try to move the patients in their beds down a hall. The smoke is getting to them too. She sinks down one wall, helplessly watching the nurses collapse one by one. There is no way for her to save the patients that surround her. Mia... where is Mia?? She had failed. If this was it, at least she had found Mia and the rest of the council. For a bright moment, it was nice to be important.

It is hard to keep a train of thought. The smoke is getting to her. She can't breathe it much longer. Her mind turns back to her home. The lakes. If only she could go back... the vision comes so strongly, the caress of the water, the breeze, the smell. The memory is making the present moment even more unbearable.

The entrance doors splinter and crash open. A group of warriors dressed in black move inward led by a tall dark amazon. McKenna... There is hope after all. She tries to shift upward. McKenna runs over to her. She is conscious of the troops moving from bed to bed, unhooking patients and carrying them out through the flames. The hazy world isn't fazing them as they act with precision.

"Calder," McKenna barks, trying to pierce through her cloudy consciousness. She has to tell McKenna. She can meet McKenna's eyes for only a moment... "They have Mia..." she manages, then passes out.

Orange.... her vision is orange, cloudy, but orange... She looks down at the bodies lined up on the floor. They are deathly still. She crosses to the first one and checks their pulse again, just to make sure. She's still alive. They're all alive. Thank the Goddess... One of the boys starts to stir in his sleep. She rushes over, trying to wake him up. She needs help. She's all alone. What made her think she could ever be a hero? These people will probably die, and it will be her fault. Suddenly, there is beating on the door. "Mia sent me," the voice claims. Her heart is pounding in her chest. What should she do??

"Brisa? They've started a fire. We have to get them out. I swear, Mia sent me." The faint smell of smoke enters the chamber. She pulls furniture away from the door, and the smell of smoke grows stronger. The scratches that the dresser legs cut into the wooden floors mark her final struggle. As soon as the door opens, she sees a young dark-haired nurse.

"I need help to move the dresser all the way," she gasps. Without a word, the nurse works her way through the door, pushing the bureau aside, leaving the door wide open. The nurse moves out into the hall where there is a gurney waiting.

"We have to get them out of the building," The nurse says definitively as the gurney enters the room. "Do you think we can get two of them on here at a time?" It will be a tight fit. Quickly, she moves to help the woman. Between the two of them, they can move people up onto the gurney. They push them down the hall until they reach the stairs. There is no good way to transport the gurney down. Suddenly, they hear a pounding coming from the closet nearby. She moves quickly and opens the door. Sprawled on the floor is a security officer, tied and gagged.

"We can't leave her here," she comments. What if the guard attacks? What if she wants the fire to burn them all? If only Mia was here to read her. There really is no choice. She moves down and unties the woman. As soon as the guard is free and on her feet, the woman grabs her and slams her against a wall.

"What is going on?" the guard snarls.

"Fire, we have to save as many patients as possible," she gasps. The woman smells the air.

"Did you see a nurse and a security guard near here?"

"No," she lies, kinda. She hadn't seen a nurse or a security guard. She had seen Mia and Calder. "There isn't time for this. Are you helping?" She struggles and pulls away from the guard. The woman looks down the hall and sees the nurse standing next to a gurney.

"Off load them here," she calls. The nurse and security guard look at her oddly but comply. "Go see if you can reload, I have an idea." They head down the hall. She moves into the first hospital room. Pulling hard, she dislodges the mattress from the hospital bed. It is too bulky to move easily. Once it is off the frame, it is easier to pull. She shifts the mattress onto its side to slide it through the doorway. In the hall, the nurse arrives with two more thin females on the gurney.

"Brilliant," the nurse breathes. Smoke is flowing up faster. They position the mattress at the top of the stairs and load all four of the first patients on top. As soon as the mattress is full, they guide it as it slides down the front stairs to the main doorway. The security lady takes the gurney back for more patients. She and the nurse both grab an arm and pull each of the patients through the door and onto the porch. The two of them are on the second patient when they see the van slam into a black stretch sedan. Time is running out.

They run inside, leaving the two patients. They offload the other two in the foyer and then push the mattress back up the stairs. The smoke is thicker. The entire place is heating up. The security guard had already offloaded two more patients at the top of the stairs. The guard was leaving the end room with a full gurney. The nurse helps her repeat the process as before. When they reach the bottom of the stairs, they move the patients outside. Everyone is gone outside. The lights on the wrecked cars can still be seen. It is a good sign. Before they are able to enter the front door again, a group of black-clad warriors filter in from the dining room. The nurse screams, but she only sobs. They are saved.

A burst of white dots appears before her then settles into a warm brown. Pain lances through her arm and shoulders as she slowly opens her eyes. The sky is black above. A haze allows the light of only a few stars through. The large brick mansion is on her left, lights blazing. Smoke pours out the windows. The past few hours flood back in. Mia... with a groan, she sits up. Shot... I've been shot... Blessed be, it hurts... she looks around fearfully... they are probably long gone... the cars are still there. Everything is where she remembers it. How much time has passed? She staggers to her feet, then stumbles towards the sedan. The man who shot her is lying on the ground. All the men that had been pouring out of the van, are slumped over and littering the area. What happened? Everyone seems to have passed out at the same time.

Next to the shooter, she spies a pair of dark blue scrubs... Mia... she stumbles forward ... the scrubs seem so far away... the throbbing of her left side is begging her to stop, but she can't. She has to get to... Mia... closer... her attacker is only a few feet away. He is starting to recover... she topples down onto the ground, next to Mia's prone form.

She checks for a pulse... it is still strong. The shooter is moaning. With what little strength she has, she pulls Mia into a sitting position. Taking a deep breath, she puts one arm under Mia's legs and places Mia up onto her good shoulder... She just needs to get Mia away from them... she moves slowly... falling down to one knee, then pushing up again... They are almost to the trees. She just needs to get Mia to the trees. They can hide there... in the earth... just a little further. She heads towards the left of the mansion where the waiting forest beckons. A mop of dark red hair on top of a pale face approaches them... Colin? Colin could get help... He tries to call but fails... Colin is running towards them, looking over his shoulder...

"Damek! They're waking up," he says quickly. "Give Mia to me, I'll take her." She nods. As much as she doesn't want to let go of Mia, she must. They will have to save Mia together. With the burden lifted, she can keep moving. Soon the shadows of the forest swallow them. They are safe. "I couldn't see everything that happened. I saw you get shot, and Mia scream, then everyone collapsed!" Colin rambled. They continue deeper into the woods, until the trees completely obscured them from the road.

"We're going too slow. Find the others," she rasps. "Warn them about the people out front. I'll watch over her here." She hunkers down against a tree.

"What if they come in to find you?" Colin wavers.

"I'm a Gnome, Colin," she sighs. "They will never find us here." With a nod, Colin heads to the rear of the mansion for help. She pulls Mia up to her side, placing her arms around Mia. Then she reaches out with her mind. The warmth and pulse of the tree. She allows herself to meld with the bark and welcomes the embrace of the surrounding tree. She says a prayer to the Goddess, hoping that Mia will be obscured in an earthly embrace. Then she falls asleep.

Purple... she can see through the clear purple to a light on the other side. "Mia?" she yells looking through the woods desperately. Nothing. It never occurred to her that Damek could hide Mia from the rescue party too. They had searched the section of woods where she left them.

"Maybe they moved farther in, towards the manor?" She turned to look at the rest of the search party.

"Worth a shot," came the reply. They started searching back towards the house, still on fire.

"Mia?!" No response. Only the sounds of the search party.

CHAPTER TWENTY-NINE

It was approaching midnight when Mia awoke. Her arm was throbbing, and her throat parched. Her eyes fluttered open at the trudging of feet through the leaves around them. Someone called her name. The voice sounded like it belongs to Colin. The moon filtered through the canopy above them. She had always felt a connection with the moon, and now she thanked it from the bottom of her heart. Regardless of all else, she had made it out alive. Her mouth opened, but she couldn't make a sound come out. Water... her throat was too dry. Suddenly, she realized she wasn't leaning against a tree like she thought. She was leaning against a person, Damek. His eyes were closed, and blood covered his entire left side.

Oh my God, what happened? Calder, Brisa, the fire, the man in the suit, Damek being shot. Damek should have left her. This was entirely her fault. Mia attempted to yell for help, but the effort produced barely a whisper. Panic set in. She screamed, but only a high-pitched squeak emerged. Tears welled as she screamed again and again. No one could hear her. Nothing was around that might make a noise. She searched her pockets... the cell phone... she dialed McKenna, and the call was quickly picked up....

"Mia?? Where are you?" demanded a worried voice.

"Scream," Mia whispered.

"What?"

"Scream," she managed to say in a coherent voice, then put the cell phone on speaker.

"*Mia*??" McKenna demanded loudly.

"Over here!" Came shouts, hearing McKenna. "Where are you?"

"She's over here!!" McKenna shouted through the phone speakers. It was working. Tears of relief flowed as Mia collapsed next to Damek. With McKenna attracting attention, Mia checked his pulse. It was still there, but faint. The searchers were getting closer.

"Stay with me," Mia whispered, grabbing Damek's hand so he could hear her. *You can't leave me… you promised… stay with me…* she repeated over and over again. Soon, the searchers were upon them. Colin caught Mia up in a tight hug.

"We were so worried," Colin half laughed and sobbed at the same time.

"Damek," she whispered. A doctor was already tending him with the help of a full medical kit. Mia dropped to the ground, taking his right hand again. Colin knelt behind her and put an arm around her for support.

"I brought a med team with me. He was lucid when I left for help but… he's a Gnome… he must have set up your camouflage before he passed out. We have been searching for almost an hour. I've been by this spot at least five or six times. I could sense you were near, but I wasn't strong enough to find you," he confessed. His frustration and embarrassment were easy to read, but Mia had no words to sooth him. Her entire throat was aching.

"Water?" Mia croaked.

"Does anyone have water?" Colin said louder to the assembled search party. They passed a bottle forward. Mia drank eagerly, feeling the refreshment travel through her chest. "I need to call McKenna. She, Calder, and Brisa have been frantic with worry. They are helping the doctor's team treat all the Sylph. A group of mansion nurses are helping us."

"The men who tried to take me?" she rasped.

"They are gone," he confirmed. "By the time we were able to spare some people to follow after them, they were long gone."

"They are headed to the airport," Mia stated. "I don't know if that would help."

"I'll tell McKenna and Brisa. Maybe they have a connection. But with this much time having passed, I don't think it will be much use." He grimaced again as he stood up to make the call. The doctor had cut open Damek's shirt, exposing the bullet wound.

"Will he be okay?" she asked tentatively.

"It was a through and through, so that's good. He's lost a lot of blood though," the doctor answered. "We need to watch him. If we could get him a transfusion, that would be best. It's a drive to the real health center. As soon as we can get him in a car, that's where we'll take him." She dressed the wound. The other members of the search party had returned with a stretcher. As Damek was lifted and placed on top, a low grown escaped him.

"That's a good sign," the doctor nodded. "Okay, let's get him to the trans-port." Mia held Damek's hand and walked alongside him while they rounded the mansion. She continued to send him positive messages, pleas, and bargains. In the underground garage was a large semi-truck. Inside, the kidnap victims were laid out. Lights were suspended across the top. Jules had her arms wrapped around Vi and she was not going to let go anytime soon. As the group approached, Brisa came flying down the drive to greet Mia with a huge bear hug.

"You're okay!" Brisa cried. Tears came unbidden to both she and Mia as they sobbed with relief. "We got everyone out, but... with the blood loss and smoke inhalation, I don't think they'll all make it," Brisa indicated the truck. "It isn't ideal transport, but this was how they were going to transfer their 'patients.' We will use it to get everyone to the care center." Mia watched as Damek was loaded into the truck. "We're about to leave." Brisa met Mia's gaze. "We will get him help." Right then, Calder walked up. He sported a makeshift sling holding up one of his arms. Mia ran over and hugged him, quickly releasing him at his groan.

"I'm sorry! I'm so sorry," Mia cried.

"Totally worth it," Calder gave his signature jaunty smile, despite the pain. "It seems to be a clean break." His arm was broken... like in her dream? Visions of smoke and pain and mattresses?? Could she have witnessed what the others had been going through?

"Calder, did McKenna find you in the middle of a hall in the basement?"

"Yes... I couldn't stand-" Mia turned quickly to Brisa.

"Did you get the people down the stairs using a mattress?"

"Yes," Brisa quirked her head to the side.

"It was a genius move, Bri," Calder congratulated her, slinging his good arm around Brisa's shoulder. "Amazing."

"How did you know?" Brisa asked Mia.

"I... I dreamt it... I watched you, and McKenna and Calder, and Damek while I was passed out. I don't believe it." Suddenly the world tipped a little sideways. Brisa took hold of one of Mia's arms as Calder grabbed the other.

"Let's get her on the transport," Brisa said.

"We need to stay with Damek," Mia muttered. In agreement, Brisa and Calder supported her as she stumbled towards the truck. As soon as Mia attempted to climb aboard, the combined agony of those on board struck her. She fell backwards. Thankfully, Brisa and Calder caught her.

"I'm following in the van," Calder offered. "It's a little less jarring. Why don't you come with me?"

"Damek?" Mia replied weakly.

"I'll stay with Damek. Just as he stayed with me," Brisa swung herself up and settled down next to Damek. Brisa cradled his good arm in her lap and gave words of encouragement. *They are good together*, Mia thought wistfully.

"Mia, come on. Let's get you to the hospital." Leading with his good arm, Calder escorted her to the van.

"Calder," Mia pressed. "Thank you. You saved me more than once tonight."

"We're a team, Mia," he gave her a knowing smile. "No thanks are necessary." After they boarded the van, Mia allowed herself to relax in Calder's embrace. The screams of those on the truck were fainter but still assaulted her. The pain was almost overwhelming. But she was alive to feel it. Nothing was said as they sped along the highway towards help. There was too much to say to start and no words to express their turmoil.

When they arrived at the care center, the worst victims were treated first. Which meant that Damek was among the first assigned a bed. All but one of the rescued made it to the care center alive. It would have been cruel to say out loud, but the dead may have been better off. The patients rescued from the basement were all in bad shape. The care center immediately started transfusing their own blood into the Sylph. Local Sylph were called in to donate and create a supply. Despite the taboo, Sylph started showing up at one in the morning. Cailleach Ilma was among the initial wave of help, carrying several batches of homemade cookies. By daybreak, Sylph were arriving in droves. Most came to donate. While others asked if they could stay and assist. The new council soon found themselves superfluous as better rested teams replaced them. Cailleach Ilma tended to every single patient.

The Salamanders, who were still at the center, donated their time and expertise with technology. They posted pictures of those who couldn't share their identities to a website where Sylph across the United States could check and find their loved ones. Boreas warned all the other tribes, having them check as well. Since so many of the Sylph were gaunt and ill, they used pictures from Dave's confiscated cellphone. Family members were calling before noon, booking flights to come and take care of their loved ones. Before dusk of the next day, every person had been claimed.

By the second night, the Sylph had organized food and additional supplies for the overwhelmed facility. Blankets, cots and pillows were among the items donated. A steady stream of letters arrived: messages of love, and prayers for all of those trapped in the middle of this horrible ordeal.

All the patients rescued from upstairs, as well as their friends, came through the experience. They were terrified, but intact. With little care, they could transfer to the Sylph community in Alpharetta where willing families took them in. Until they knew the full extent of the damage caused by their experience, everyone agreed to stay together for extra support.

The patients from the basement were another story. The farthest gone were almost disconnected from their Elements. Luckily none of them were as completely unlinked as Tana was. A steady dose of transfusions was ordered, which helped and calmed them. But none, as of yet, had regained consciousness. Mia knew that soon she would have to touch their minds and see how they were. She secretly hoped the donations would help before she made the attempt.

Thirty-eight Sylph had been recovered. Twenty-two had been on the upper floors. The deceased Sylph was a young teen named Anila. They planned her funeral for four days from the recovery. Fifteen Sylph remained in comas.

Damek remained unconscious but was resting comfortably according to the doctor. Damek's sleep was fitful, his face contorting with whatever dreams or nightmares he was stuck in. Colin and Brisa picked up a change of clothes for the entire group. Calder was x-rayed, his arm was set and now he was sporting a fancy new cast and sling. The bullet had to be retrieved from McKenna's shoulder, followed by stitching of the wound. Mia, McKenna, and Calder then set up house in Damek's room while they waited for him to wake up. They slept in shifts. Once Colin and Brisa returned, they took turns taking showers and cleaning up in the small hospital bathrooms. Brisa and Mia stayed at Damek's bedside, holding his hand as if attempting to be an anchor to life. It was noon on the second day before Damek came around. Mia had fallen asleep holding his hand again. The growing strength of his grip as his hand clasped hers woke her with a start.

"Damek?" she whispered, as his eyes fluttered open for a moment. They closed again. "Guys, his eyes opened!" The entire crew gathered around the bed. *Damek?* She asked silently, watching his face for any reaction.

Mia? The thought came faintly.

"Damek!" she exclaimed out loud.

"Come on, dude," Calder urged. "Talk to the rest of us too!" He was grinning widely.

"Why?" came Damek's weak reply. They all laughed, pushing and shoving each other in relief. Tears came unbidden to several faces. Damek's eyes slowly opened, taking in the sight. Mia couldn't stop smiling. "Can't a guy take a nap in peace?"

"No," McKenna told him. "Not when you're on duty, mister." She sat down on the edge of the bed.

"Well, since you're all here, I take it everyone made it out okay?" he asked, closing his eyes with a smile.

"We got lucky," McKenna admitted. "If we hadn't enlisted a group of Salamanders, it would have ended differently."

"Where are your band of merry men?" Mia quipped.

"I sent them home," McKenna gave Mia a weird look, then sighed. "We will have to attend their marking ceremony. The Sylph are grateful. The Sylph elders approached me and asked if, after their memorial for Anila, we can all meet again to honor those who helped save the others. So, perhaps the Salamanders will be marked in front of the Sylph people. "

"Nice unity moment," Colin commented. "We as the new council stand for a new age of unity amongst the Elements. Salamanders risked their lives for Sylph. The Sylph honor them. Have you ever heard of anything like that happening before?" They all shook their heads.

"Well, I'm not going anywhere soon," Damek joked weakly. Mia squeezed his hand.

"Don't pity him, ladies. He's a Gnome. He'll be out of bed in no time," Calder teased. Mia realized Damek was staring at her face. Without thinking, her hand reached up to check for anything stuck to her. She immediately felt the swelling around her eye and mouth.

259

"It's pretty bad, huh?" she acknowledged. His right hand reached up, grazing her where she was now black and blue. The man in the suit must have worn a ring which caused a cut across her cheek where he struck her. Her other cheek sported a rug burn from the car. Bruises had formed under her chin, perhaps from the manhandling she had received or maybe from her fall on the stairs.

"No," Damek finally replied, having inventoried all her pain. He then examined Calder. He didn't look much better. Calder's face was black and blue, too. "Broken?" Damek asked, referencing his arm. Calder nodded. Next, McKenna. The swelling from her fight at the Agon was the worst of her visible injuries. A few fresh cuts had been added down one of her arms, which was in a sling to keep her from tearing out her stitches. Brisa looked okay, only exhausted. Colin was the same. "Looking at you guys, I can't believe we won," he snorted. Tears were welling up in his eyes as he viewed his own shoulder.

"King Boreas is on his way. He should be here soon to debrief us," Brisa piped up.

"Several Sylph are still missing. Fifteen in comas… Are we considering this a win?" Calder asked.

McKenna started, "The missing were some of the first taken. More than likely they have already passed. We found the kidnappers. We stopped them…."

"For now," Mia finished grimly, remembering Doc's taunt.

"We still don't know who orchestrated this; Who 'the Master' is," Brisa admitted.

"I'm not sure there are any leads that will shed light on that one," Calder frowned.

"We discovered how the Sylph were being kidnapped and that they wanted their blood," Mia met each of their gazes as she spoke. "We have sent out the warning signal. We have reunited thirty-eight Sylph with their families. And we have answers for those who have lost their loved ones," she hesitated, "It isn't perfect. We didn't save everyone but… yes… we call it a win." Mia looked up and watched them mull over her words. One by one, the others found truth in her comments.

"We call it a win," McKenna repeated as Calder nodded.

"A win," Brisa agreed and Colin smiled.

"We call it a win," Damek gasped, then let himself fall asleep. Now that Mia knew Damek was okay, she let Brisa stay with him while she headed to the lake house. As soon as Mia arrived in her room, sobs and tremors ripped through her. She crawled under the covers and stared at the familiar ceiling until she could get herself calm again. Then she slept. She slept for most of the next two days.

CHAPTER THIRTY

The recovery was slow. The nurse that had aided Brisa and the basement nurses shed light on the mansion's procedures. The nurses had been told the patients suffered from a rare blood disease. Their blood was being processed with hemodialysis. Most of the patients didn't even realize they were ill. The doctors at the facility were supposedly working on a cure while treating the contaminated blood. The doctors had referred to the disease as Coro. The nurses had truly believed they were helping the patients. At least until the suits showed up on the day that the new council attacked.

It shocked the survivors when they learned how long they had been in the facility. For the first few days, they were a little loopy. Even when the survivors' muddled minds cleared up, they could not pinpoint when they had lost friends, or when they had become 'sick.' The time blended together for them. Vi tested the blood of the survivors and couldn't find any foreign substances in their blood. She hypothesized that the kidnappers gave them the very drug their blood was being used to create, Coro. How some Sylph had lasted longer than others, Vi also couldn't tell. She proposed it was based on the strength of the Element within them.

Anila's funeral was one of the largest that had been seen in quite some time. Every Sylph who had survived joined with the community to honor one of their own. In addition to Anila, each of the Sylph deemed lost was recognized and lauded.

After such dark days, the Sylph community decided to celebrate the rescued Sylph's homecoming. Sylph poured in from neighboring states for the ceremony. Local hotels were booked, every Sylph home hosted relatives as well as the victims and their families. Other tribes from around Georgia, and those that had arrived to claim a loved one, were invited as well.

King Boreas arrived the night before the festivities. The Sylph people praised him. His efforts brought the new council to them. Instead of sending a representative, he had worked to help his people personally. Everyone respected and honored that.

The celebration was set for two weeks after the Sylph funeral. During that time, three of the Sylph from the basement awakened from their coma. They were weak, but recovery was assured. An upswing of hope and joy swept through the entire community.

Luckily, Elementals heal pretty quickly. Damek, though weak, was able to attend the festivities. Calder still sported his cast, but his face had regained its handsome smile. Brisa was back to normal, though she had kept the haircut. McKenna's black eye was gone. Even Mia resembled her old self. The dark rings under their eyes caused by the last few weeks disappeared and they all felt better. Though the new council acknowledged their success, the weight of what they had failed to do sat heavily on their shoulders. It was the elephant in the room, putting a damper on their excitement for the celebration. They left the care center together and headed north towards the Alpharetta community.

As they turned on to the street that led to the community entrance, they saw the Salamander van on the side of the road. They pulled beside it. McKenna opened her window and leaned out to talk to them. The other council members rolled their windows down to acknowledge the Salamanders.

"Did you guys break down?" McKenna teased.

"Nah," the Salamanders replied. "Didn't feel right going in without you," their spokesperson offered.

"Don't tell me you're afraid of a couple Sylph," McKenna mocked.

"A couple… no," Flint replied. "A full community…." Both vans were laughing.

"Okay follow us in." McKenna retreated into the van. The new council looked at each other.

"It's a celebration. They've found their family. We need to be happy for them," Damek suggested.

"Right," McKenna confirmed. "Celebrate the victories as you get them."

"I'm always up for a party," Calder smiled.

"It was kind of them to want us to join them," Colin commented as they arrived at the gate. The gate was festooned with dark yellow ribbons, complimented by a silver circle in the middle. Ribbons representative of every clan led to it and then weaved together. Brisa gasped.

"I don't think they just invited us," Brisa murmured as the gates parted. Inside, Sylph lined the sides of the road, five to six people thick. As soon as their van entered, a huge cheer arose.

"Oh my God," Mia mouthed. People were pointing and clapping, yelling and cheering. It was like being in a parade. Mia noticed a little girl who was waving at her. Mia automatically waved back. The cheers became louder. Joining Mia, the rest of the council waved out of the windows. They drove slowly down the main street to the park they had visited only a month before.

The Sylph had decorated the entire community. Yellow ribbons and balloons covered almost every surface. However, in the middle of the traditional golden wash, and for the first time, the Sylph had worked in the colors of every other clan in honor of the new council. As the vans pulled up, there was a large group of people in front of a dais in the park. Each had wrapped bands of beads around their arms.

"It is a tradition in the Sylph community to create a personalized bead necklace to give to those who you honor and thank. It is a great honor to receive them. It is a sign of the greatest respect," Brisa said quickly, filling them in.

McKenna jumped out of the van to explain the tradition to the Salamander crew. As the new council members advanced toward the crowd, Neil pushed Vi towards them. Vi grabbed Jules' hand and pulled her into the group. They were followed by the medical response team that had volunteered the night at the mansion.

Then a young lady approached them. She must have been seventeen but appeared far younger. Mia tried to place the familiar face. Suddenly, the image of the girl as one of the many barricaded in the mansion's last room popped into Mia's head. A memory of Brisa moving the girl down the stairs on a mattress filtered in. As the girl advanced, Brisa recognized her as well.

The rescued girl stopped in front of Mia, who was at the center of the crew.

"I thank you and honor you for saving my life and returning me to my family," her voice quivered. "Please accept this token of my esteem." She placed the necklace around Mia's neck. It was a hand-painted collection of pink beads, large and small. A white pattern adorned the biggest bead, designed to resemble the tattoo on Mia's arm. Mia sensed the emotion radiating off the woman and promptly bowed in respect, the same way Mia had seen the Salamanders do for McKenna. She placed her hand on the necklace.

"Thank you," Mia managed. The girl enveloped Mia in a hug. The rescued girl moved on to Damek standing right behind Mia. He had refused to use the wheelchair once he saw the crowd. He was doing okay but Mia would have to keep an eye on him. When she faced forward, a man was holding out a necklace.

"I thank you and honor you…" It was surreal. All the faces Mia had seen, lying in hospital beds, through the eyes of others. The Sylph were all there, alive and thanking her. Tears streamed down her face. The rescued were in tears as well. The rough and tough Salamanders were no less affected. They bowed respectfully to every person who approached them and accepted each hug and necklace. The necklaces were building up on Mia's neck. Soon, an older lady approached her, a necklace in her hand.

"I thank you and honor you for saving my daughter…" she began, and thus a new wave of people approached, all offering necklaces. Mia almost lost it when a young tearful girl held up a simple necklace she had obviously crafted herself.

"I thank you and honor you for giving me back my sister…" she whispered, just as shy as could be. The young girl then threw herself at Mia for a hug. Eventually the crowd thinned out. At some point, someone brought Damek a chair which he reluctantly accepted. As the new council stood in front of the dais with King Boreas, however, Damek joined his companions again.

"When the new council was founded, I doubted," Boreas addressed the whole crowd. "What could a group of six teenagers do to solve our problems? I wondered." The crowd murmured in response. "But no one would help us. And we were losing those that we loved. The Moirae marked them as our saviors. I knew the big and brave heart of my niece, Brisa. And I reasoned, if the rest of the council was half the person she was, then there might be a chance." He paused. "I must say, they have exceeded my every expectation." His audience roared their approval. "For the first time, in my very long memory, different clans have worked side by side to help each other. Malta said it would be the beginning of a new age. I may have doubted then, but I believe now. I thank you and honor you for taking on this challenge, for fighting for our people, and bringing our children home." With those last remarks, he stepped off the dais and went to each council member, Salamander, and medic, thanking them and giving them a necklace made by his own hands. Each Salamander was treated as royalty and the treatment obviously overwhelmed them.

When Boreas arrived at Brisa, he bowed to her and offered his necklace. At her accepting smile, he swept her into his embrace. "You bring great honor to our family, Brisa," he whispered. "You are the best of us." As he pulled away, pride in his niece was shining from his face.

After Boreas released Brisa, he turned to Mia. "I have made you two necklaces, Mia, Leader of the new Council. For I am doubly in your debt. First, for standing up and saving my Brisa. Not only on the day of Samhain, but by helping her find herself again in the weeks since. And secondly, for saving our people from a horrible foe. We may not know who they are, but thanks to you, we know how to protect ourselves from their unspeakable evil." He bowed, and Mia returned the gesture.

"I thank you, King Boreas, on behalf of the new council. Despite your doubts, you gave us a chance. For that, we are in your debt."

"You have more than paid it, Mia," he grinned, "I would say I am still in yours. Should you need the support of the Sylph in the future, you will have it." His face crinkled with a smile. Mia could totally see why Brisa had a crush on him when she was younger. He was like a rugged prince charming. The two necklaces from King Boreas were placed on top of the pile on Mia's chest. His were a deep burgundy glass, interspersed with gold pieces that she suspected were real.

As music started to play, the celebration began in earnest. A long line of Sylph assembled to meet the new council. The members were escorted to a long table, and given seats, to Damek's relief. A wide variety of foods covered the table, and soon the feasting commenced. Tables had been set up all along the street, flanked by chairs of every shape and size. Despite most homes having donated their tables and chairs, there were still people left to picnic on the nearby lawns.

Several different tribes provided food of their heritage. People mixed and mingled, asking questions and making connections. Everyone felt welcome.

Mia looked down the table at her fellow council members. They were overwhelmed, but happy. She understood the feeling. Every fiber of her being quivered with joy. The weight of the necklaces around her neck was a bit much, but she would never dream of taking a single one off in front of the Sylph. As the tables were being cleared, the priestess from the last celebration approached Brisa and whispered something.

"The Sylph Cailleach would like to run the marking ceremony for the new council and the Salamanders. She asks if you would be willing to read the marks." Mia looked at Brisa in a panic, grabbing her hand.

I have no idea how to read the marks.

Uncle Boreas brought his own priestess. Defer to her. Mia breathed out a sigh of relief at Brisa's suggestion.

"I believe King Boreas has brought his own priestess. I would not usurp her place. We are in the Sylph home and their priestess should preside," her eyes opened a little wider to Brisa. *Was that right?* Brisa nodded. The priestess bowed.

The people gathered around the dais and the new council, the Salamanders, and the medics were ushered in front of the assembled masses. A hum of anticipation worked its way through the audience, but silence fell as soon as King Boreas' priestess reached the edge of the platform. She started to talk, but Mia was distracted by the stares she was receiving. Most of the crowd was watching the priestess, but several males were staring blatantly at Mia. They didn't shy away when she returned their stare either. Mia touched Damek's hand. *The men are sizing me up again.* Damek's eyes scanned the crowd.

Keep holding my hand until they call us up, he replied, reassuring her with a smile. Mia tried to focus in on the priestess. She was wrapping up her speech. The Salamanders were called up. They bowed in deference to the priestess. Then the assembled crowd kneeled and put their hands to their mouth, releasing their breath towards the Salamanders, in the same way they had to Brisa at Samhain. A wind arose. The Salamanders' eyes widened in surprise. In front of the crowd, black tattoos appeared on their arms. However, unlike their other tattoos, there was a pale-yellow shadow to it. The priestess went before each one and announced what the symbol meant. All were variations on bravery and selflessness. Different members of the crowd would stand as she spoke, mainly the rescued. When the priestess concluded each one with "he or she is a friend of the Sylph", everyone would stand, then kneel again for the next person.

Why are they standing? asked Mia.

Each tattoo is a symbol of who we are and what we have accomplished. Each clan has their own ceremony where the tattoos are placed by the Goddess. I have to say, this one is definitely longer and more poetic than the Gnomes.

The standing? Mia repeated.

The priestess announces to the crowd the symbol and its meaning. Those who can attest to the veracity of the pronouncement stand.

The priestess finished her way down the line. The Salamanders bowed to the assembled Sylph, then returned to their seats. The process was repeated with the medical crew, Jules and Vi. Their symbols related to compassion and selflessness. Then the new council was called up. They stood in a line across the front of the small stage. Again, everyone kneeled, raising their hand to their mouth and releasing their breath towards the stage. A strong breeze rolled around them, surrounding and caressing each of the new council members. Mia's eyes closed at the gentle yet powerful touch of the wind. When she opened her eyes, she realized she was about a foot off the ground, lifted by the air. As she sank back down, Mia could feel the placement of her tattoos, just as she had during the Samhain council meeting. She examined her arm. Under the silver double triangle star, a golden yellow triangle with a line through the top had appeared. The priestess moved to the first in line: McKenna.

"McKenna, daughter of Aiden, of the family Ognyan," The priestess lowered the top of McKenna shirt exposing the top of her spine. Fortunately, it was below the collection of necklaces. The priestess touched the mark. "McKenna is marked at the top of her spine with heart. She will be a great leader due to her care and understanding of others." The Salamanders behind the priest all stood along with the rescued.

"Calder, son of Maris, of the family Kallan," the priestess lowered his shirt. "Calder is marked with intelligence. He will be a great leader due to his insight and vision." The Salamanders and the rescued stood.

"Colin, son of Alma, of the family Nuelle," the priestess lowered his shirt. "Colin is marked with courage. He will be a great leader because he is willing to take on any challenge." The Salamanders and the rescued stood. Colin looked like he could be bowled over with a feather.

"Brisa, daughter of Boreas, of the family Aeolius," Brisa's eyes turned to her uncle with a questioning smile as he claimed her into his family. Her uncle nodded with approval. "Brisa is marked with strength. She will be a great leader because of her drive, determination, and inner strength." The Salamanders, the rescued and most of the Sylph stood.

"Damek, son of Delphi, of the family Delphin," the priestess lowered his shirt. "Damek is marked with wisdom. He will be a great leader because of his analytical mind that is tempered with compassion." The Salamanders and the rescued stood.

"Mia, daughter of Triana, of the family Raegan," Mia was surprised at the announcement of her family. Mia smiled. She was more Triana's daughter than Alain's, the father she never knew. Mia felt the priest lower the neck of her shirt and her warm hands touch a spot she had felt tingle before. The priestess' hand withdrew quickly, as if sparked. "Mia is marked with power." The priestess whispered, but it could be heard throughout the entire square. "She will lead the council and all Elementals into a new age. Mia's power will come from her heart, her intelligence, and her unlimited potential." From the middle of the crowd, Tana's family stood first, then the rescued and the Salamanders. Then King Boreas stood, as did every person in the square one by one. *I'm not the leader of the council,* was all she could think. *How am I supposed to face everyone with a pronouncement like that over my head?* She studied the crowd. Their faces reflected awe and faith. The other members of the council appeared... proud of her. This was way too much to process.

The priestess held up a hand, and the entire crowd immediately fell silent. "Finally, all members of the new council have one additional mark. The Goddess has named them not only a member of their own clan, but of the Sylph people. They are marked with the wind." She nodded to the council, and they raised their arms to show the golden tattoo resting under their silver clan mark. Brisa now had two. Her silver air clan mark and a yellow one below. At that proc-lamation, the crowd went wild. Mia looked to her friends who were grinning, laughing, and full of pride and joy. Their arms remained in the air to show proof of their newest affiliation. Soon, the crowd swept the dais, shaking hands, marveling over the marks, congratulating and praising.

When there was a lull, Cailleach Ilma pulled Mia aside. The last few weeks had taken a toll on Cailleach Ilma, but she still had a warm smile. "Well, little Cailleach, it seems," Ilma chuckled.

"Oh, no… I could never hope to.."

"Ahh, but you will. I took some time to consult my stones and my cards. I was able to tell two things. First, that you will have a dangerous road ahead of you. People will try to push you to be what they want. You must follow your own path." The words reminded Mia of the warning from Triana, the night she was marked. "Second, you will be a Cailleach… one day… and when you are, your teaching will save the traditions that have started to be lost." Cailleach Ilma handed a worn cotton bag to Mia. "I have something for you." Mia pulled out a book with a dark purple cover. Mia opened it, noticing the pages were blank. She looked quizzically at Ilma. "It is a grimoire… your grimoire… as you learn, write it down here so it will always be with you. But Mia," she leaned forward and placed her hand over Mia's. "Learn everything you can and record it all. I am privileged to give you this book because it will become more important than you could possibly realize at this time."

"Thank you," Mia stuttered, holding the precious book to her chest.

"Now don't treat the thing like it's costly… Get it dirty and fill it up. Breathe life into it. That's what it's for." Ilma smiled and pulled Mia into a warm embrace. "Be careful child, and I will be here when you need me." Ilma winked, and then quickly hurried away.

Mia wasn't sure how much time had passed since the start of the celebration. She enjoyed watching the young people of the different tribes breaking down the barriers between them. Eventually, a small group came forward. Their dark skin contrasted with their light brown hair. Two of the saved were with them. The rest of the Sylph gave them a wide berth but were respectful in doing so. An older woman regally draped in yellow fabric addressed Mia.

"We did not want to miss our opportunity to thank you for returning our young ones. Nor did we want to reject the hospitality of those who welcomed us. This ceremony has been a… unique experience." The older woman addressed

Mia. "Our traditions are very different; we have no necklace for you… only our true respect and our debt."

"There is no debt," Mia replied quickly. "Your respect is more than enough to thank us." The woman paused, then bowed her head slightly.

"We are the storytellers of the African Tribe. We keep our history from centuries before and will continue to create our stories for generations to come. The tale of the new council and how they saved our children, that story will be told for the rest of time."

The lady focused on McKenna. "I admit, when they told me Akuji was a member of the council, it was easy to dismiss it," McKenna bristled. "However, perhaps the Fire should rename you…. For you have shown yourself to be a Candace…" McKenna blinked, clearly confused. The woman didn't explain but began to leave. Each of the African contingent moved forward and delivered a mix between a bow and a curtesy. The council bowed in return.

As they left, Mia whispered, "What did she mean?"

"I have no idea," McKenna whispered back.

"McKenna, when I was passed out and saw the battle in the… mansion… There was a warrior named Semmy?" Mia asked.

"She is a warrior who helped us with the breach… but then disappeared. I don't know who she is." McKenna was puzzled. Long after the rest of the council returned to the celebration, McKenna remained deep in thought.

A sea of faces had gone by. Little kids slouched in their seats. Many had already been taken home. People started to disband. Mia was dizzy from the onslaught of emotions she had been exposed to all night. Her vision was blurring. She sat in a chair, keeping a smile on her face. Brisa walked up with her uncle. The rest of the new council gathered around them.

"Brisa says you must leave," Boreas smiled indulgently at his niece. "I leave you all with a final thank you." He approached each. They bowed and accepted his clasped handshake. When he approached Mia, she got to her feet, but she was woozy. "Mia, I must say that the Aether were correct. You are worth a king's ransom," he took her hand. "The Sylph will put in their bid for your dower. I hope one day you will truly be a member of our clan." He brought her hand to his mouth and kissed it. Mia and Brisa shared a perplexed expression. Clearly, Brisa did not understand what he was talking about. Thank you, Brisa mouthed with a slight shrug. What is a dower?

"Thank you, your highness," Mia replied awkwardly. With a final smile, he gave Brisa a huge hug. Mia watched as Boreas and Brisa moved away, talking about something Mia couldn't quite hear. Finally, he whispered something in Brisa's ear to which she nodded, kissing his cheek. Then Brisa returned to the council. "We may have a problem," Brisa said, focusing on Mia. "Apparently the Aether are taking bids for Mia." The members all looked at Mia.

"What?!" Mia screeched. All the appraisal by the men. The dower... a dowry? She looked wildly at her friends, who seemed taken aback. "I think I need to sit down," she whispered... It was too much... she took in a deep breath... the wooziness returned... All Mia could think was she had a promise to herself to keep.

Mia stood on the front porch watching the final moments of the setting sun. Once it was gone, she no longer had an excuse to stay there. Her breath sped up. Before Mia could knock, she heard the door open behind her.

"Mia?" Mia turned to see a familiar silhouette framed by the foyer light. "Mia, is that really you?" the voice cracked.

"It's me," Mia confirmed. Tears came unbidden to her eyes. "Can I come home?" she choked out. The silhouette moved forward. The rising moon highlighted Triana's face.

"Yes, thank the Goddess! Yes," Triana wrapped her arms around Mia. They stood, crying and holding each other. "I've been so worried." Triana finally pulled away. "Come in." Mia followed Triana into the house but stopped at the front door. Mia looked back at the way she had come. It had been a long, hard road. Mia sighed. She had to close the door on it. So after a final glance, she did.